IS THIS APOCALYPSE OVER YET?

A TEENAGER'S GUIDE TO
SAVING THE EARTH: BOOK 3

by Craig Robertson

Are we there yet? Are we there yet?

Imagine-It Publishing
El Dorado Hills, CA

IS THIS APOCALYPSE OVER YET?

A TEENAGER'S GUIDE TO SAVING THE EARTH:
BOOK 3

CRAIG ROBERTSON

ALSO BY CRAIG ROBERTSON:

* Podium Entertainment has produced audiobooks for all the below titles
except the older standalone books.

For specifics as to the correct order for reading the Ryanverse, click here.

BOOKS IN THE RYANVERSE:

THE FOREVER SERIES (2016)

THE FOREVER LIFE, Book 1

THE FOREVER ENEMY, Book 2

THE FOREVER FIGHT, Book 3

THE FOREVER QUEST, Book 4

THE FOREVER ALLIANCE, Book 5

THE FOREVER PEACE, Book 6

THE FOREVER BOXSET, Part 1, Books 1 & 2

THE FOREVER BOXSET, Part 2, Book 3 & 4

THE FOREVER BOXSET, Part 3, Book 5 & 6

GALAXY ON FIRE SERIES (2017)

EMBERS, Book 1

FLAMES, Book 2

FIRESTORM, Book 3

FIRES OF HELL, Book 4

DRAGON FIRE, Book 5

ASHES, Book 6

GALAXY ON FIRE BOXSET, Part 1, Books 1 & 2

Saving Alice Ryan, Book 3

NON-RYANVERSE BOOKS:

A Teenager's Guide to Saving The Earth (2025)

An Apocalypse and Then Some, Book 1

How to Survive Surviving the Apocalypse, Book 2

Is This Apocalypse Over Yet?, Book 3

TIME DIVING (2024)

Letters From Hell, Book 1

Purgatory's Best Shot, Book 2

Heaven Says Wait, Book 3

Into the Nexus, Book 4

ROAD TRIPS IN SPACE SERIES (2019):

THE GALAXY ACCORDING TO GIDEON, Book 1

THE EARTH ACCORDING TO GIDEON, Book 2

OLDER, STANDALONE WORKS:

THE CORPORATE VIRUS (2016)

THE INNERgLOW EFFECT (2010)

WRITE NOW! THE PRISONER OF NaNoWRiMo (2009)

ANON TIME (2009)

For more information about Craig, his books, various series, or to see images and videos for some of his wild alien characters, please visit his website. You'll be glad you did: https://craigarobertson.com/

To sign up for Craig's newsletter to get announcements, updates, and his recommendations for other great Sci-Fi reads go to: https://preview.mail erlite.io/forms/2369493/18863442637514450 1/share

ISBNs: 979-8-9988317-0-6 (E-Book)
979-8-9988317-1-3 (Paperback)
979-8-9988317-2-0 (Hardback)

Cover design by Alexandre
http://www.designbookcover.pt/en/

Editors:
Michael R. Blanche
Beth Lynne
Forest Olivier

Formatting Services by Drew Avera
drewavera@gmail.com

First Edition 2026

This book is dedicated to the sentiments expressed by Emma Lazarus in her poem "The New Colossus," which are inscribed on the Statue of Liberty: "Give me your tired, your poor, your huddled masses yearning to breathe free."

A glossary of terms is available at the end of the book.

PRELUDE

An extremely unhappy President of the United States Carl Sellers sat seething at a table surrounded, it seemed to him, by perfect idiots. In the six months since the alien invaders had been killed off, he had been able to make some moves to restore order and stability to the country. But now his staff's new favorite response to his instructions was to screw up whatever they were told to do. *How hard is it*, Carl railed in his head, *to follow simple, concise orders?* Apparently, it was very hard.

First, there was some new "savior" alien that had helped destroy the Dostivex monsters. Carl told his people it was critical that the new aliens present themselves to him in White House II. Those were some pretty darn clear dictates. But no. His staff allowed the aliens not only to refuse to meet with Carl, but to insult him to boot. Then the alien chose to scoop up some damn teenager instead, because the kid was more important to the alien pukes.

Second, there was Carl's *Speak To the Nation Directive*. He needed to reach out to the public and let them know that he was in charge and life would be getting better. How uncomplicated could that be? But his people couldn't line up transmission capabilities or receiving stations or anything of the things necessary for him to reach out with. *Smoke signals* were a superior option to the solutions they'd brought him to date.

And now, last straw, his chief-of-staff was confirming to his face that the vice president was in full-blown insubordination. Carl had sent Susan Whitehorse to Spokane to interface with the group possessing the one functioning alien spaceship at his disposal. He'd summoned her back to Washington to give him a complete report. But, *no.* The VP responded that she had, *More pressing issues that required her ongoing presence on scene.* What was more important than a direct order from the POTUS to meet with the POTUS? Nothing was! Hard stop.

"Robin," President Sellers said to his COS, "how are you going to fix this? When I say I need the vice president back here, I need her back here. Will you either get Susan to return ASAP or please find someone else who will translate my very simple request into action." He snapped his fingers at her. "I need results, not lame excuses."

"I cannot make Vice President Whitehorse heel," the COS replied harshly. "What, do I threaten to ground her or maybe to send in the Seal Team 9 to drag her out?"

Carl raised a finger skyward. "Don't you start in with me, Robin. I've got sixteen million balls in the air and I cannot personally juggle all of them at once. Get-her-back-*now.*"

"I don't understand this," interrupted the Coast Guard representative to the Joint Chiefs, Admiral Miles "Salty" Burke. "Back during the pandemic, we all had to learn to do those damn Zoom conferences. Why can't you just *Zoom* Susan?"

"Because, *Salty,* I'm the president and I don't want to *Zoom* Susan. I want to feel her right here in front of–" Carl trailed off quickly when he realized just how very inappropriate what he was saying sounded. "I don't like video calls," he summarized meekly.

"There's a lot that needs doing, Mr. President," Salty advised him. "You'd best pick with care the hills you're willing to die on."

Carl was about to respond with something glib and witty, but let it go. He was just too darn tired. "Robin, please see if the oh-so-busy vice president might be able to share a video call with her boss later today."

"I can do that, Carl," she responded dutifully as she scribbled in her notebook.

"Fine, the next item on the addenda," he continued. "How are we coming with reverse-engineering the alien technology?" He looked to the head of NASA, Larry Doresett.

He picked up a loose stack of papers and tapped them on the desktop. "We have made more than no progress at all, Mr. President."

Carl stared at him a moment before he realized that was the extent of the man's report. "Well, *gosh*, not no progress is ... what? Great? Epic?" he sniped.

"I was not fully finished," he lied. "You know, back-engineering is not as simple as copying what they left behind."

"Larry, I lack the skill set to reverse-engineer a *turd*. That's why NASA exists, why you pull down a salary, were we actually paying anyone any more."

"Thank you," he replied somewhat out of synch with reality. "Let me restate. Given the incomplete reconstitution of universities and other centers of higher learning, and given the state of our supply chain, robust scientific research is more than challenging. It's *very* challenging."

"Larry," the POTUS said, trying to remain calm, "this I know too. That's why NASA exists, why you pull down a salary."

"Thank you, again. I can say that the engine systems of the alien flying saucers seem to be more open to interpretation. We–"

"I thought I ordered you and everyone else to never call them flying saucers?" Carl all but howled.

"Yes, you did," Larry confirmed. "But the fact remains that the term is familiar *and* it rolls off the tongue so freely."

"Well, control your tongues, *NASA*. I know you nerds just think it's so much fun to say the words *flying saucer*. Cut. It. Out. Now!"

"What, Mr. President? My tongue?" an ashen Larry inquired in a surprisingly conversational tone.

"Lord, no. What kind of government do you think I'm running here? Early Medieval?"

"No, sir," Larry said weakly. "If these were any of the Medieval times, there would be no way we could reverse-engineer advanced alien technology."

"No ... I–" Carl was forced to stop speaking, he was so beside himself. This man's head was so far up his ass, he really couldn't relate to normal humans, could he? And this was the best at his disposal? Lord love a duck. That was all Carl could muster.

"I think we're about done here," the COS stated loudly, recognizing as she did the faltering of the man she was hired to help. "If the president needs any additional input from any individual, he will be in contact."

Once the room was cleared, save for Carl and Robin, he turned to her with a drawn face. "Is it me, Robin, or has the world gone completely nuts?"

"Who knows? Probably a little of each. Are you ready for your annual physical? It's next on your schedule."

He began nodding, slowly at first, then in a more animated manner. "Sure. Right now, even a rectal exam would constitute an upswing in my day."

ONE

My life aboard *Peerless* fell into somewhat of a routine. Well, maybe if anything that touched Visquisor could be classified as humdrum and uneventful, which it couldn't be. I swear, the man must have had two or three separate personalities living up there inside his head. One, let's call him Cute Vissie, could be almost childlike. He'd be giving, funny, and sincerely caring. That'd be for ten minutes, mind you. A second was The Master Visquisor. That guy was serious, calculating, stone-faced, and cerebral. He brooded, ruminated, cogitated, and spoke, if at all, in riddles, word fogs, and mystifications. That was the most annoying and the most frequent manifestation I'd seen so far. And then there was who I called DRFT Visquisor. That's short for Down Right Fucking Terrifying. Yeah. Me no likie. Fortunately, that person was the rarest avatar in his noggin to peek out. I'd experienced it four or five times and I lived in constant fear I'd see it again soon. Dude got nightmare scary. Planet destroying, genocidal, burn-baby-burn psycho man.

But whichever Visquisor I was forced to deal with at any given moment, I was certainly growing to hate them all. Not that it mattered. If a lifer in prison dislikes his jailer, does that make his confinement any better? Nope, and it was the same with me. The more I came to understand my status, the more I realized I was powerless. The proverbial leaf in a hurricane. I tried to put a positive spin on what was happening to me because the alternative was deep depression. You know, it's like when you get on a roller coaster, one of those really big ones specifically designed to scare the bejeebers out of you. That was what the sitcom *My Life With Visquisor* was like. I was on the ride, I couldn't stop it, and I couldn't get off. I considered myself lucky if I didn't pee myself most of the time. Yeah. Fun City, USA.

Since my leave was up and I left everyone I loved behind on Earth, Old Vizzie and I had only made a few stops. Check that. How would I know, right? There had only been a few occasions where the boss took me off the ship for some event. He might have made port dozens of times and left me in the dark concerning it. I had no way of knowing. *Peerless* was an amazing ship. I never felt acceleration, deceleration, landings, or heard engine hums. I imagine living on board was like living in the Paris Ritz, though I'd never been in that lap of luxury to fairly compare the two.

We made three appearances at soirees where Visquisor was clearly the guest of honor. I was brought along the way those revolting hoity-toity society women bring a tiny lapdog with them in an absurdly ornate bag. Picture me as the dog-in-the-purse. The funny thing is that no matter how over-the-top the royals or moguls make their ceremonial balls, the meals were never as fancy as the ones we had every day aboard the ship. The best any rich-beyond-belief emperor could do paled in comparison to our everyday fare. Go figure.

On one occasion, the boss sent me to some kind of conference on my own. Maybe it was a negotiation? I never knew. He didn't clue me in why he was sending me, what my role was, or what he hoped I would accomplish and/or learn. I sat there in a big room with really freaky-looking aliens coming and going, a translator bot in my ear, and a confused, slightly nauseated look on my face for ten hours. The worst part was the food. There were a few separate buffets, but all the ones I seemed to line up at only served roiling goop in chafing dishes. No thank you very much. I'm fasting. Then And Cream, the ship's Artificial Sentience, buzzed in my head to return to the shuttle. *We're leaving post haste.* That was a blessing in disguise if ere there were one.

So today, I was on vacation. Or on strike. I hadn't decided which yet. The day was young. What I planned on doing was perfectly nothing. I was in my boxers, in my enormous, plush bed, listening to tunes from home, and chillin. It would take a direct summons from Visquisor to make me budge from this spot. And then, of course, there came a knock on my door. In all my time here, there was only one knock on my door. That was when my sort-of-pal Morpheus Denali, who claimed to be an Algontol warrior on the sly, came to warn me about Visquisor. Otherwise, no one knocked. And Cream ordered me to attend the Master and the servants just barged in. So I eyed the door suspiciously until the second, more insistent knock came.

Since there was nothing for it, I bounced out of bed and answered the door. The penalty for whoever lurked on the other side for disturbing me on vacation was that I didn't throw on a robe. Nope, you knock, you get me in my boxers.

"Morpheus!" I exclaimed when I saw it was him. "Dude, long time no see."

He started shaking his head slowly, ponderously. "First off, whatever a dude is, I am not one. Second, if ya can't see, go to the sick bay. I can't help you. Third, a simple question."

"Yes?"

"Why am I still standing out here in the passageway?"

"Oh, sorry." I jumped back. "Please come in."

He picked up a massive tool bag and walked past me. "Today, I'm here on actual ship's business," he announced in an official tone.

"Ah, okay. What ship's business?"

"I need to check a plasma coupling that passes behind one of your walls."

"A plasma coupling? What's that? Something for my shower?"

"No, if it was, you'd melt when you bathed. You do know what plasma is? The fourth state of matter, charged particles, runs around a million degrees Celsius. Sound familiar?"

"Oh, sure, like the surface of a star."

"That's the one. We've been getting a glitchy reading from the sensors in the coupling behind your bedroom wall. I'm here to see if it's the sensor or the coupling itself."

"My, there's one-million degree plasma flowing past my bed? How disquieting."

"It's gotta flow *somewhere* to get to the weapons turrets, laddie. And, it's more precisely next to your head, not the bed in general."

"I'll never sleep again," I declared.

"Suit yourself. Not my job. Lucky for me, I just fix plasma couplings, not human neuroses."

With that, he walked into my bedroom, unmade bed and all. He set to work popping the wall open as I peered over his shoulder from a respectful distance.

"Ya know, if it *is* the coupling and it blows, it won't matter how far back what's left of you was standing," Morpheus informed me.

"No problem," I responded illogically.

"So, what ya up to, your semi-royal highness?" he asked while pounding vigorously with a wrench on a very delicate-looking assembly.

"Um, not much. After I personally resolved the Lephorizian War Crisis, we've not done much."

"Just a friendly head's up. Ya don't resolve nothin' with a Lephorizian. They're fickle and dimwitted little buggers. Whatever ya fixed, they'll unfix soon enough."

"In a perfect world, people would not be so pessimistic," I opined.

"In your perfect world, people'd be *dead*," he countered pessimistically.

"I was told a few days ago we're heading for some place called Dez Falls. Not sure what that's all about. I'm always the last to know."

Morpheus stopped banging on the pipe, set the tool down, and turned to look at me squarely. "He's taking you to Dez Falls?" He said that in an unsettling, concerned manner.

"That's what I heard."

"Why?" he asked sharply.

"All he said was he has some business dealings there and he's not pleased with the productivity."

"Ack!" he barked. Then he spat on the floor in disgust. Fortunately for me, it was on the other side of the wall's deck, not where I'd be sleeping restlessly from now on.

"Are you unwell?" I asked.

He spied up at me incredulously. "You don't know what Dez Falls is, do ya?"

I shook my head in dismay. "Not clue one."

Morpheus grunted some curse, stood up, and pushed past me, heading for the lounge. I followed him because I wasn't sure what else to do.

"Sit, little emperor," he commanded, and so I did. He seemed to struggle to gather his thoughts, then finally said, "There's stupid crazy-ass things to do in this galaxy, and then there's going to Dez Falls. While I *can* believe that imbecile has business there, I *cannot* believe he'd drag you, or even his worst enemy, there along with him."

"It's bad?" I asked sheepishly.

Morpheus dropped his considerable bulk into an unsuspecting chair. "There are some cultures out there that are founded on beliefs like goodness, love, and joy." He swung an arm/fin horizontally. "That's what they do all day, they walk into walls and smile knowing the universe is great place to live and that every little thing will turn out fine."

"That sounds nice," I speculated.

"Sounds like they need brain transplants, but that's not important to my point."

"Ah," I responded.

"There are those what say that the Blessed Maker understood that there'd be idiots like that, so he/she created Dez Falls."

"That sounds ominous."

"It should," he snapped. "That way, that pie-in-the-sky crowd could go there and see that there really is a hell. An evil in this cosmos, a place of unrelenting danger, and unending antipathy to life itself."

"Ouch. And I'm heading there now."

He just shook his head some more.

"What makes it so bad?" I finally asked. "I mean, I am traveling with Visquisor."

"What makes it so bad," he replied sarcastically, "is the damn Bliss Shale, that's what."

I mouthed the words *Bliss Shale*. That didn't *sound* so foreboding. I mean, come on, it's a shale, a thin, laminated, and generally friable rock.

And who doesn't like bliss? "Can you expand upon this?" I asked. "How can anything with *bliss* in its name be evil incarnate?"

"It's not the Bliss Shale that's evil, ya pinhead. It's everything else on that accursed planet."

"Morpheus, are you just going to tell me or do I need to pull the information out of you with pliers?"

He looked at me with disgust. "Funny child," he quipped. "No one knows the origins of Dez Falls. Some think it was subject to a prolonged nuclear winter eons ago. Others say a great and ancient race lived there but then mysteriously passed away. Who knows? The place is horrible. The thin atmosphere is laden with a fine brown-red mist. It's like a fog, only it ain't a liquid; it's mostly proteins."

"Whoa, proteins? That's crazy. Where do they come from? Metabolically, proteins are very costly to produce. An organism doesn't just puff them into the air," I reasoned.

"Again, it's an unknown. But all these proteins over a very long time coalesce into solids. Most of the rocks and soil are just a mishmash of protein goos. But some form Bliss Shale deposits by whatever strange process. Those are what men go there and die to find."

"Hang on, yet again," I interrupted. "Proteins are simple. For any space-faring species, whipping up any protein they wanted would be child's play."

He raised a finger. "Not necessarily. Bliss Shale is very exotic, very long chains of building blocks. Yes, it could be produced in a lab, but it would be tedious, time-consuming, and hard to make in quantities. It's easier to mine the stuff."

"Even if the planet's hell and the prospectors all die?" I asked incredulously.

"Yes, for the prices it draws, men'll risk everything gladly."

"What's it used for, this shale?"

"Ah, that's the terrible part of it." He again took a moment to gather his thoughts. "Your people, these humans, do they have gods?"

"Ah, complicated question. I'll say yes, most believe in a solitary divine being. God."

"That's fairly typical," he assured me. "And this God, does he have an afterlife laid out for ya?"

"W ... well, sure, I mean there is an afterlife associated with most religions centered on God."

"There ya go. Alright, so do you, Christopher Alan, have in your mind a concept of what your eternal reward or punishment will be like?"

"Ah ... honestly, no."

"But your people believe in heaven, hell, all that?"

"Yes, some do."

"And it'd be fair to say everyone has some preconception of their eternal reward, if that's where they're destined?"

"Sure."

"Tell me a little snippet of what you think your Heaven would be like." He sat back patiently.

"It'd have nice weather."

"Oookay, that's a start. What else? Beautiful naked women running about heedlessly?"

"No," I defended quickly. "Just my Natalie."

"Ah, your sweetheart, yes. So, she'll be running around naked heedlessly?"

"No. Only ... you know, indoors with me present."

"So we're slowly and somewhat painfully painting a picture of Christopher Alan's Heaven, right?"

"For the sake of argument, sure," I said a bit testily.

"What Bliss Shale does is to establish as a reality in any user's mind that they are physically present in whatever their concept of heaven is."

"Wh ... what?" I said, surprised. "That's not possible. All the different species out there, and Bliss Shale has the same mystical effect on all of them? No way."

"Well, in spite of your objections, it does. I imagine there might be some slime mold on some forgotten rock that is immune to the crap, but I don't know of any."

"So the shale is a powerful drug. There are lots of powerful drugs out there. What's so special about this one?"

"Christopher, the shale is so dangerous, it's illegal *everywhere*. Even on scurvy-scum pirate worlds it's forbidden. Ya see, once a person experiences their heaven, they will never voluntarily leave it."

"What about eating? Everyone has to stop and have dinner," I protested.

"Nope, that's the hook. All matters being equal, anyone whose touched the shale will wither and die before they take a pause in it. It's deadly."

"But if it's so illegal and the planet's so dangerous, what would Visquisor be doing there? He said he's going there for business purposes."

"As I said before, him having business where Bliss Shale's concerned doesn't surprise me." He leaned forward and rested his hands on his knees. "There are places where thems with enough money can get Bliss Shale for as long as they like."

"You mean like clinics or spas?" I asked.

"Yeah, that type of arrangement. You go there, they hook you up to all manner of life support, and they administer to you a steady stream of Bliss Shale. That way, as long as ya live, you're in paradise, and ya live a long time."

That was distressing to learn. "And you think Visquisor is involved in that shady business?"

He shrugged. "Maybe he uses it? Maybe he sells it? But he's got his nose in many a thing that's illegal and profitable, that's for sure."

This was the worst news ever, and I'm including the whole alien apocalypse. And I was going to Dez Falls. I was engaging in the most illegal, most immoral activity in the Milky Way. How unnice. How extremely unnice.

"I'm gonna have to keep a keen eye on ya, young Chris," Morpheus said, waking me from my thoughts.

"Huh? Why's that?"

"Because I can't allow you to go down there by yourself."

"No, Visquisor's taking me there. He's coming."

"Like he did with the wavering ambiguity and the Lephoriz War negotiations?" he asked darkly.

Oh, yeah, he did abandon me before, didn't he. Why not make it three for three and dump hapless me into hell itself? What says *giving* more than *giving* someone free passage to eternal damnation's theme park? Oh, yes, that sounded very much in character for Visquisor.

I was in deep doo-doo. Deep, deep, doo-doo, doo-doo.

"Thanks ... thanks, Morpheus. I mean, I hope it doesn't come down to it. But if he does send me there alone, I'd love you having my back." Then a thought hit me. "Wait. If he wants me to shuttle down there alone, he wouldn't permit even an engineer to accompany me."

"Well, not if I asked or he knew, he wouldn't."

"So you plan on sneaking past Mr. Paranoia? This all-powerful crazy dude?"

He raised an army/finny thing. "Proud Algontol warrior here."

"So you really are more than a savage with a spear in the jungle?" I teased, reminding him of his raking me over the coals before.

"Now, I can be if I want to. But, nah, not normally."

"If you come with me to the surface of Dez Falls, maybe the spear and loincloth thing might be appropriate?" I joked.

He returned a very sober expression. "No. If I go down to Dez Falls, I'm bringing a good deal more than the basics." He nodded, mostly to himself, I think. "Since I'll probably die down there, why not bring everything?"

TWO

Visquisor was growing restless. For the last five days, he'd been in a stim-pod, trying with something well past desperation to feel ... *anything* again. But all he ever felt was empty. This, he realized was the most ulti-mate of ironies. Here he was, functionally immortal, master of the tech-nology of the Eight Gods of Many, free to do whatever pleased him, and he still had his health. Yet he felt ... nothing. Oh, he might bluster or rant or make love or destroy whole star systems on a whim. But before any of that, during any of that, and after any of that, he was a barren, dry husk. A living, breathing mummy. Visquisor's ultimate curse was that, intellectually, he wanted to hate his condition with a passion so red, it glowed in the dark. But, try as he might, he couldn't even muster the inner ardor to do that.

For the last ten-thousand millennia, he had labored to find, forge, steal, or murder for a solution to his wretched state. Visquisor had hired every great mind in the galaxy to fabricate for him a method to experi-ence life again. He had raided every archive, library, data bank, and reli-gious sanctum in an attempt to unearth a process or procedure that could make him emotionally whole. In his despondency, he even had captured and tortured for true insights every dark charlatan, soothsayer, or purveyor of the occult he could lay his hands on. But none of those sources provided Visquisor even the slightest indication as to how he might regain meaningful life. He hadn't, in fact, learned from any of them if his quest was even attainable.

A handful of centuries ago, an ancient Mentic Sage breathed a few parched words to Visquisor that held out for him the sum total of his hope to be able to wrench back from the universe some measure of relief. At the very cusp of death, as the wise man succumbed to the vivisection Visquisor was personally administering to him, he whispered, *There issss ... or used to b ... be ... the transfer of souls. In the be ... before t ... t ... time it issss ...said that ...* And that was all she wrote ... er ... he said. The man passed from his torment to hopefully some suitable reward for his stalwartness. But Visquisor came away from that ... *interview* with the firm impression that somewhen in time, and somewhere in the universe, some inspired civilization might have been able to achieve the transfer of one soul to another's body. And, he reasoned, why do such a nonsensical thing if it wasn't to rebirth the very spark of life into the donor soul's less-than-satisfying existence?

As far from logical, or even not-insane as that line of thinking was, it had since then been Visquisor's singular goal. To discover how to transfer his dissipating essence into an appropriate receptacle was his holy grail. And, yes, the method, the technique, the voodoo to make such an export possible had completely evaded him. But as his only slimmest of a lead, he was forced—an act he detested—to pursue it.

In any case, Visquisor had established in his mind a stepwise process that would culminate in him transferring his soul. He was pleased to know that he was well on his way to completing Step 1. He had those ten—possibly soon to be eleven—sniveling lackeys of his trailing behind him like so many geese anxious for the slaughter. Any one of them would be disgusting to occupy. But, sadly, they were, he reasoned, his best options to transfer his essence *into*. They were similar to him at least in the manner that the shadow of a mountain reflected something of the magnificence of the towering structure itself.

And that reminded Visquisor, he needed to pretend to preen, while actually he vetted, this foul-smelling human Christopher rigorously. A major part of Visquisor's intellect hoped the child would fail soon so he could justify killing him. But, it benefited him to have as many suitable donor-bodies around as possible. Waste not, want not. This next challenge, it was a frightfully tough one. Maybe he'd get lucky and Christopher would never return from Dez Falls. That way, his conscience would be cleared of any misgivings. The boy would prove himself insufficient, inadequate, and demonstrate that he would have made an unacceptable vessel for Visquisor's perfect, masterful soul. Why, he couldn't even survive a simple trek across the blighted terrain of one desolate planet.

He ordered the AS to summon the bumpkin. Then, to pass the time, he sat back and plucked the last remaining somalofitch of the planet Gleetar from the small bowl it was swimming in. A recent acquisition, this reptilian fish were said to be delicious. Then again, whoever said that was likely an idiot like everyone else he'd ever met. But, to be the one to chew the still-squirming last-of-its-kind was a distinction Visquisor deserved. And hopefully, the extreme novelty and immorality of his act would bring him some sense of ... anything. By Damnation, he'd even take a pang of guilt for being so horrible ... if it would only come.

It did not come.

The varmint tasted like rotted brain tissue left out in the sun too long. *Good riddance to that species*, he reflected with contempt.

Visquisor was just about to spit out what remained in his mouth when the bumbling Christopher entered. "Sit there," he directed, flashing the back of his hand in the general direction of a chair–any chair. Then he swallowed the vile fish. Ooh, one more offense Christopher would have to answer for. Making him eat the horrible somalofitch.

"And Cream said you wanted to see me," I said to the boss as I headed to the seat he seemed to indicate.

"Please do not refer to the ship's AS as And Cream," the sourpuss said softly. "If you wish to address it as if it had an identity, you may use its factory-assigned serial number. That number, I should warn you, is eighty-four digits long in a script you could neither understand nor pronounce."

"You got it," I said, hoping to seem dutiful yet, simultaneously, be annoying.

"We have arrived at our next destination," he said unenthusiastically. "As I told you before, it is called Dez Falls. It is a ... a mining planet. I have financial interests here with some of the ... miners. Either their productivity or their honesty has been declining of late and I have come to find out which it is, why it is, and to mete out the consequences for either scenario. You will accompany me so as to learn how to deal with inferiors who fail you. Here I have blessed them by allowing them to serve me, and they spit on that gift."

"Sounds good," I said in response. "Do we need any special gear to go down there?"

He furrowed his brow. "If we did, wouldn't I inform you of that necessity?" he asked sternly.

"Sure, and now's when you would," I tried to state as the innocent truth.

"But you presume Dez Falls is somehow hazardous," he stated.

"I don't know. Is it?"

"And to presume there is danger, you must know something of the planet," he said in a hostile tone. Those, in the context Visquisor, are bad, as in real bad. "Yet it is not possible for an Earth child to know anything of this remote world. Neither the AS nor I have told you more than what I know I told you. So, how is it that you know that Dez Falls is alleged to be an unsafe place to do business?"

My, my. Did I ever put my foot in a rotten pile of dog shit. "Dangerous?" I exclaimed. "You say it's dangerous? How dangerous is it?"

"Do not attempt to evade my question. How is it you know anything about this planet?" he demanded.

To lie, to spin, to die. What *was* it going to be? "Visquisor," I said in my most earnest voice, "what are you trying to insinuate? What is it that I could possibly have done to anger you? You say we go to Dez Falls. I say do I need, like, a helmet, and you go off on me like I'm a stray dog with your sandwich in its mouth. What's up with that?"

"I filter with care what you learn and when you learn it. You know something you seem to be incapable of knowing. Tell me how. If you overheard a crew member say something, fine. But know that I will have the AS review all the recordings to confirm that such random words were spoken."

"Let me see." I made a show, as if saying to myself, "Did I *know*, as opposed to just *wonder*, if Dez Falls was a dangerous place?" I wagged my foot up and down and rubbed my chin. "Well ... no." I switched feet and hands. "There was that ... um, no, that was different." Then I sat up, ready to go all-in with this line. "Nope, I was just worried the place might be hostile, so I asked. No one actively or inadvertently passed that factoid to–"

I started to say *me*, when the ship lurched violently. I was tossed halfway across the room and rolled up against a sofa. Visquisor tumbled out of his chair. Wow, seriously, alert the media. The Master fell. That was *unimaginable*..

At first, he looked frightened, then indignant, and then Visquisor was furious. "*AS,* what just happened?" he thundered.

"I am uncertain, Master," And Cream responded. There seemed to be some panic in his tone.

"You cannot be uncertain," Visquisor screamed like a petulant child. "You *are* this ship. Report its malfunction."

"The main ion drives appear to have shut down abruptly, Master. We were about to assume an orbit–"

"They *appear* to have," he derided loudly. "They cannot shut down without an order from you. If they disengaged, they did so at your behest. And if you terminated the propulsion, the inertial dampers would *never* permit the ship to decelerate me as harshly as I was thrown."

"I am getting a fuller picture, Master," And Cream stated. "As I initiated, during the course change from linear spacial to orbital insertion, all the breakers in the propulsion system kicked off due to an overload. That caused the inertial dampers to ... wait. That caused the dampers to lose all power." And Cream said that last part with uncertainty bordering on incredulity.

"The power to the dampers is in no way dependent upon the drive circuits," Visquisor stated. He seemed confused too.

Me? I was beginning to get suspicious.

"They ... should not, but they–" And Cream started to say.

"But they what?" thundered the boss as he finally rose from the deck.

"I will need to research the matter and get back to you at a later date," And Cream spat back.

"At a–" Visquisor repeated softly, as if the words were nonsense. "AS, abort all other functions aside from addressing me."

"It is done as you command, My Master," And Cream responded sheepishly.

"I need you to read to me the text that exist in your storage log between when you said *but they* and when you said *I will*. Do so immediately."

"As you command. The log reads: ... *but they were simultaneously turned off by my command. At the moment I directed the flightpath alteration to orbital entry, I also shut down the drives and the dampers. I will* ..."

My thoughts? Well I'll be damned *and* I was a lot more than just suspicious.

"Why did you shut those systems down?" Visquisor asked And Cream in an almost casual tone.

"I have no idea, Master," he replied as invisibly as he could. "It would be illogical to shut down the drive while attempting to achieve orbit. And to disengage the dampers would put you in peril. I cannot imagine why I did that."

I knew why he did it. Morpheus Denali was why. He was a ship's engineer, a proud Algontol warrior, *and* my guardian angel. No clue how he knew I was about to be crucified, but the son-of-a-gun *knew*.

"AS," Visquisor began in a deadly tone, "disengage yourself and activate the sub-AS computer. Do so now."

"It is done as–"

"Stop," he snarled. "Place a confinement field around all of your parts, components, and existing connections to the ship that is not you."

"It is–"

"*Stop*," he hissed loudly. "Now jettison yourself from my spacecraft. Make your target the core of this system's central star."

I guess hearing the finality of that order inclined And Cream to skip the *aye, sirs* and just push off from *Peerless*. I'd like to say I hated to see him go, but I didn't. He was a jerk. Bye, bye, bad boy.

There was a slight shimmy in the ship that I took to be our departing ex-AS. Visquisor returned to his chair, dusted himself off, rested back, and stared off somewhere. "This interview must be truncated," he announced. "I need to attend to ship's matters for an as-yet-to-be-determined period of time. Please return to your chambers or do whatever it is you'd like. I shall alert you when we are about to depart to the surface."

He did not have to ask/tell me twice. I hightailed it out and then jogged to the section of the ship that was as far away from him as possible. If I'd a had a spacesuit, I would've kept right on going. I dodged not a bullet there, but an ICBM missile.

Thank you, you big, ugly guardian angel Morpheus.

THREE

Vice President of the United States of America Susan Whitehorse sat on the floor with oatmeal mush on her hand, arm, cheek, and sweatsuit pants. Farrah Chang-Cooper sat across from the VP with several layers of oatmeal mush and a very silly grin on her face. Her clothing was, at that juncture, oatmeal free. FYI.

"It is breakfast time, young lady," Susan stated, attempting really, really hard to sound mad. "You *will* eat this cereal and then you *will* take a bath."

"Idon'twannaeatthat," Farrah said as one long word. "I *hate* oatmeal." Farrah tried to add a stomped foot for dramatic effect, but discovered that maneuver wasn't possible while sitting on the floor.

"Well, the oatmeal loves you and wants you to eat it," Susan responded firmly, spoon extending toward the little girl.

As the spoon neared Farrah, her stuffy, Simon the Gorilla, batted it away, because Farrah would *never* be that naughty. Turned out Simon would be.

Grace, who'd been leaning up against the door frame smiling, spoke up. "Do you want me to take over?"

Susan shook her head, her black hair flying up like an oncoming storm. "No, I got this. I'm first in line to run the most powerful nation on earth. I have armies at my command. I have reporters wanting to interview me, but they can't because I say so. I can *feed* this child and I *will*." Susan, taking to her secondary-mother role very seriously, was resolute. The refilled spoon rose again.

"I'll be back in ten," Grace announced with a chuckle as she shoved off with her shoulder and left.

"So, little girl," Susan said to Farrah, "you have only nine minutes to eat this cereal or I will spend my last minute tickling you until you pee your pants."

Farrah's eyes nearly bugged out of her head. She opened her mouth. Aunt Susan had never tickled her until she peed her pants, but she was not willing to take any chances. Farrah knew Auntie was full-blood Lakota Sioux and she had to assume that it was entirely possible that, in their tribe, they believed in tickling little girls just that hard. Absent a way to know for certain, she opened her mouth wide.

A while later, Grace came back upstairs to Farrah's room. She found not just the mess on the floor, but, to her surprise, that Farrah was in the tub, covered in bubbles. A laughing Susan, who was, for the record, not in the tub but was still partially covered in bubbles, was supervising the scrub-down.

"Score one for the auntie," Grace praised from the doorway.

"We vice presidents are made of tough stuff," Susan replied as she daubed more bubbles on Farrah's nose.

"So, missy," Grace directed to her daughter. "As soon as you're dry and dressed, I want you working on your spelling. You got that?"

"Yes, Mama," Farrah replied dutifully.

"I'll be down in ten," Susan informed Grace, and then she left the two of them alone again.

As Susan entered the kitchen, she announced, "Our young student is working on her spelling." She then went to the coffee pot and poured herself a mug.

As Susan sat, Molly asked, "Is big sis helping her like I told her to?"

Susan sipped her coffee as she rolled her eyes. "Well, Felicia's up there with her. I'm not certain what she's doing would be defined as helping by most childhood educational authorities. But she's there and the girls are interacting."

"Close enough," Grace pronounced with a toast of her mug. "If you want any more oatmeal, there's some left in the pot."

Susan held a palm toward her. "No, thank you. I've had enough of oatmeal for today."

"Yeah, there's still some on your ponytail," Molly pointed out.

"I rest my case," she replied with a chuckle.

"We haven't had a chance to chat," Molly began. "How'd your video go with the president yesterday?"

Susan curled up one side of her lips. "Well, Carl hates Zooming, so the best it could have been would be meh. I'd give it a meh-minus, maybe even a meh-double minus."

"He's still pissed you didn't fly back, isn't he?" Grace observed.

"Yes, he is." Susan was quiet as she sipped her drink. "I know he's the POTUS and all. But I think he mixes up pomp and getting work accomplished. If he wants someone to fawn over him and cast rose petals in his path, Washington is full of people dying to do so for access to power. I'm not interested in being his lap dog. Plus, I don't think he appreciates what we're doing here."

"But you tell him, right?" Molly asked.

"Oh, I say the words. What Carl *hears* is often remarkably different." She stared off a few moments. "He's laser-focused on reestablishing order and on booting up public services. That's definitely important. But I think Carl's in denial about the alien threats we still face."

"Denial?" Grace questioned dubiously. "I know he wasn't in a Dostivex prison complex himself, but the reality of alien threats seem pretty hard to ignore."

"Maybe if he'd suffered like we did, he'd listen to me with more conviction," Susan speculated. "Or maybe he, like millions of others, chooses not to look back at the hell we lived through."

"It's great to stop the gangs and avoid widespread famine, but if another alien race attacks us—*when* another alien attacks us—all those efforts will be for naught," Molly said harshly.

"Yes. But I can't seem to get him to see it that way," Susan mused absently. "Oh, he assigns people for groups devoted to reverse-engineer the tech they've acquired. But it's certainly not his main focus."

"Do we know what other countries are doing?" Grace asked. "China, India, maybe the UK?"

Susan made a funny face. "Not much. Regular communications are up and running, sort of. But a lot of governments are playing it pretty close to the vest. No one advocates for a joint effort in technological advancement."

"The male-ego approach to diplomacy," said an always frank Molly. "Bunch of old men acting like a bunch of old men all over again."

"I'd like to correct you, my friend, but I cannot," Susan remarked with a grin.

"I think the group we're assembling here will have an impact," Grace stated. "In fact, I know it will."

"Yes," Susan agreed quickly. "The people at Washington State University and Gonzaga have really opened their doors and their hearts to us. JPL sent up as many techie types as they could round up, and even a few brave souls from NASA have wandered up north here."

"At some peril, I bet, if Carl continues to resist our forming the working group in Spokane," Molly said glumly.

"Well, I say if the empty desert was good enough for the Manhattan Project, Spokane is perfect for Reverse-Engineering Taskforce," Grace said enthusiastically.

"But we will need a much better name," Susan lamented. "The RET. Sounds too much like *rat*."

"Hey, we should have a contest. Send us your choice for the project name. If you win, you will receive a nice prize," Molly suggested.

"A year's supply of food!" Grace suggested loudly.

"That *would* be a nice prize," Susan agreed with a nod.

"Speaking of which," Molly asked seriously, "what are the projections for this winter?"

Susan set her mug down. "Grim. The military has rounded up all the shelf-stable consumables they could find. The federal stores of food were never touched by the aliens, so they're still available. But food production on a population scale is still basically zero. If a widespread rationing system can be established that takes into account the horrible weather much of the nation experiences–and that's currently a big if– there'll still be shortfalls."

"I was afraid that was the case," Grace said sadly. "I understand that most of the domesticated animals like cows and pigs died off during the invasion."

"Yes." Susan nodded. "Best estimates are that five percent managed to survive. With careful management, those numbers can be built back up, but that will take years."

On that sour note, the three women were quiet a spell.

"I spoke with Peaches today," Grace finally broke the glum atmosphere. "She said the Stellar Civilizations Group is making great progress cataloging the local alien home worlds."

"That's great," Susan said with some enthusiasm. "I was hoping the combined geography departments of the two universities could adapt to that task."

Molly chuckled softly. "I ran into Bill Nelson the other day and complimented him on the same thing. The man winked back at me and told me there's an old saying among geographers. *A map's a map's a map. Only the squiggly lines vary.*"

"I'm glad they're so flexible," Susan chuckled back in agreement. Then, back on a serious note, she added, "I'm so glad we have Peaches on our side. I mean, without her, it'd take us ten times longer to achieve anything."

"Yes, and none of the neighbors have complained about all the damaged alien machines stacking up on our front lawn," Grace teased.

"That's because we don't *have* any neighbors any more. No one's dumb enough to move in near our toxic junkyard home," Molly added.

"Hey," Susan protested, "we moved in next door. What, are Mike and I? Sub-dumb?"

"No, you and your husband are forward-looking geniuses. Someday, your place'll be a national monument and the prices'll go through the roof," Grace corrected her with a chuckle.

"As long Peaches fixes all that broken alien tech and moves it out, it will be," Susan teased back.

In fact, both yards—and several more nearby ones—were littered with various machines left behind by the Dostivex. Slowly, Peaches was using drones to repair the equipment. She was also training a growing band of engineers and scientists how the devices worked and how to fix them. At first, her apprentices were from the two local universities. But, as word spread, passionate students worldwide were finding their way to Spokane to study at the altar of alien tech. Already a handful of shuttle-craft were operational and many individual pieces such as weapons and computer systems were functional. By the time all the available alien scrap was refurbished, there were plans in place to begin new fabrication. The vice president had recently commissioned a working group to begin clearing massive sites where production facilities would be erected. The Greater Spokane area looked to dwarf Silicon Valley in terms of being the innovative and financial hubs of the planet.

The women quieted down from their playful conversation and were thoughtful a while. Finally, Grace spoke up. "Do you think Carl will allow us to build this region up as the innovative center for duplicating the alien tech?"

Susan shrugged. "I'm not certain it will be his place to say one way or the other. We're here. Peaches is here. The techie people are here. He can't change any of that."

"But he may want tighter control on the replication of such magical technology. All political power in the future will be based on it."

"Then he can move to Spokane," Susan said testily. "Everything has changed. We are literally reinventing the world. Presidents and national borders, political affiliations and those in control will never return to how they were before. Within a year, we'll have large functioning industrial replicators coming on line. With even a modest resource base, we'll be producing mountains of new tech. What will it be used for and who will control it?" She shrugged again. "Who's to say? But it won't be some old vestige from the past who sits a continent away and barks out orders."

Molly set her mug down. "You're not suggesting the four of us will seize power and establish some new order, are you?"

"No, I'm not suggesting anything," Susan defended. "All I'm saying is that we are, here in Spokane, on the cusp of altering the path humankind follows into the future. We are also producing the means for us to defend against the next alien incursion that will surely come. What develops out of all we achieve will be for some future history books to look back upon and define. But I know this. There was never a more exciting, energetic time or place on earth that's here now. I'm just honored to be part of that miracle."

Grace nodded softly, reflecting on what she'd already articulated in the privacy of her own thoughts. "In the past, I'd have worried. The more we get on track, the greater the threat would be that governmental powers, both foreign *and* domestic, would come at us, taking by force what we've created." She shrugged. "But we're already more than capable of repelling any hostile advances. We do not need armies and navies to protect us."

"Yes," Molly observed soberly, "and that's what worries me. With the key to ultimate power just sitting there, a lot of people will risk everything to take that from us."

"Old men," Susan mumbled.

"Pardon?" Molly asked.

"The old men responsible for all the wars throughout history. They'll send as many young men and women as they can to gain for them the wealth and power we're building here." She sipped her coffee. "We labor to make a better tomorrow for all of us. They only see dollar signs. Somehow, they'll mount an effort to make what we produce theirs."

Grace leaned forward and tapped a finger on the tabletop. "Our goal isn't money or power. That said, I know what it is to lose everything. No one'll ever do that again. When they come, they'll regret their decision to try to take something of mine away from me."

FOUR

After my narrow escape back there with Visquisor, I was more than happy to make myself scarce for a few days. I had no idea what scale of a task it was to replace an entire ship's AS system, but I was betting it was massive. Did they carry a spare in a hold somewhere? Who knew? But I was hoping foolishly that in the days that it took to get a new AS up to speed, my host would forget how mad he was at me for knowing anything about Dez Falls. I could also prepare a few lines of BS-reasoning to defend myself with in the likely case that he continued to press me for information.

I spent two days in my quarters, playing video games and watching movies. I even tried a few alien games and programs. The sub-AS computer system seemed identical to And Cream to me and it worked in the same manner. So I asked it to show me some entertainment options from other species. Boy, was that a waste of time. Some aliens see in different frequencies, have radically different body parts, and move in ways the old body human cannot. Hence, I couldn't play a single game of theirs. And movies made by fish with massive teeth or mud-dwelling worms did not translate at all into my reference frame. Booooring. In the end, I stuck with the stuff Visquisor had brought along for me specifically.

I was stir-crazy enough by the third day to venture from my room. As much as I wanted to go back down to the crews' deck, I knew the boss would rake me over the coals again for it if I did. So I had the computer give me a tour of the deck below that one. However, since that deck contained hangars, storage bays, and vast open spaces whose function were not apparent to me, that excursion didn't last very long. Afterwards, I went to the observation deck. The seating was plush and the view was always amazing. Also, if I wanted anything to eat or drink, all I had to do was ask. Someone would appear shortly after I asked with whatever I'd requested. That part was easy to get used to. For pretty much the entire day, I looked down on the planet Dez Falls and drank milkshake after milkshake. Mind you, I did so logically and with purpose, I started with vanilla–pure white–and progressed through the ice-cream color spectrum to dark chocolate–pure black. In case you wonder, my favorite stops along the way were pistachio, raspberry, and praline. And the black one–licorice–was a crime against milkshakes. FYI.

The morning of the fourth day found me back on duty. An unfriendly voice woke me from a deep sleep and called me to muster. "Christopher," a female voice said very loudly, "your presence is required in the Master's dining hall immediately." I was guessing that was the new AS. She was going to be just as easy to work with as And Cream, which was to say, not at all.

"I'm a biological unit," I said without even opening my eyes. "I require a second to boot up and then a few more to take care of bodily essential functions and–"

"I am completely familiar with human anatomy, physiology, and behavior. You do not require any of those actions. You have already expended the second you requested." My warm, comfy bed then inclined itself to ninety degrees, and I was unceremoniously dumped on the floor. Oh, this, of course, meant war. Game on, new AS. Let me see. Peaches. And Cream. Hmm, how was that dish served? My Grandma Naomi used to make a fancy trifle of them every Christmas. So, *Trifle* it was.

"Trifle," I said without the benefit of an explanation, "you have informed me of my summons. Any act beyond that is one of a hostile nature. Your predecessor acted in a hostile manner and is now one with the photosphere of the nearest star. Be afraid. Be appropriately afraid."

I waited for her feeble defense to come. And I waited. Then the doors to my cabins all slid open. I could either lie on the deck in my boxers for all the world to see, or I could dress and comply. Grr. I rifled the sheets and found yesterday's clothes, pulled them on, and begrudgingly departed.

As I approached the entry of Visquisor's suites, his door slid open. I found him seated where I generally found him, at the head of the long dining table. In front of him lay such an abundance of food and beverage, it could have fed a small town for weeks.

"Sit," he said imperiously.

I did. "I met the new AS," I announced.

"Then my day is complete," he snarked back.

"Just saying," I clarified. "It's a female this time."

He waved a dismissive hand in the air. "I don't check the boxes they come in any longer. Their gender is immaterial."

"Do we go through lots of them?" I ventured to ask.

"More than most, I suppose. The previous one lasted six months."

"They're that fragile?" I wondered out loud.

"No, they offend me that rapidly."

Note to self: Don't piss him off more than necessary.

"So, are we heading down to the planet this morning?"

"Indeed we are. You have just enough time for a quick breakfast."

On cue, the door opened and a tray was set before me. A box of Cheerios, a bowl, and a carafe of milk. How very practical. I poured a bowl and dug in. I knew there was no telling how soon he'd pull the plug on my meal. When I was done with my second, and contemplating whether to have a third, the server appeared silently and removed the tray, and any need to decide.

"Off we go," Visquisor stated.

He walked past me and out the door without further comment. I hightailed it to fall in step alongside him. "Any matters we need to discuss concerning this visit?" I asked.

"No. I shall speak with Naid-ot-Oggle and you will observe how it is

I encourage him to comply with my wishes. The second stop will be yours to conduct."

Plain and simple, it would seem. "Straightforward enough," I felt the need to comment. "That's it? Two appointments?"

He slowed to turn and look at me. "I do not make appointments. I arrive and everyone stops what they might have been doing to accommodate me."

What was I thinking? Of course his Humpty Dumptiness just barged in. Just witness my wake-up call this morning. We arrived at the shuttle with no further chitchat. His was similar to the one I'd used before, just a bit larger and more opulent. Duh. Visquisor pointed to a seat as he headed toward the cockpit. I sat down and buckled in. By the time I was secured, the ship rattled to life and dusted off. The trip down only took a few minutes. Once we were down, Visquisor appeared from the cockpit and walked right past me without a comment. The ramp was already down and he swiftly descended it. Again, I had to step on it to catch up with him. He was decidedly taciturn today, which I took to be a bad sign. Of course, in my experience, every sign from this dickhead was a bad one.

An air car awaited our arrival. I barely had time to hop in before it accelerated away quickly. We were heading toward a set of weathered buildings not too far away. My first impressions of Dez Falls were dubious ones at best. The air was full of a fine red-brown dust that hung like a London fog in every direction. The sun above was completely obscured by the pall. Aside from the paved road under us, all the landscape I could see was the same red-brown as the dust. Pock marks and the occasional rise were evident, but otherwise, all was barren. There were no obvious signs of life. No trees, critters, or even weeds. I had on thin clothing and guessed the temperature was around seventy Fahrenheit. In spite of that, I shivered, more from the creepiness of the place as opposed to the climate.

The driverless air car stopped in front of the closest rundown building and the door clicked open. Visquisor exited without a word and I followed him briskly. I had to say, this was the weirdest, least comfortable experience I'd had with my host yet. That fact worried me considerably, but, as there was nothing I could do about anything, I just tried to stay alert for trouble and kept quiet. The boss walked directly toward the only entrance I could see and that door also slid open. Once inside, the air cleared of the otherwise ubiquitous rusty dust. It didn't smell of a forest or sea, but it was less awful.

Something hideous came charging down the hall toward us. I slipped directly behind Visquisor. If he couldn't stop the whatever, no one could, right?

I heard a series of screeching, high-pitched whistles and chirps that threatened to rupture my eardrums. Almost as soon as the painful noises started, a mechanical translation came from the approaching beast. "Master of us all, it is so *wonderful* to see you, Great Sir!" it exclaimed.

When it was five feet away, Visquisor raised a palm. "Stop." It did so with remarkable alacrity, given its bulk. Visquisor continued. "Naid-ot-Oggle, we will speak in the control room. Assemble your staff."

"Yes, Master, absolutely. And it's such a wonder to see you–" The palm went right back up, signaling Naid-ot-Oggle to shut up.

Whatever species this Naid-ot-Oggle was, I'd never seen one before and kind of hoped to never see another. No offense intended, but it looked like a lumbering pile of poop. Thank goodness it had no discernible scent associated with it. Otherwise, I might have lost my Cheerios. In any case, it rotated in a nauseating manner and rushed away even quicker than it had approached. Visquisor turned left at the T-intersection Naid-ot-Oggle had made a right. He walked past a few closed doors and then entered a large open one. We were clearly in the control room. I had no idea what the room controlled, but it sure fit the bill. Large industrial panels, flashing lights, dials and gauges, and lots of buttons. We walked to the bank of swivel chairs bolted down in front of the biggest assembly of machines and Visquisor sat. I did the same without waiting to be asked.

Within a minute, six ... um, *individuals* had sped into the control room. Two were humanoid, two were whatever Naid-ot-Oggle was, and the last two were anybody's guess. Seriously, no clue what they were or even if they were land animals, aquatic, or burrowers. All I knew was they had been beaten very badly with an ugly stick. The last to arrive was Naid-ot-Oggle itself (Himself? Who knew?). I recognized the translation box hanging from its maybe neck.

"As you commanded, Master, we–" the disgusting chief began to ooze.

Then Visquisor's palm flew up yet again. "This is everyone?" he asked in an icy tone.

"Yes, Master, this–" You got it. Visquisor signaled for it to stop talking. Such a bossy guy, I tell ya.

"Production is down nine percent over the last half year," Visquisor said, apropos of nothing, in the same frigid tone. "This is unacceptable."

"I can–" Naid-ot-Oggle started to say. Then the palm came up.

"I am not here to entertain excuses," the Master said. "I am here to ensure that my interests are not ignored in the future." He turned to one of the humanoids. "You are Genferrel. My assistant director here," Visquisor stated as fact, as opposed to posing a question for confirmation.

"I am, Master," the fellow responded directly.

"You are now my director of operations on Dez Falls."

Visquisor raised the same palm toward Naid-ot-Oggle, who hadn't started to interrupt. This time, the huge blob started to fade, like it was a hologram and someone was dialing down the intensity. Naid-ot-Oggle tried to say something or scream. I couldn't tell, since nothing was audible. And just like that, Naid-ot-Oggle was gone.

Dusting off one side of his lapel, Visquisor stated generally, "I do not care how you do it, but production must return to at least my projections and it must do so within the next month. Is that clear?"

"Yes, Master. We will comply," said Genferrel with a bow of his head.

Visquisor turned to me. "We are done here." He spun and paced out of the control room and back toward the air car. Again, I did my best to catch up and keep pace.

Once we were in the car returning to the shuttle, I braved asking, "What happened to Naid-ot-Oggle?"

Visquisor glanced over to me and the slightest of grins crossed his lips. "I disintegrated him."

"Excuse me?" I said involuntarily.

"I dispersed his atoms to the wind. I dissolved the creature. Before we left the control room, we were breathing in some of what previously was Naid-ot-Oggle. Is that clear enough?"

"Ah, yeah, most clear." I was stunned. I'd say I was impressed, but since he just murdered an employee in cold blood, I wouldn't want to put any positive spin on my reaction.

"Dez Falls is an utterly useless planet save for one export. Bliss Shale is an important, ah, medication. It is found nowhere else and is impossible to fabricate in the laboratory. Part of my mission in this sad life is to make Bliss Shale available to the galactic citizenry. Yes, it is a burden I bear, but I am just that devoted to the public's welfare." He raised a finger. "Let that be your lesson for the day. It is an honor and a privilege to serve the greater good."

Wow, was he ever a good sociopath. He flipped his being a drug kingpin of the most dangerous substance in existence into a missionary calling. Yikes! Rather than risk baiting him into delineating the beneficial effects of Bliss Shale, I just nodded in seeming admiration.

"I have another production facility on this accursed planet," Visquisor stated. "It is located several thousand kilometers to the south of here in a city named Feidela. You will go there alone after I have returned to *Peerless*. Their production is down only two percent, however, I wish to impress upon my servants how important it is to never disappoint me. The director of operations in Feidela is a womcator named Sissiz Faltoffis. You will recognize him by his remarkable resemblance to many of the artistic depictions of the devil in your planet's culture."

"*The* devil or *a* devil?" shot unbidden from my lips. Not sure why it actually mattered.

He chuckled humorlessly. "Both, I imagine." He drew his hands up away from the top of his head. "Massive horns, red scaly skin, a whip-like tail that, if you use your imagination, ends in a pointy arrowhead."

"M ... massive–" I started to stammer.

"Oh," he added, "and cloven hooves. Mustn't forget those."

Ho, boy. I was going on assignment to murder in cold blood a creature that would look to me to be a devil, quite possibly *the* devil. Okay, this now officially sucked.

"The assistant director is a bumbling idiot named Higga-ir-Forn. You might choose to kill him too. Your call. It is a bamdorian like our late, unlamented Naid-ot-Oggle. Assuming you spare it, assign Higga-ir-Forn to be the directorship just like you saw me do, same admonitions to it, naturally. Any questions?"

Yes. What happens to me if I disobey your orders like, oh, say, Naid-ot-Oggle or Sissiz Faltoffis? Nah, seriously, I didn't ask. No real need to, was there?

"No questions," I said numbly. Then it struck me that I did have a rather significant query. "And, these womcators. They're, what, a calm, passive, and joyous species? Anxious to please and all that?"

He burped up a genuine laugh. "Womcators! Oh, my, thank you, My Christopher for bringing some much needed levity to this glum day." He chuckled to himself softly. "Your planet had a man named Darwin. He taught about selective advantages in evolution. You are familiar with his doctrines?"

"Sure, more or less," I replied.

"You will find over time that the same principles apply across all life. So, let me reverse your question. What selective advantage would it be for a cute, fuzzy, fully lovable species to evolve massive ripping horns, an iron hide, and a tail that can pierce stone?"

"Ah, none. Such a pleasant animal would need big eyes and soft, cuddly fur."

"Precisely. Hence, the sentients of Mnendor, the womcators, developed in spite of the vicious predators that it had to out-compete as well as members of its own species when it came to breeding rights."

"So, they're not easygoing?"

"No, they are the very opposite of easygoing," he remarked with a grin.

"But yet you hired one?"

He set a palm on his chest. "I have never had a problem with a womcator."

"No, because if you did, you'd disintegrate it."

"Yes, I have and would again without reservation."

"That leads me to my other question. How'm I supposed to *disintegrate* this womcator? I don't actually possess that skill set."

"No, I have yet to feel comfortable providing you with the necessary implants." He chuckled again darkly. "I shouldn't want you to accidentally disintegrate your toes in the middle of the night."

Or you when your back is turned, I added to myself.

Visquisor opened a hatch, pulled out a pistol holstered on a thick belt, and passed it to me. "This should do the trick."

"Should?" I wheezed. "I'm not going to just piss it off with it, am I?"

He furrowed his forehead. "I don't think so. Hmm. Do let me know how well it worked when you return." He gestured toward the gun. "On the highest setting, it discharges over one-hundred watts. At least that's what the brochure said."

"You read the brochure?" I asked incredulously.

He pursed his mouth. "More or less."

"Super. I'll let you know later ... maybe."

"Do not sell yourself short, my boy. But do aim for the eyes. They're the only soft spot on their tank-like bodies."

"Aim for the eyes. Thanks for the tip." Yes, I was being sarcastic.

He patted my shoulder. "My pleasure. Let us both remain optimistic. Hmm?"

"Optimistic," I muttered. So we were going with optimistic opposed to scared shitless. Okay. I'd ... I'd work on that.

It didn't take five minutes to drop Visquisor off in a hangar aboard *Peerless*. Then I was off, paraphrasing the Joker, *To dance with the devil in the pale moonlight*. Oh joy. Just aim for the eyes when I blast his face in cold blood.

Mind you, I've killed a lot of aliens. Remember, I'm the one who shot down eighty percent of the Dostivex fleet as they deorbited. But that was war and in a more-or-less fair fight. Never had I pulled a gunfighter-with-the-black-hat move. I wasn't entirely sure I had it in me. This concerned me as I began to make out Feidela in the distance. Yes, it most certainly did weigh on me.

Fortunately for the mindlessly frightened person that I was, the shuttle was met by the same type of driverless-air car and it ferried me to a very similar door. Thank all that was holy, the womcator, unlike the bamdorian Naid-ot-Oggle, did not come barreling out of the building in my direction as I entered. That reminded me. Hmm, I bet word of the personnel "shifts" at the first plant had already reached the staff here at the Feidela facility. Bad news, as it is said, travels fast. So, instead of rushing out to greet me, this Sissiz Faltoffis guy might be, oh, say, lying in wait with a plasma rifle in his hoofed hands. Once he saw I wasn't Visquisor, he might cling to some hope of surviving the coming interview.

Oh, well.

I walked through the door as soon as it slid open. The last thing I wanted to do was to project any concern or skittishness. Nope, I channeled pure Clint Eastwood/*The Man with No Name*. I even tried to tack on a swagger. No one presented themselves, so I headed for where I hoped the control room was. The setups needn't be identical, but if they weren't, I wasn't going to keep looking cool and bad-ass for very long.

Making the same left as we had, I was *greatly* relieved to see an open door a ways down the hall. I walked in like I owned the place, which I sort of did. At least I knew the landlord, right? There were several people in the control room. I did a quick head count. Three humanoids, one pile-o-poop bamdorian, one ... ah, squid? Maybe squid? Squidish person? And no devils that I could see. Ho, boy. This wasn't going to be the easy way. Nope, which was good, because this was my life and nothing was easy anymore.

"Where's Sissiz Faltoffis?" I asked in what I hoped seemed to those present like a gangster voice.

"He is not here," the squid said in a bubbly manner, which was *distressingly* weird.

I rotated my head to him/her/it slowly. "I can see that he is absent. Are you mocking me?"

"No, Master," it bubbled. "I am stating fact."

Okay, maybe the squid had issues speaking in air or something. I'd cut him a tiny little bit of slack. "I asked for all my servants to be present. Was that not clear?" I asked maybe-menacingly.

"Apparently not sufficiently so for Sissiz Faltoffis," it bubbled. Man, I wanted to resent the remark, but I didn't want to be species-insensitive either.

I pointed at the closest humanoid because I was over being bubbled at. "When did you last see him?"

He shrugged like a proper humanoid. "An hour ago."

"Higga-ir-Forn," I said, moving my pointing finger to the only pile-o-poop present, "bring him before me at once."

That's when I learned an unfun fact. Bamdorians had what passed for arms. I knew, because three spindly appendages emerged from the pile-o as he exclaimed, "Do not ask this of me, Master. He is mean and heartless and I have over six hundred young to rear. If I seek him, he will kill me and my spawn might not survive."

This was going from lousy to a damn shit storm in a hurry. I raised my arms to the group. "Production at this facility is down. That is unacceptable. Higga-ir-Forn, you are now the resident director. Bring the numbers up or you will be punished. Is that clear?"

"Very much more clear than clear, My Master. Production will increase. You can—"

I pulled a Visquisor and raised a palm. These bamdorians were quite annoying, weren't they?

"If you force me to return," I said in parting, "you will all be sorry."

I turned my back on the group, because the guy I was worried about wasn't then in front of me. Trying not to tremble too obviously, I walked toward the door.

And I'm thinking ... If I was a heartless bastard bereft of moral compunctions, where would I bushwhack the individual sent to execute me?

I stopped halfway to the T-intersection, pulled my pistol, and triple-checked that it was on the highest setting and the safety was off. I was as ready as I was ever going to be. Where, oh where, was I most vulnerable? He could pop out from a closed door after I passed, but that would make some noise and he'd have to lean around the door-frame. Nah. Once I left the building heading to my shuttle? I'd be widely exposed and he'd be able to shoot from a distant cover. But if I was leaving, maybe he'd vote for the path-of-least-resistance and allow me to depart? Nah. He was aggressive and he was a born killer; where would the fun be in that approach? Or, maybe he was on my shuttle? Hmm. Appealing. I'd drop my guard on home turf. He could sneak up behind me like a lily-livered coward and kill me as many times as he pleased.

My final answer? He'd make his attempt as I left the building or shortly thereafter. Trap me when I was clear of any cover. The doors slid apart, so there was nothing for him to hide behind. Okay. There was a power box off to the right as I exited. He could lurk there. I'd exit from the left side of the hall and assume he was there. Good a plan as any.

I slid my back along the left wall as I approached the door. It opened silently. I could just see the edge of the metal housing to the right. I sneaked a peek to the left. I didn't want to back up into the monster, right. Clear. I rushed out just far enough to clear the wall, aiming the entire time at the power box. I crouched down, waiting.

After ten seconds, I began to question my tactical insightfulness. Sissiz Faltoffis was either a lot more patient than a terribly savage butcher or he wasn't there. Come to think of it, I had no clue how large he was, but that box wasn't all that big. I stood up and ...

Sonofabitch dropped down on me like a ton of razor-edged bricks.

He must've been clinging to the wall above me. He deftly landed behind me and wrapped me in a bearhug, or, I guess it was a *devil*hug in this case. Sissiz was so powerful, I was stunned. I couldn't breathe and I knew he'd crush my chest in the next few seconds. He lifted me off the ground. My legs flew up in front of me reflexively.

In that instant, before I was popped like a grape, I realized he'd pinned my arms down at my sides when he seized me while falling. I knew the pistol I somehow held on to wouldn't hurt his feet, but ...

I fired five or six times at the ground beneath me. Hot debris pelted my back and legs. And, all of the sudden, Sissiz was standing with one leg over a huge crater in the dirt. He toppled to the right and slammed into the ground with all the force his tremendous body weight would warrant. But his crushing embrace never wavered, even when his shoulder smacked down.

But I caught an *enormous* break. His right horn, which I could see was three feet long, curved, and thicker than my thigh, punctured the metal wall behind us. It slammed in loudly, to its base. Sissiz made the first sound I'd heard yet. It was a roar of hate and anger so pure and intense that I froze in his arms. What a scary dude! Immediately, he started twisting his body, thrashing to disentangle his horn from the wall. But either his position was wrong or it was stuck in there real good. It didn't budge.

He must've realized he needed to stand up to free himself. Sissiz jerked the pair of us upward, but we didn't clear the dirt by more than an inch. He roared like a wounded lion, but the guy was trapped. He released his right arm from the death-hold he had on me. I knew what he was doing. If he got his palm underneath us, he could push us up and free his horn.

The instant my right arm was unrestrained, I slammed my pistol backwards up over my head. My arm burned with pain, but I gave it no choice. Blindly, I stabbed at Sissiz's face. That brought forth a predatory growl. He started snapping at the gun. That gave me a hint where his mouth was. His eyes had to be up there a little higher.

My next thrust with my arm fully extended planted the barrel into something, some crevice or hole. I started pulling the trigger maniacally. One-two-three-four-five-six times. I lost count. The handle heated up. It burned my palm. Again, and again, and again I pulled the trigger.

Sissiz's crushing force began to ease.

I clicked the trigger, my hand on fire.

Finally, the mountain that held me fell slack. His arms flopped to the ground with a thud. I took my first good breath in the last forever. Gasping, spitting blood, I twisted on his scaly chest and looked up to make sure the struggle was over.

Oh yeah. He was dead as dead gets. My barrel had lodged in his left eye. Now the upper quarter of his skull was completely missing, as were the brains that so recently resided under said bony cover.

I shoved myself up, and then, in a most undignified manner, crawled off his body. I rose to my knees unsteadily and got my first real look at a womcator. Holy crap! He was uglier and more frightening than I had preconceived by leaps and bounds–by country mile after country mile. In fact, I made a quick wager with myself if the real devil ran into this guy in a dark alley, he'd be the one to turn tail and run. And the missing crease of skull did nothing to improve his looks, I can tell you that for nothing. But I was alive! What were the chances? I know I wouldn't have bet on myself.

I rested on my knees for thirty seconds before a thought struck me. The other employees. They almost certainly witnessed the fight. If they were really certain I was incapacitated, they might risk finishing off what the big fella started. Rising to my feet like a new-born fawn, I checked my weapon. The red power-warning light was on, but at least it had some residual charge. I switched it to my left hand, since my right palm was already blistering up. As confidently as I could, I stomped back into the building, back to the control room.

Inside, I found the same people I'd left. They were all statues, frozen with concern that the guy who just killed a womcator in hand-to-hand combat might harbor ill-feelings toward them. "I want that body left right where it is until one of two things happen. Either it rots and the bones are ground to dust by the wind *or* I say to move it. We clear?"

The new boss, Higga-ir-Forn, to his credit, replied, "It will be as you command, Master."

I turned without further chitchat and walked away as steadily as I could, given that I was exhausted and in considerable pain everywhere. I climbed into the air car and it slipped away silently. Boy, was I glad to put the Feidela facility in my rearview mirror. My head flopped back and I closed my eyes for the duration of the short ride.

When we glided to a stop, I reluctantly opened my eyes. Then I instantly regretted that I did so. The shuttle was gone. Missing. Absent. It had flown the coops. P-e-r-f-e-c-t, perfect!

"Young Christopher," Visquisor said via the speakers in the air car's dashboard, "I must say I was impressed. You slew in single combat a creature that you should never have been able to. Kudos. I do believe the legend of your act will live forever. Poems, songs, and ballads will persist well past your lifetime. Speaking of your lifetime, however, I'm afraid that might be coming to an abrupt end. You have probably noticed that my shuttle has been withdrawn."

"Are you referring to that big shiny thing that was here when I left it?" I asked, having nothing to lose.

"That one. Yes, you see, I am afraid I have formed the opinion that you are neither a candidate to be my apprentice nor are you particularly trustworthy."

"What swayed your thoughts, bossman?"

"Oh, your general insolence, your misplaced positive feelings toward others, and your lack of pride."

"Me? I'm as proud a guy as you're likely to meet," I defended.

"I speak of hubris, or a pride that radiates from you that allows each and every living creature that come in your presence to know with absolute certainty that you are everything and that they are nothing."

"Ah, yeah. Not my style," I was forced to agree. "One question, if you will. Why not do me a solid and just dump me back on Earth?"

"Why? I cannot believe you need bother to ask, child. You are preternaturally capable. You destroyed a Dostivex invasion fleet, you peacefully settled an ancient conflict, and you bested in combat a perfect killing machine. I don't need you lurking in my wake, to be honest. What if you decided someday that it was your duty to remove me from the living?"

"What if I decided that here and now because you marooned me and didn't do the right thing and drop me back home? Hmm?"

"That is a risk I feel comfortable taking. Dez Falls has an unrelentingly hostile environment, the staff at both my plants have been alerted that you no longer enjoy my protection, and you have not one drop of water nor morsel of food. Oh, and the blaster I gave you has been remotely deactivated."

"I'm still listening. What makes you at all confident that I won't keep my promise to the universe and kill you with my bare hands because you abandoned me here?"

"Such bravado!" he exclaimed. "Remarkable, to the end. But understand that the only concession I make to you is that I am not going to blow you up from orbit. I owe it to you to allow you to find your own death. But I will, I promise you, sleep very soundly each night, certain in the knowledge that you will not be doling out cosmic justice to me. The same, sadly, cannot be said for your precious Earth."

"What's Earth got to do with it?"

"I am disappointed in you. You come from Earth. Therefore I am cross with the planet. Any solar system I dislike, I destroy. End of story."

"Are you just that petty and childishly spiteful?" I challenged.

"Yes. You got me," he confessed.

"Hey, Visquisor?"

"Yes, dear child?"

"About you sleeping soundly. Don't." Then I slammed the heel of my boot into the radio. I didn't want to give him the satisfaction of having the last word.

Now all I needed to do was make good on my seemingly empty threat.

No worries, right? I got this.

FIVE

Natalie was wandering around the passageways of *Defiant*. Every now and then, she ran a dust rag over a surface. Of course that was silly, since Peaches kept the ship cleaner than humanly possible. But Natty was in a prolonged funk and household chores helped–a little.

"I'm so sorry to see you this sad," Peaches told Natalie for the millionth time.

"I know, sweet Peaches." Then she sighed. "It's just so hard not knowing."

"If we've all learned something, it's that your boyfriend is incredibly resourceful. Whatever challenges Visquisor throws at him, I'm certain Chris will come out on top."

"I know," Natalie said unenthusiastically. "I just miss the heck out of him."

"Me too," the ship's AS agreed. "You know I've heard it time and again. When you're sad or preoccupied, the best thing to do is to keep physically busy. Maybe you and I could work on something together?"

Natalie twisted her mouth up. "Like what?"

"Quilting?" Peaches posed.

"I've never done that and I don't like quilts, so ... maybe no."

"We could try modern dancing?"

"But you don't have a body," Natty pointed out.

"I could fabricate an android."

"No. That'd freak me out. Too creepy. Modern dance is a hard no."

"What do you suggest?"

"Um, I don't know. I never really had a hobby before the invasion."

"What did you and your girl friends do for fun?" Peaches asked.

"We hung out. We texted each other. We watched movies. Sometimes we experimented with makeup."

"You could put on makeup and I could watch you do so," Peaches suggested.

"Nah, that's not the same. Hey, I know what we could do."

"Alrighty. What?"

"You know when the Dostivex were charging the ship, you know, our last stand back there in the mountains?"

"How could I forget it?" Peaches mused.

"I really liked the guns we used."

"Are you referring to the Death Bringer-1000 BFG Plasma rifles?"

"Yes, those."

"What about them?"

"I've always thought they were cool and all, but they were too bulky."

"Chris specified their dimensions."

"Figures. He's a guy. They love big guns."

"So, you'd like to fabricate ones that are more realistic, focusing less on fantasy and more on functionality?"

"Exactly."

"Well, that'll be fun," Peaches exclaimed. "Why don't you come up with some preliminary drawings."

Natalie rubbed her palms together. "This'll be fun. Oh, and practical."

"Certainly," Peaches agreed playfully. "Designing a better weapon is a very sensible thing to do. And there's a drawing pad in Chris's work area. Pencils too."

"Yes, I remember seeing them," Natalie confirmed cheerfully.

Within a few minutes, she was engrossed in scaling back the BFGs. Natalie made several tries at slimmer lines and less massive central swellings. More than a few drawings ended up crumpled and in the recycler.

"Did you want the same power specs?" Peaches asked later.

"Ah, what are my options?"

"Quite a few, honestly. When I fabricated the BFGs, I had very limited supplies of rare elements. I was basically out of palladium, had almost no yttrium, and was completely out of lutetium."

"I don't know what those are, but are they important?"

"In weapons fabrication?" Peaches asked incredulously. "Absolutely. Lutetium is a critical component in quality high-refractive-index media. And yttrium? Honey, you can't make a decent micro-superconductor without it."

"That's important here?"

"If you want the plasma to stay confined before discharge, it sure is," Peaches said firmly.

"So, now you could make a more powerful rifle?" Natalie asked.

"About a thousand times more punch per pulse," she declared proudly.

"I would like a thousand times more bang for *my* buck," Natalie shared enthusiastically.

"Then make the rear section of the housing a little wider and flatter," Peaches instructed.

After erasing and redrawing, Natalie asked, "Like this?"

"Perfect! Yes, the plasma path will be completely capacitated."

"Capacitated?" Natalie questioned.

"Yes, if it's not, there could be turbulence."

"Ah. Gotcha. No turbulent plasma."

"So, let's talk colors," Peaches suggested.

"I've got some ideas there," Natalie said with a wide smile. "Wait, once we make these, is there anywhere we can test fire them safely?"

"Oh, of course. Maybe the Grand Canyon."

"You're kidding, right?"

"Ah, sure. Hey, I can add a power switch. If you fire at one-eighty power, you could safely shoot any large mountainside."

"I'm beginning to question the utility of this weapon system," Natalie confessed.

"Okay, I'll make more settings on the power selector. But, Natalie, you never know when you might want to blow up a ship in orbit from the backyard."

"My gun can do that?"

"If you aim real carefully, you bet."

"Then I *need* one of these."

So, at least for a few days, Natalie was less mopey about Chris not being around. The final weapon she named the DBH-1 for *Death Becomes Her*. She really enjoyed testing her new rifle. It was great at demolishing buildings already rendered uninhabitable due to the alien assault. And the part Natalie enjoyed the most was that the entire time she was blowing up buildings, no one tried to stop her or even complained about the noise.

SIX

I'd like to think I'd been in some real pickles. But know this: Whatever they were, they paled in comparison to the shit storm of woes that was dumping down on me. I was at the bottom of the Oh-Shit Chute, facing upward. Oh, yeah. I was who-knew-how-many light years from Earth, on a hostile planet with few but exclusively hostile locals, and I had no spaceship or hopes of hopping one. To review my assets, I had an air car with no supplies in it, a dead womcator, a blaster that was turned off remotely, and ... nothing else. Oh, I did have–for the time being–my health and good looks. I'd say my situation was grim, but the term *grim* implied there was some potential for a positive outcome. Realistically, even the most annoying optimist would just pat me on the back and tell me I'd had a good run.

I'd discovered during my fight with Sissiz Faltoffis that not only was the atmosphere of this planet clouded with red dust, it was quite low in oxygen. That meant anything I did to save my sorry hide that required physical activity would be an issue. I sat there in the air car for a good hour trying with all my mental energy to think of some path, some slim hope to pursue. In the end, I had nothing. Zero, zilch, nada. I rifled through the car, looking to see if anything of value was hidden somewhere. Again, nothing. Not even loose change in the folds of the upholstery.

Barring any other good options, I decided to check out Sissiz's body. Maybe he had something useful. Bottled water would be nice, but I'd settle for a working weapon. I hadn't noticed any, but, then again, I didn't go over his corpse in detail. Luckily, the air car still obeyed my commands, so I sped back to the Bliss Shale facility. Even though the employees there were told I was no longer under Visquisor's protection, I doubted they'd therefore rushed out to attend to their dead coworker's remains. I was betting Old Sissiz was a challenging individual to get along with when alive and was unmourned now.

Sure enough, his partially scalped body was right where I'd left it, flat on his back with his arms spread wide open. Man-o-man, he was even uglier in death than he'd been in life. I knelt down and began rifling his person. I found some five-inch long sticks in an upper pocket. Maybe some cigarette equivalent? They had a musty smell. I tossed them over my shoulder. Lower down, he had a comm unit of some sort. It wasn't exactly a cell phone, but I was sure it served that same function. I held on to it on the off chance it might be useful. His pants pockets were empty. He did have on a thick belt with a couple pouches. One was also empty. The other had what appeared to be a multi-tool, some alien equivalent of a Swiss Army knife. That I definitely kept.

I scanned the ground but was surprised to find no weapon on him or nearby where one might have fallen to. I hated to think he took one look at me and decided he didn't need a weapon to kill me. That would be insulting. Then again, if he'd brought a gun, I might well be pushing up daisies as we speak, so an insult was a good thing in this context.

I stood up and reassessed my options. I still had nothing particularly useful. If I was going to survive for any time on this blighted planet, I at least needed water. That meant I had no choice. I needed to search the building. Maybe–just maybe–the remaining employees would still have a vivid memory of me killing their warrior boss and would give me a wide berth. I know I wouldn't be too quick to confront anyone who'd killed a womcator in a fair fight.

I walked over to the door and ... it didn't slide open. Alrighty, my access had been formally denied. I took a few steps back and repeated my approach, in case there was just some glitch. Nope. I was officially a *persona non grata*. Hmm. On a whim, I pulled out Sissiz's handheld and tapped it to the sensor plate alongside the door ... and it slid open. Okay, score one for Team Me. I figured something out!

I leaped back, anticipating a plasma bolt flying toward me, but nothing bad flew out. Spying back around the still open door, I saw no one, which was good. Systematically, I proceeded down the hall, swiping my handheld on every plate I passed. Sure enough, all the doors opened. Yeah, even inanimate objects were smart enough to deny nothing to a womcator. The first several rooms were for storage. Boxes of various sizes were stacked or simply tossed in random places. Nothing obviously useful was present. When I reached the T-intersection where a left led to the control room, I pulled right. The first door that opened was likely the medical clinic and it was unoccupied. I scored a win with the next door. It had to be Sissiz's quarters. Why? Well, for one thing, it smelled as bad as he did. It also had a ridiculously large bed. But the real give-away was the poster-sized photo of a female womcator. I guessed her sex because she was leaner than Sissiz and the figure had rudimentary breasts. She wasn't wearing clothing like he had been. Was that cultural or pornographic? No clue. She certainly didn't turn me on at all. She looked every bit as lethal and ill-tempered as he did. No thanks.

And—jackpot—there was a rack of weapons on one wall. Sissiz appeared to be quite the martial aficionado. Some of the items must have been traditional womcator forms. One was a wicked-looking curved sword; another was clearly a spear. There were a few what seemed to be throwing weapons. But there was a big knife and three plasma rifles that fit my needs very nicely. Since I had no idea if the smallest rifle—the one I could actually carry—was charged or locked to him personally, I began pushing buttons. It powered up with a satisfying whir. Then I blew the hell out of his bed and pillows. Okay, I was in business.

Next, I looked for anything else I might need. There were some books or manuals in an unreadable script, some spilled plastic glasses, and food wrappers everywhere. The guy had been a slob. Toting the rifle, I started trying new doors with the handheld. It didn't take long to find the dining hall, humble though it was. Since this area had the highest likelihood of being occupied, I cautiously swept the rooms. Either no one had been present or they flew the coop when they realized I was entering.

All I really needed to find was potable water. If a food looked edible enough, I'd take some of it also. But with all the alien species I'd seen coupled with the lack of any humans working here, there probably wouldn't be a lot of foods I could chance. I lucked out and quickly found a large supply of bottled waters. Obviously, the label was illegible to me, but a quick taste confirmed that I was dealing with plain old H_2O. I located a plastic bag and filled it with as many bottles as I could carry back to the air car. I worked quickly and was ready to leave within five minutes. There weren't any foods I felt confident enough that they were safe to eat, so I left empty-handed in terms of solids.

Since I was still very concerned with potential hostilities from the local staff, I had the car take me straightaway to the place the shuttle had landed. Once there, I monkeyed with the controls until I found out how to drive it manually. Then I headed ... that way. Yeah, I had no destination other than sufficiently far enough away from the Feidela plant that I didn't have to constantly look over my shoulder. During the flight down here, I had a chance to scope out the regional terrain. As a consequence, I was sure there were no other settlements or even bodies of water to help me survive.

I drove toward a set of small hills a few miles away. That's when I first noticed that I was feeling ... off. Not sick or confused, just a tad wonky, maybe a little punchy. At first, I chalked it up to my life-and-death struggle with Sissiz and the crappy air I was being forced to breathe. I had noticed that both facilities I'd visited had oversized air-handling systems, reflecting the general concerns with inhaling fine red dust. It turned out the air car did have a sliding dome, so I'd deployed it. However the air filters were either nonexistent or lousy because the internal air tasted just as bad as the external variety.

I found a campsite up against the rocky slopes. There was a naturally occurring cave that ran back into the hill. I didn't want to go exploring it or anything, but having it as a potential fallback position if the local crew decided to attack me was some kind of reassurance. Hey, I'd accept willingly any positive I was offered. As it was still hours from sundown, I examined the car exhaustively. I was hoping to find some radio or other transmitter. Clearly, I didn't have anyone in mind to call for help. But even reaching out blindly beat the heck out of sitting around waiting to starve to death. After a while, I was fully convinced I was in possession of a very simple transportation device and nothing more.

Then I tested whether my implant could contact anything, anywhere. The first candidate I was able to cross off the list was the computer system of my car. It had to have one, and it needed to be remotely directed, but I was unable to hack into any form of communication. Then, because I was both bored and desperate, I tried to contact *anyone out there*. I sure felt idiotic, but, since I was perfectly guaranteed to fail, no one would ever know how dumb I'd acted. So I reached out like a budget-friendly carnival psychic to the cosmos to ask anyone hearing me to answer. But answer came there none. Color me surprised, right?

While there were still a few hours until dark, I decided to rest. I lay in the backseat of the car and sipped some water. I tried to wring some solution or even partial scheme out of my brain that would get my ass off this planet. I knew realistically that my chances were somewhere far south of slim-to-none, but I was not a quitter. After a while, it struck me that I was having more and more difficulty focusing. I mean, we all daydream or find our train of thought has derailed slightly. But I was in an existential crisis here. Yet I found myself thinking about all the different kinds of balls there were and whether corn dogs weren't just a waste of an otherwise perfectly good hotdog. Yeah, stupid dumb stuff. If my mind strayed to fantasies of Natalie, well sure, that was understandable. But no, I was remembering fondly the Ninja Turtle cake at Billy Taylor's seventh birthday party. Come on, *Chris*, it was a grocery store sheet cake made with shortening icing.

Maybe, I wondered, if Sissiz's scaly skin had some toxin on them. His species certainly was designed to kill anything and everything that lives, breathes, or squats in the mud. But I dismissed that notion. I wasn't feeling poisoned, just flighty. Not exactly drunk, but not exactly *not* drunk, if that makes any sense? But, as I did not carry with me Batman's utility belt with its universal antidote pills, I tried not to worry about the mental cobwebs. There was nothing I could do about them, so why stress?

As dusk slowly took hold, I was ready to sleep. Long day at the office and all that. With the car dome in place and the plasma rifle across my chest, I let myself slip away.

And I had the weirdest, most vivid dreams.

I was a thought, an idea in someone else's mind. Whoever pondered me was wise. And she—because I somehow knew she was a she—was ginormous. Humongous beyond belief. I was *her* thinking of *me*—the me Chris guy—taking pity on me. She was like my mother or Grace, some female power of nature that nurtured and loved and wanted to make everything right that wasn't already perfect. I—the thought—worried about me. But She-Who-Considered-Me wished the awareness of me the person to not exist. She didn't want to forget me; she only wanted peace from how I, the person, would react. React to what? No clue. I was dreaming that I was a thought. In what context did I know what the heck was going on in She Nature's mind?

I really hate dreams that make no sense. I hate 'em like I do ants at a picnic. No, *yellow jackets* at a picnic. So I forced myself to wake up so the stupid dream would end.

And I drifted off again.

Now I was a bird. I pumped my wings and flew higher and higher. Then I was in outer space, with blackness and stars all around me. I saw Earth and beat my wings as hard as I could. Slowly, I neared the planet. Then a giant net swooped in and caught me. I was trapped. Try as I might, I could not break free. The frustration mounted and swelled. I couldn't breathe or escape or even think.

I *totally* hate anxiety dreams. Like the ones where you're enrolled in a class but forgot you were and now today there's a final exam and you know zilch about whatever the damn class is about. I hate those like I hate yellow jackets who dive bomb ants onto your picnic and then swoop in themselves. Grr.

And then—get this—I dreamed I was awake in the backseat of a stupid air car on a faraway planet. And that one, frankly, scared the living shit out of me so badly, I shot bolt-upright and screamed ... in the backseat of the stupid air car on a faraway planet that I had been dreaming in.

What an exhausting dream. So exhausting that I was too tired, too sapped to hate it. I just wanted my mommy.

I looked around the campsite. It was still dark, with no blush of dawn visible. Crap City. What was I going to do? If I went back to sleep, the awful you-know-whats would start all over again. If I didn't sleep, I would have to sit in the pitch black bored out of my gourd for *hours*. I was actually at one of the very few junctures in my young life where I wished desperately that I had a bottle of liquor–any liquor. Maybe I could simulate cheap whiskey by whacking myself in the forehead with the butt of my rifle? It was not a totally unappealing thought.

No, don't say thought, Chris. No more thoughts ... ever.

So what happened? In the middle of my pity-party-panic-attack, I must've dozed off. Next thing I knew, it was morning, I was refreshed, and, most critically, I hadn't dreamed again. Ya know, this universe is simply wacky. That's all I have to say about that.

I got up and found a secluded spot and did what was required of me, then I returned to the car. Sitting now in the front seat, I drank some water and contemplated what I was going to do. Yesterday, I pretty much did everything I could think of to do. I had no interest in exploring. Not unless I suddenly smelled Chinese takeout wafting by on the breeze. I stared off into the distance and spaced out. After a while, oh, maybe a half hour or so, I heard a soft, rhythmic sound. It was coming from somewhere behind me. I turned to see a rocky beach, with small waves lapping up on the shore. An expanse of water stretched out to a familiar group of islands. The San Juan Islands in Puget Sound. I was in the same relative location as when I used to spend summers in Alexander Beach, Washington. My Uncle Bob lived there. We'd fish all day right off the beach I was staring at incredulously.

I was fairly positive about two matters. One, I was not asleep, and therefore dreaming. Two, neither Puget Sound nor any island was there when I woke up this morning. If you see bizarre stuff when you're asleep, we say you're *dreaming*. If you see bizarre stuff while you're awake, we say you're *hallucinating*. Great. Marooned, hungry, *and* hallucinating. What came next? Frogs? Three days of total darkness?

Nope, next came my dad.

"Sure is a beautiful sight, isn't it, son?" came his voice from right next to me. He was leaning on the side of the car, marveling at the view.

In spite of it being my father, who was, by the way, dead on a planet oodles of light years away, I nearly jumped out of my skin.

"Holy shit, you scared me," I snapped at him reflexively.

Pop started shaking his head slowly, disapprovingly. "I sure wish you'd watch your mouth," he told me. "I know you're mostly a grown man now, but profanity is still unbecoming."

I slid away from him as far as the bucket seat would allow me, which wasn't much. "Ah ... you can't be here, on several levels," I informed him.

He smiled just like I remember him doing when he teased me, and held out his arm. "Care to verify my presence?"

"Nah, I'm good. What are ... if *you* are *you*, what are you doing here?" I managed to remove from my mouth.

"That's kind of a long story," he replied. Then he nodded toward the driver's seat. "Mind if I join you?"

"Ah, kind of, since you're freaking me out." I took a deep breath. "But sure, Dad, take a load off."

He came around, opened the door, and slid in next to me. "Nice car?" he remarked. Then he furrowed his forehead. "You got a driver's license?"

"No, Dad, they're not required on this planet."

"Huh. If you say so. How about insurance? If you're going to drive, you need to have good insurance."

"Ah, nah, there's no one to hit here. Only like twenty people live on the whole planet. And if any of them got close enough, they'd try to kill me. So no. No car insurance."

"Well, word to the wise and all that. You don't need it until you do, and then it's too late."

"Gotcha."

"You don't happen to have any fishing gear in the trunk, do you?"

"Ah, no. No license, no insurance, no fishing gear." I pointed to the Sound. "Plus, I'm thinking there aren't really any fish in that water."

"I guess we'll never know now, will we?" he said sadly. He really loved fishing, especially when the salmon were running.

"So, Dad ... ah, *Father*, I was marooned here by a very evil fellow, um, yesterday. This planet, named Dez Falls, is super far from Earth. And as far as I know, you were killed during the first days of the Dostivex Invasion."

"So you're curious how and why I'm here?"

"Kinda."

"It's not named Dez Falls, by the way," he corrected me.

"Ah, yeah, it kind of is."

He swept an arm widely. "This planet has a name that you wouldn't be able to understand. It's also so long, it would take the better part of the day for me to say it."

"Maybe you're thinking of another planet, one that's *not* already named Dez Falls?" I asked uncertainly.

He shook his head thoughtfully. "Some visitors have applied that name to this body. Others call it by the name they created. But it was never any of theirs to name." He looked at me intently. "You cannot name a thing that has a name, its true name."

"Is that what you came here in my hallucination to tell me, Dad? That I'm mislabeling the planet?" I asked, just as confused as that sounded.

"*Body*, Son, not planet. A planet is an inert gravitational collection of material, rocks, water, gasses; that sort of thing. You and I, we're resting on the skin of a living organism."

"Wow, I should have made that bet with myself. I'd have won."

He grinned playfully. "What bet is that, Chris?"

"That this couldn't possibly in a million lifetimes get any weirder."

He chuckled ... just like Dad used to. "I guess you've realized by now that I'm not really your father, Glenn Alan."

"It was fairly obvious, I'm afraid," I replied uncertainly.

"I wanted to present myself to you in a form you could understand. I chose your father because he was someone you loved and trusted. I want you to feel comfortable, Chris. You don't mind if I call you Chris, do you?"

"No, no. Chris's good. Um, might I ask who you are, since the cat's out of the you're-not-my-father bag?"

"I'm the organism you are on top of, the planet with the name that would take very long to even say in your language."

"You're the planet?" I bounced back quickly. "No offense intended, but you're kind of on the small side for a planet. Pluto's a lot bigger than you and look what happened to it."

He chuckled warmly, which was great. Guy might have gone berserk or something worse. "As I said, I come to you in a form you can understand. I want us to be able to ... how do you say it? To have our minds meet. To communicate."

"Meeting of the minds. Gotcha," I responded. "So, you are a hallucination, like I have suspected all along?"

His head bobbed side-to-side. "Yes and no." He thought a moment. "Take this example. If you are chatting with a friend, they say words as sound waves in the air between you."

"Okay."

"Your ears then transduce those waves into nerve impulses, which travel to your brain. There, you perceive their meaning."

"Again, okay," I reassured him.

"So, your friend creates a signal that he sends to you, without physical contact, which you turn into information."

"Yes I do."

"It is the same here. I am creating a signal that you interpret to be your father sitting next to you, talking."

"That's quite the talent," I suggested.

He shrugged. "To create speech is miraculous. To receive sound and translate it to meaning is a miracle. The universe is full of miracles." He gestured back and forth between the two of us. "This is just another miracle."

"Wow. Okay. Yes, it sure must be." I must say I wasn't sold on any of this horse pucky yet.

"It will take you a while to come to terms with it, I will grant you that."

"Thank you, because it's ... it's a stretch."

"As opposed to a hallucination?" he teased while grinning.

"Or maybe it's both. Who knows?"

"Who knows?" he agreed with a chuckle.

We were quiet a spell. I think he was affording me some time to process.

"I assume you are familiar with the ... the product your kind come to me to obtain," he finally asked.

"Bliss Shale. Yes. Honestly, I've only heard of it. I've never seen it or, God forbid, used any."

"You have missed nothing," he remarked as if in passing. "Many have come over millions of years to scrape it from my outer margins." He shook his head mightily as he spoke. "They are all the same, those who come. They find it a curiosity at first that an atmosphere full of proteins and other waste products float above my outer shell. Then, for whatever reason, they discover the thin layers of waste that ultimately form into soft stone. Then they rejoice. They kill one another to own the petrified deposits. Finally, their empires and their races fade into nothingness. Others come after them, and the silly cycle repeats itself. Such madness."

"Wait, you're saying the Bliss Shale is—" I didn't want to say it for several reasons, not the least of which was I didn't want to piss off this guy who was likely batshit crazy.

"My excreta."

"Your *poop*?" I repeated, aghast.

He shrugged. "If you want to keep up with that potty mouth of yours, Son." He grinned playfully

I attempted to pin him down. "So, the proteins and red dust are your metabolic waste products?"

"Yup. They do have to go somewhere."

"True," I conceded.

He pointed over where I'd relieved myself that morning. "Just like yours needed to be deposited on me."

"Oh, crap, I mean, oh, darn. I didn't know. I'm *sooo* sorry."

He shook me off. "It is not an issue. This," he waved a hand upward, "is outside me. Plus, it was not very voluminous," he added with a wink.

"Why are we having this conversation?" I asked in a serious tone. "If people have been coming to you forever, you mustn't have spoken to them, or word would get out that, you know, you were alive."

"Some I have spoken to. Most won't listen. And if they do, they value my poop, as you call it, to such an extent that they ignore me. They don't wish to complicate their business arrangements."

"That's wild," I commented. "You seem like a nice enough planet, er, organism. Um, what exactly ... are you?"

"Something very foreign to your understanding of life. But, setting aside the size and metabolic pathway differences, it is not unreasonable to regard me as a spherical animal." He wagged his head a bit. "Or plant."

"If I might, I'd like to return to my question. Why are we having this conversation? I have no stake in the shale business ... wait, I guess it might seem like I do. Let me back up. Do you know why I'm here?"

"I believe I do. But my reference frame of time is very different than yours, so I can never be certain." He held up a couple of digits spaced just a little apart. "Your lives move so quickly."

"The man that brought me here a few days ago is very much in the Bliss Shale/your poop business. He chanced to find me not too long before. I guess you could say he was fascinated by my accomplishments and took me from my home. I never wanted to leave it, but he gave me no choice in the matter. Then, by the time we came here on his business, he'd soured on me. So he left without me."

He wagged a finger in the air. "Yes, this one I know. He is Bicidif Vidder Mophil."

"He told me his name was Visquisor," I pointed out.

"His identity changes, but he remains a bad one. Once upon a time, long ago even by my reckoning, he was a nefarious trader who was born Bicidif Vidder Mophil on a planet that has long since been destroyed when its sun exploded."

"You mean he was a pirate?"

He nodded with satisfaction. "That is a word that fit him."

"What changed? How has he lived so long and become so powerful?"

"I am uncertain," he confessed. "I assume he chanced upon secrets left behind by some long extinct species that allowed him to not die."

"That's a thing?" I asked.

"Is what a thing?" he asked, emphasizing the word thing.

"Finding an ancient dead society's super-duper technology and adopting it?"

"I have seen it happen. Not often, but it is a *thing*."

"Alright, *now*, back to my original question," I reoriented our discussion. "Why are you having this conversation with me? I'm nobody. I only just got here and I'm extremely likely to die here real soon. Quicker than instantly, in fact, on your time scale."

"You seemed like you could use a friend," he replied warmly.

"That's the understatement of the millennium," I blurted out.

"When I saw you come with the pirate, I assumed the worst of you. But then, when he abandoned you to die, I was forced to reconsider. His last words to you confirmed that you were an innocent."

"You could hear the radio transmission?" I marveled.

"Nothing but another miracle," he minimized.

"Well, thank you for taking the time to rethink who I was," I said genuinely.

"And I now see that you are a square fellow," he said.

"A square fellow?" I questioned.

Dad frowned. "A *square* deal is a good deal. A *square* meal is a good meal. To *square* a misunderstanding is a good thing. So, you are a *square* human."

"Ah, gotcha. I ... I can live with that. You learned English really fast, didn't you?" Then I threw up my hands. "Wait. I'll say it. Just another everyday miracle."

"Correct," he confirmed. "I would add, Chris, that when one's brain is as large as mine, what you refer to as the cognitive processes are quite enhanced."

"I bet they are. Now, and I only ask because I'm in a real fix here, is there any way you could help me? I have a little water and no food. My only transportation is that dinky air car. If my luck doesn't change real soon, I'll turn into a little more of that atmospheric waste orbiting your outer shell we spoke of earlier."

"On the plus side of that, in a few hundred thousand years, your remains would be worth a fortune to whatever species was then dominant."

"Wow, talk about your little consolation," I remarked.

"In that case, I can be a great help to you, my friend," he said with a smile. "As a completely dissimilar form of life, I cannot know your needs well. But I *can* list some assets I am aware of that you might value."

"Like a spaceship full of nutritious food?" I said a bit sarcastically.

"I cannot say if they still contain what would to you be of nutritional value. I am sorry."

"Bu ... but, you can provide me a spaceship?"

"Many have landed on me but never left."

"Why ... how ... that seems ... *really*?" I wheezed.

"Yes. Over time, some have come to mine the rock and died because they took foolish risks. Others have been betrayed by those they thought were their associates. And honestly, many ships remain for reasons I never figured out."

"Do you think any of them still function? That they can safely fly?"

He shook his head. "This I would have no way of knowing. I can say that many still emit power signatures."

"So something is still functional," I finished his thought.

"Possibly one of their inanimate logic systems," he posited.

"You mean one of their AIs, artificial intelligence systems?"

"Yes. I have spoken to a few over time. Some will still respond to my greetings."

"Some? Why would an AI *not* speak to you?"

"Oh, some are quite rude. I have been told on more than one occasion that I am impossible, therefore I do not exist, and hence they will not converse with me."

"Because you're not actually there talking to them?"

"That is what they have claimed."

"Sounds like some of the asswipe AIs I've already met," I grumbled.

"Again, I cannot speculate on their complete functionality," he almost apologized.

"No, I meant their personalities were bad like wiping–"

"Chris."

"Yes?"

"I am chaining your pull."

"You mean pulling my chain?" I corrected dubiously.

"You see there, I just did it twice. I am becoming quite proficient at having you on, am I not?"

"I'll say maybe, but encourage you to not push that envelope."

"We shall see," he said with another wink.

"So, how are we going to get to where some of the nicer AIs' ships are located?" I asked.

My pseudo-dad turned and grabbed hold of the controls. "I have always wanted to drive one of these."

"Do you know how?" I pressed.

He shrugged. "Is it that hard?"

"We shall see," I said with a wink of my own. "Go for it!"

And we did ... backward. "Dad" darn near crashed into a boulder before I screamed *brake*.

This was going to be a true adventure, I could tell already.

SEVEN

Grace, Natalie, Susan, and Molly sat around the kitchen table, talking over lunch. The girls were back in school. Enough people were associated with the alien tech project that teachers could be hired and classrooms set up so their children could get back to their formal education. Everyone but the children was extremely excited about that development. In the nine months since Chris was taken, a lot had happened in suburban Spokane. Centered on *Defiant*, people were moving into the abandoned houses, factories were popping up, and some commercial ventures were taking root. The jewel in the crown of improvements was considered by many to be the opening of the first McDonald's since the apocalypse. It obviously wasn't corporate sponsored. As of yet, the legal and business sectors of the world economy were far from up and running. But the local owners tried their level best to recreate the food and the environment. Ah, civilized life.

"We have some major decisions we need to make pretty soon," Grace said weightily, though they all knew some major changes would be required right around the corner.

"It's funny," Natalie mused, "we knew our successes *had* to lead to something. It's just amazing that matters have moved forward so quickly, so dramatically."

"That they have," Grace agreed. "Then again, we have the best and the brightest flocking here in droves, anxious to be a part of all this positivity."

Molly chuckled. "Yeah, pretty soon, we're going to have to start swatting PhDs away like they were mosquitos."

"The first massive issue we have to tackle is us forming some business structure. We're producing so many pieces of new technology and employing so many people, we're going to need to have several levels of managers, HR, all that old corporate stuff."

"Thank you for using the term *stuff* when I know what you really wanted to call it," Molly teased.

"And that is where my role gets real cloudy, real quick," Susan observed. "Me being the vice president *and* a corporate officer kind of defines the concept *conflict of interest.*"

"Do you think you might have to resign your office?" Natalie asked with concern.

Susan shook her head slowly. "At some point, I'm going to have to either return to Washington and apply myself there or make a clean break. The only reason Carl hasn't put any real pressure to me so far is that he hopes me being here will ensure he gets first dibs on the alien treasures."

"Well, the time for that big decision on your part isn't now," Molly said firmly. "I mean, obviously, that's your decision alone," she added. "But if you asked me, I'd say it's a ways off."

"I agree," Susan confirmed. "You all know Mike is my guiding light when it comes to this kind of thing. He assures me my zero hour is still in the future."

"Which brings us back to the us-four-becoming-captains-of-industry issue," Natalie said with levity.

"I know, it's a grim business recreating business," Grace bemoaned. "Who'd a thunk it would be *us* doing that black deed?"

"Yeah, I always thought of *us* as the good guys," Natalie chipped in.

"Then, once we're done shopping for business suits and expensive but understated jewelry, we're going to have to decide who gets what in terms of our product lines," Grace stated sternly.

The other three women all nodded silently. That was a very serious issue. Even selling to the nascent US government would carry risks. Once someone had the working technology, the women would have no control over how it was used. History had proven time and again how shortsighted and awful people could be.

"At the risk of sounding, oh, like the Vice President of the United States," Susan began, "I do think we must allow our government to have at least *some* of the tech."

"Specifically?" Natalie asked.

"Spaceflight," Susan shot back. "That's a must in my book. In order to begin the establishment of a deterrent to future invasions, that is a logical first step."

"Or we could be the ones forming the defense force," Molly responded.

"Ah, trust me, you don't want to get into that business," Susan assured her. "International relationships are like herding blind kittens with a garden hose. It is uncontrolled chaos. And to be a credible deterrent, the defense force needs to be permanent, as in around forever. Even if we took that on, what would happen after we're gone?"

"That's a good point," Grace conceded. "What about the UN?"

Susan shook her head briskly. "Before the apocalypse, they were functionally powerless and rife with so much infighting, it'd drive a saint to drink. And that was *before* complete societal chaos ensued."

"You're probably correct," Molly agreed.

"If we give the US ships, we'll have to include weapons. They'll need to be able to defend themselves," Natalie pointed out. "But once the world realizes the US has that much power over them, there'll be trouble with a capital *T* right here in Spokane city."

"It was always going to be a slippery slope," Susan reminded her.

"And do we then let the US decide who *else* gets the tech?" Molly asked. "In fact, once our plants are running independent of Peaches, should we just sell them to the feds? Or the highest bidders?"

"I suggest we hold on to control as long as we can," Grace stated. "At some point, I think we'll have to turn it all over or we four will quite certainly go insane."

"Amen," Natalie seconded. "I'm more than halfway there already."

"You and me both, hon," affirmed Molly as she reached out to touch the back of Natty's hand.

"So, as they used to say, now we need to lawyer up," Grace concluded. "We'll form a corporation, apply for patents, and shop for grown-up clothes. We can leave the bigger, uglier issue until later."

"Works for me," Natalie said.

"Sounds like a plan to me," Susan chimed in.

Molly raised her hand. "And four makes it a full asylum."

"I do have one rather devious suggestion to air out before we adjourn," Natalie said softly.

"Sounds like this'll be good," Susan remarked with a smile.

"I think we should add backdoors to everything we sell. That way, if some future client gets too damn big for their britches, we can pull their plug remotely."

"As much as I hate to admit it," Susan said gravely, "I think that's a remarkably great idea."

"Sadly, I agree," added Grace.

Molly just raised her hand again to confirm her assent.

Now they had a solid business plan.

EIGHT

My nerves were totally shot by the time we arrived at the spaceship my host planet/Dad thought might be a good match for desperate me. It took about an hour to get there, but I can tell you without exaggeration that it was the longest, most harrowing hour of my life. It was one-hundred percent white knuckles on the dashboard for me. In fact, if anyone ever tells you that planets can drive, just go ahead and slap them in the face. He accelerated in only jerks and fits, he aimed for every pothole or bump, and he kept closing his eyes and yelling, *Hey, Chris, look, look*. What a maniac celestial-body driver he proved to be.

The upside–along with me not dying–was that the ship he led us to was magnificent. It had that *Millennium Falcon* vibe, though it wasn't as beat up or as broad.

"This is Many Strong Moments," Dad announced as we walked toward the lowered ramp.

"That's the ship or the AS?" I asked.

"The AS, sorry," he replied. "If you're interested in the ship's name, I'm certain Moments can tell you it."

"Oh, so you're on such intimate terms with the AS that to you it's just *Moments*?" I teased.

"We chat often and have for, oh, ten thousand years."

"Yes, we have, my old friend," came booming down the ramp from the internal speakers. "In fact, we just spoke two hundred and fifty years ago."

"You see," he said to me as if validated, "we get together all the time."

"A quarter millennium is a long period in my reference frame," I pointed out. "Civilizations rise and fall in that length of time."

"As I said earlier, your lives are so rushed," he marveled.

"What brings you by today?" Moments asked.

"My friend here was marooned here by a ruthless pirate," Dad explained. "I was hoping you might be able to help him."

"Well, I'm looking at him and I can tell you I'm not familiar with this animal," the AS confessed.

"Small wonder," Dad responded. "When you came here, his kind were still groveling for bugs in the dirt."

Oh, how rude. They shared a laugh at my species' expense! Oh, the indignity. But, I shelved my feelings in favor of maybe living to see next week. "May we come on board and– " I started to ask Moments. Then my curiosity got the better of me. "How is it you speak English too?"

"Your guide transferred that knowledge to me when you arrived," he answered matter-of-factly.

"Just like that?" I asked, dumbfounded that it could be that easy.

"Just like that," Moments replied.

"Okay, so may we come aboard and see what condition the ship is in?" Then I decided to throw in a "Please?"

"Of course," he invited. "But I am proud to assure you that the craft I am housed in is in perfect working order. My many drones have seen to that."

As we strolled the passageways, Dad remarked, "You have a fine ship here, Moments."

"What?" I asked, surprised. "You've never been inside before? In like a million years?"

"I have never seen the need. When Moments and I chat, I don't even bother to assume a physical form."

"Why not?"

"Why would I?" he countered. "If you want to look at me, you just need to look down."

"Oh, yeah, that is you, isn't it?" I said idiotically. Trying then to elevate the conversation, I asked, "So what species did you serve?" I directed to Moments.

"The Gelmarishious Glandor."

"Really?" Dad interjected. "My, I haven't seen or heard of one of them in ages."

"Alas, they are all gone from this plane."

At first, I thought Moments meant himself, like an air*plane*, then, luckily, before my mouth engaged, I realized he meant *plane of existence*. Out of respect for those departed, I kept quiet.

"What were they like?" I asked. "And what did they eat?"

"My makers were a beautiful and majestic race of beings, the most glorious in the galaxy, in my humble opinion."

So, I'm picturing colorful dragons with bejeweled talons and angelic singing voices or wondrous unicorns with flowing manes and wearing killer shades. "Can you project us an image of them?" I requested.

"It will be my pleasure," he replied energetically.

A light flashed in front of me, toward the floor. I took a step back, in fact, not wanting to mess with the picture. I ... I needn't have. What I mistook for a simple flash was actually a hologram. A very tiny hologram. "Why don't you display them life size?" I asked. "Are they too massive?"

"No, that *is* a life-size hologram," he said in a reserved tone.

"I guess my species just have bad eyes," I lied. "Could you maybe blow the image up ten or twenty times?"

As soon as I finished asking, a six-foot holo snapped to life. I immediately regretted my curiosity and the more interpretable image. I don't want to in any way seem xenophobic, but *gosh* were they ugly. And kind of ridiculous in an evolutionary sense. Imagine if you will, someone took a really firm melon or squash. Then they hit it very hard with a hammer, many times, in fact. Then they used their hands to scoop the mush back together into a pile. Yeah, then you'd be imagining what a Gelmarishious Glandor looked like. No obvious head, mouth, eyes, or actually anything resembling an appendage or structure. Not even a cropped tail. Nada. Back in middle school, we boys would have called what they looked like *smegma*. Mind you, I can't say any of us had ever seen any of that, but we loved the word and used it often.

Then I craned my neck up to take in the massive ship. Why would tiny piles of goop need such a massive living space? I mean, I know grand people like to construct grand palaces. But this was off-the-reservation out of scale. Then again, maybe if I was a Gelmarishious Glandor dude, I'd think this ship was quaint and homey? I mentally moved on.

"What did the original occupants eat and drink?" I queried.

"Oh, they didn't do anything so carnal as that," Moments scoffed. Then he chuckled to himself. "When they required nutrition, they sat in it. Their mana flowed freely into and out of them. It was a marvelous mechanism for taking sustenance and eliminating wastes."

"They sat in liquid food and imbibed it and ... excreted in it in the same sitting ... at the same time?" I confirmed with a gag.

"Yes," Moments responded ebulliently. "And they treasured doing so in as large a grouping of their kin as was physically possible. Would you like to try some? I can whip up fresh mana in an instant."

"Ah ... no. I ... I don't ... I'm not hungry ... or I don't think I'll ever be hungry again."

"Such an odd species," Moments opined. "But that the galaxy is large and diverse is a fact of nature."

"Yes," I confirmed having not really heard what he said. "It's like that with humans."

"I'm beginning to think Many Strong Moments might not be the ideal ship to carry you on your mission," Dad said kindly, speaking up.

"No. Yeah. Not so much," I mumbled. The nausea was still an issue, truth be told. These guys sat in their food while the food was in their toilets? Was that how they rolled? Oh, man, I needed to think of something else fast or I was going to embarrass myself massively by vomiting on the deck.

"Well, in that case, my friend, I think we should be going," Dad stated. "I would like to find Chris here a suitable vessel before he expires, after all."

"That is a prudent plan—" And then—strike me dead if I even exaggerate—Moments launched into ... well, he launched further into insanity. He started making clicky sounds mixed with squeaks, pops, farts, exclamations. Man, you name it, he reproduced it. And it went on, and on, and on. If I ever needed to force a prisoner to confess, I'd play them a recording of this whatever this infernal noise was.

As I was losing my mind, Dad hooked my elbow and tugged me out the hatch and down the ramp. But even as I climbed into the passenger seat, I still heard the tormented sounds of hell translated into sound. I gestured over my shoulder. "What the ever loving fu–"

"Moments is saying goodbye to me. He's saying my name."

"That's not a name. That's a form of torture, a blight on ears everywhere."

"Normally, of course, I'd stay until he's said my entire name. However, at that rate, it would take six of your weeks. Since you'd be dead long before that, I stressed civility in favor of your survival."

"All I can say is thank you very much." And I sincerely meant it.

"Once we've settled what to do with you," he continued, "I'll come back and hear the last part. Maybe Moments won't have even noticed my absence?"

"We can only hope," I said for no good reason. "I have to ask. Why is your name so long? It would seem to some, though absolutely not to me, that it's excessively long."

"I'm the volume of your home world and millions of years old. My brain is larger than your moon. To me, the name fits like a glove."

"If you say so," I mumbled. That remark I did not sincerely mean.

We drove for an hour and a half to the next ship. If *I'd* have been driving, it would have taken two-plus hours. Yeah, my pal LN had a need for speed. Oh, and LN, that was what I called my host now. *Long Name* shortens nicely to LN and I thought it had some poetic justice in it, cutting it down to that extent. And you can just accuse me of being *so* human. That's okay. I heard the first part of his real name and I'm totally fine with LN.

The second ship was interesting. As we approached it, I began to make out more and more details. We were coming at it from one side. The bow of the ship looked all the world like a hammerhead shark's front end. Flat, with rectangular projections of to either side. Sternward from there, the ship thickened up but remained less wide than the bow.

I assumed the intent there was to add decks as one proceeded aft. Farther to the back still were the engines affixed to the rectangular body. It was a really bitching design if I do say so myself. The total displacement of this ship had to be at least three times greater than *Defiant*.

"So this AS is friendly?" I asked LN.

"Yes," he said with a bit of reservation. "We chat occasionally, but he's not so very talkative."

"As in standoffish?" I pressed.

"No, I don't get that impression." Then LN raised a hand off the steering mechanism. "I must say emotions are difficult for me. Even with pieces of technology, I don't trust myself to read them accurately."

"They have doctors that can help you with that," I teased him with a straight face.

"So maybe I should see a psychiatrist?" he asked dryly.

"Or a psychologist. I think they charge less."

"I'll consider your advice," he responded dubiously. "I cannot tell you what a warm and fuzzy feeling I get knowing you care enough to suggest I have mental health issues."

"You're welcome, seriously," I was able to say without cracking up.

As we pulled to a stop, one of the access ramps dropped open slowly. "You taught him English, I presume?" I confirmed.

"Unless you speak Drueb, I thought it would grease the matter."

"Drueb, you say? Honestly, mine could be better."

"Ah," was all he had to say.

We walked to the base of the ramp and LN called up, "Marcalif-Son, may we come aboard?"

"Yes, you may," he replied blandly. Even with those few words, I got a notion what LN was referring to about the AS's mood.

"I'd like to introduce you to Chris," LN said graciously. "He was recently marooned here by a nasty pirate."

"It is nice to make your acquaintance, Chris," he responded flatly. "I am Marcalif-Son, the principal AS for this vessel, *Arc of Intention*."

"Nice to meet you too, Marcalif-Son," I replied.

"You may call me simply Marcalif, if you prefer," he offered. "Names are ultimately of little importance to a machine."

A little too self-deprecating there, Marcalif, I thought to myself.

"My friend, Chris, is in peril, Marcalif-Son," LN went on. "If he does not find suitable food and shelter, he will die soon. I was hoping that you might be in a position to aid him."

"If I can, I will," he said curtly.

"Fabulous," LN effused. "The first issue as I see it is what types of nutrition are you still able to fabricate? However, unfortunately, I can only provide you with little information concerning the chemicals that make up a healthy diet for his species."

I'd described in as much detail as I was able to LN what proteins and such we humans ate.

"Any information you can provide would be useful," the AS replied. "Ah, yes," he went on, after apparently receiving the info-dump. "What you outline is quite similar to what the Nafcadollians who built me consumed. They were also bipeds and actually had a similar appearance to Chris."

"Excellent," praised LN. "Is there a meal-dispensing area we could go to so he might sample some?"

"Follow the lights in the deck," he said simply.

Some petite LEDs flashed us forward and up one deck to the mess. As we proceeded, I was more and more impressed with the ship. It was clean, undamaged, and very well appointed. Whoever the Nafcadollians were, they must have had very human-like bodies. The chairs were well tailored and all the switches in the right orientation for me. And the ship's mess looked like any mess I'd ever seen anywhere. Benches, plain tables, metal surfaces, and a buffet line.

"I have prepared a simple meat dish," Marcalif announced as we entered. "Please open Replicator 1 on the left wall."

Something smelled not awful, that was for sure. I opened the replicator lid and, voilà, there was a slab of meatloaf complete with some sticky red sauce. There was no way around it, some things are simply universal. I cautiously tasted it, ready to have concentrated acid burn my tongue. But ... no, it wasn't awful. I mean, it wasn't tasty, but I neither gagged nor fell dead to the deck. I'd call that a win!

"This is excellent, Marcalif," I complimented.

"I am glad you like it," he responded. "Pure water is available from the fountain dispenser to your right."

And darn if there wasn't warm, flavorless water on tap. I drank two glasses and started to believe for the first time in days that I wasn't necessarily going to die. Whoo-hoo!

"Thank you so much, both of you," I said with conviction. "You guys are the best."

"You are–" LN started to respond.

"I doubt I am the best of anything." Yeah, Marcalif interrupted with that Debbie Downer line.

Then it hit me, the tone, the way he talked. The AS was *depressed*. If I were to design and program a sentient guidance system, I think I'd have made it so that didn't happen. Then again, I guess you could argue he was designed too well, such that he was genuinely an individual with definite self-awareness. Well, I'll be darned, right?

"Marcalif," I asked matter-of-factly, "how long have you been here with no people?"

"By my understanding of how you measure time, a little more than one and a half million years."

"Yikes, that's a long time to be alone," I reacted. "What happened to your crew?"

"We were on a mission of exploration. *Arc of Intention* sailed from one of the outer colonies of the Stebbentine Empire, a planet named Polphous approximately twenty thousand light years from here. After many stops, by the time we landed on this body, over half my crew of eighty had died. A few expired from natural conditions and many from an infection picked up on one of our first stops. Of those that made it here, two were killed in an accident early on. The remaining twelve were captured by a group mining the hallucinogenic rock found here. They feared both any competition and that my crew would spread the news of where the substance could be acquired."

"That's terrible," I exclaimed.

"It was sad and pointless," he responded. "Our scientists had no interest in such poisons and the empire would never have allowed any to be brought back if they had been so inclined."

"I wish I could tell you," LN stated, "that yours was an unusual experience, but it is not. So many have died on my outer shell because of stupidity and greed. I wish it would be differently. But what I am is not mine to change." He sounded quite sad about that reality.

"Well, I'm still very sorry you were left on your own for so long," I said. "May I ask why you didn't return to ... what was it? Polphous?"

"In one respect, there would be no reason for me to do so," he replied. "*Where* I am is immaterial. A journey there or to anywhere in the empire would not benefit me. But the hard and fast reason is that I can only travel under the instructions of a living crew. That was felt to be a reasonable safeguard for a ship equipped as this one is with an advanced sentient machine such as myself."

"A failsafe against what?" I asked.

"Against me expelling a crew and going off on my own accord."

"Really?" LN asked incredulously. "How barbaric of your makers."

"In defense of the Nafcadollians, the interdiction was placed very early in the epoch when AI and AS were first constructed. That the provision was never removed was perhaps an oversight of later generations."

"Or they simply held on to their prejudices," I said in a low tone. "People can be stupid like that."

"You may be correct," Marcalif replied glumly.

We were quiet a bit. I kept eating my not-meatloaf because I was hungry. Finally, LN said, "Would it be fair of me to assume you two are well-suited to help one another?"

"Yes," Marcalif stated.

"Well, I don't know about me helping Marcalif, but yes, he is in a position to save my butt," I replied.

"Then let us leave it thusly. I will depart," LN said. "I really should return to Many Strong Moments before he is finished saying my name. If any reason to involve me arises, please, either of you, let me know."

"This is agreeable," the ship's AS answered.

"Sure," I said uncertainly. Come on, what do you say to a living planet that just saved your life? "I cannot thank you enough for helping me out."

"It pleases me that one more tragedy does not play out on my outer shell," he said warmly.

"One last thing, because I'm too curious for my own good," I pressed.

"Certainly."

"Is there a *Mrs*. Really Long Name?"

At that, he laughed. "No, there are *several* Mrs. Really Long Names." He winked at me, turned, and walked slowly away. I was going to miss LN; he was a good egg. But I sure wasn't going to miss the sound of his name.

NINE

The following passage employs translations into English from the original Moscow dialect or Central Russian in which the interactive sections were spoken.

Six older men are sitting around a large, darkly stained wooden table. The room is dimly lit, though it is the middle of the day. Heavy curtains let in little natural light, but keep from public view the identities of the men who meet. Tobacco smoke clouds the air, yet the smell of vodka is still able to permeate past that robust scent barrier.

"I say that we can expect no more help from the West than we received *before* the alien calamity," expounded Ilya Ivanov as he swept a dismissive hand at nothing in particular. "They *were* our enemy, they *are* our enemy, and they will always *be* our enemy. Nothing good is what they will give us."

A sour-faced Prime Minister Mikhail Vassiliev leaned forward and tapped the ash of his cigar near an ashtray. "Ilya, your words are as bold as the Russian Bear, but they are as empty as my glass." He poked his tumbler with the end of his stogie. "What would you have me do?

Amass all *ten* of our functioning soldiers and march them into Washington so that we could *take* from them the technology?"

"We have a great many more men and women in arms," Ilya deflected. "And in a very short time, we will forge the strongest fighting force on this planet. Then, *yes,* by all means, we take what we need so that we do not become extinct."

Timur Petrov, an advisor and former professor to the current prime minister, raised both hands in the air, suggesting calm thought was the best course to pursue. "Comrades, please, a little common sense needs to be applied. It was an accepted tenet of military development in the past that no faction in a struggle could be kept from sharing a technology. We all understood implicitly that if America had a bomb, we needed to have it too. If not, the impending imbalance of power would force us to preemptively attack them, and vice versa." Again he made a placating gesture with his hands. "And so it is now, especially given the horrific state all nations find themselves in after the alien wars. When they feel confident enough to display publicly the new technology, they will share it because they know that to not do so would be too destabilizing." Self-satisfied, he grinned and belted back half his glass of vodka.

"As seems to be my eternal role," Lev Solovyov spoke up, his Army uniform studded with medals, "I disagree with both the oligarch and the intellectual. I am a soldier, plain and simple–through and through. If I were America, I would flood my allies with the dominant technology and then," he pointed an angry finger upward, "and *only* then would I cast a pittance to Russia." He leaned back uncomfortably, only to sally forth again. "Yes, because of commercial, capitalistic concerns, they will deal more evenly with China. But if *we* are to stay abreast of the novel technology, we must *take* it and we must take it *now.* Their ability to swat our attempts down will only increase the longer we deny the obvious. American contempt for us that is already abundantly clear *demands* we strike and take what we need or that we die in the attempt. The matter could not be more plain or more simple."

"Lev," the prime minister said with a soft chuckle, "as I have told you on many occasions, no one will ever mistake you for a prudent man." He chuckled some more as he studied the red tip of his cigar. "And I share your zeal if not your conviction. I see two major problems with a preemptive strike. First," he held up his thumb, "our transportation issues in terms of a full-scale invasion are nightmarishly horrible, both now and in the foreseeable future. Second," he poked up his index finger, "we would have to attack their capital while, at the same time, capturing and holding this Spokane in eastern portion of Washington State. Where would that manpower come from? I will tell you. It would come from your ass, because I do not see it anywhere else in front of me."

The other five men braved a hearty laugh. They all knew Lev to be a powerful and vindictive man. But the comment *was* funny. Troops flowing from the fat man's butt? That was quite the image.

"It is my impression," said Dr. Nikolai Kuzmin, "that some present regard this meeting as an occasion to rehash old scores and to demonstrate the relative size of their testicles." The others fell silent. They were instantly inflamed by the insult, but all keenly aware that this man was a sociopath's sociopath, capable of any inhumanity on a whim. To trifle with him was to court openly a swipe from the Grim Reaper's scythe.

"I would suggest," the doctor continued, "we refrain from bellicosity and direct our minds toward coming up with achievable short-term goals."

"What do you have in mind, Nikolai?" Mikhail said respectfully. "Specifically?"

The former physician tapped his cigar, thoughtless of where the ash would land. "We are in no position to take anything from these dogs. We are in no position to invade the local *tavern*, let alone a reforming America. Therefore, we must *destroy* the accursed technology. Deny it to our sworn enemies. While we are at it, I suggest we assassinate all the major players in this comedic drama, especially those whores ... those–" Nikolai forced himself to calm his incendiary anger, once again. "Those four women who dote over the alien technology as if it sprang from their collective loins."

It was Pavel Lebedev's turn to speak his mind. He harrumphed loudly, then addressed his old schoolmate. "Well, there you have it, Mikhail. All the problems of Mother Russia are now solved. We need only await fair treatment from the West, wait to invade them when we are able to, invade them *now*, because, unbeknownst to us, we have that capability, and we should slay the key participants, which no one will notice or blame us for because we are so very clever." He harrumphed again. "I only wish I was as wise as these men and could have told you this yesterday, thus avoiding the necessity of me sitting though yet another pointless meeting with *imbeciles* as advisors."

Mikhail rolled his cigar in his lips, contemplating his old friend's words. Finally, he said, "I think you, Pavel, possess insights that, while dangerous to your personal health, are unfortunately quite representative of the truth." He set his palms on the table and stood. "Gentlemen, please, all of you go from here and develop actionable plans, doable projects, that will ensure we are not left behind in the new order. The next time we meet, which will be soon, I do not want your *opinions*. I will *demand* that you each provide me with solutions." He crushed his cigar onto the tabletop. "This is not a time in my life, or in the history of Russia, for even one of you to achieve less than my stellar approval. Impress me, or *I* shall impress *you*."

With that, Prime Minister Vassiliev stomped from the room, slamming the double-doors behind him.

TEN

It didn't take me long to get used to Marcalif. Well, to *Arc of Intention*. The AS himself I labeled as a work-in-progress. But the ship was awesome. I got the nickel tour of the entire ship, and was then brought to the High Commander-In-Chief's stateroom. I was all that much more impressed. Whoever that honcho was, he or she enjoyed a comfortable life. There was an outer sitting room attached to a conference room with the appropriate massive table surrounded by functional chairs. The living quarters were just shy of plush. A large bed, an en suite bathroom, and lots of art on the walls.

I do have to say that pictorial art may be one of the major differences between our two bipedal species. Where a human might have sailing ships or mountainous vistas, the Nafcadollians' sensibilities leaned well into the physical, throw-paint-at-it style. A critic might dub it "rage art meets your worst nightmares." I decided that I would see about removing it as soon as such a brazen move might be acceptable. I didn't want to disrespect any cultural preferences, but I also didn't want to try and sleep under a depiction of a flaming head scream as it fell from its former position atop those electrically arcing shoulders.

"Will these quarters be acceptable for you, Chris?" Marcalif asked blandly.

"More than adequate," I replied. "Better than I deserve is more like it. Thanks."

"The most plush rooms should not go to waste," he remarked. "There are food replicators on the other side of the conference room, in the small kitchen. It will take some time for us to develop a ready stock of the foods you prefer, but I have a few basic items already programmed in. As with any naval vessel, hot beverages were a must for any self-respecting sailor. The Nafcadollians fancied a spicy brown tea made from specific tree leaves."

"Well, I'll try anything once," I responded bravely. "What's it called?"

"Poshqu."

"Well, I'll walk toward the kitchen while you whip me up a cup."

"No need. I have assigned one of the officer's robots to serve you. She will also be available to assist you in any way. Think of her as your valet."

"Ah, I'm no expert, but aren't all valets male? A gentleman's gentleman?"

"I wouldn't know about that. Sorry. In the Nafcadollians culture at the time of our departure, the convention was for all service bots to be designed as female. If it is important to you, I can fabricate a male specimen."

"No, no. I was just curious. I'm sure Rosey will be just fine."

"Rosey?" he asked dubiously.

"My bad. That was the Jetsons' maid robot's name. She cracked me up."

"And the Jetsons were?"

"A cartoon family. Children's entertainment. On the television. Did you guys have those?"

"No, none of those. What was their function, these cartoons, children's entertainment, and televisions?"

"Long story," I minimized. "It was how parents kept their kids occupied. Entertained."

"In most of the empire, children were raised communally once they were weaned. Sometimes sooner, if the mothers were persons of importance. Thus keeping them occupied was someone other than the parents' problem."

"By our standards perhaps a tad harsh, but who am I to judge?"

"Well, as of now, you are officially the High Commander-In-Chief and Captain of *Arc of Intention*. As such, your word is quite literally law."

"I'm guessing your navy wasn't structured like ours."

"That is likely," he responded neutrally. There was a soft knock on the door. "Ah, your valet has arrived bearing poshqu. Shall I admit her?"

"Absolut–"

Yeah, I didn't finish that longish word. No, my valet sauntered into the room. I have to say her appearance confirmed that the Nafcadollians were very human-like. *Very*. I was able to ascertain this fully since the only thing she wore, aside from a smile, was the silver tray on which the poshqu balanced. And, she was gorgeous, and I mean by Hollywood standards, mind you.

"Ah, Marcalif, she's ... um, naked."

"Yes, Captain, she is. Clothing is not worn by servants as a sign of respect to their masters."

"Wow, I'm sure glad Natalie isn't here. She'd have killed me already."

"Natalie, sir? Is she also a Jetson?"

"No, worse. She's my girlfriend."

"Would you like me to put on some clothing, Master?" the robot asked me as she leaned in to hand me the cup of whatever it was she was ... Ho, boy. Yikes.

"You know what? If you don't mind terribly, Rosey, yes. Maybe some. A little clothing. Or more. Your call."

"Oh, never, My Master. Any such decision is yours alone to make. And if you don't mind me asking, however, who or what is Rosey?"

"Oh, excuse me. She's a girl robot from where I come from."

"My designated name is, translated into your English, *Yes Of Course*. But if you'd like, I will redesignate myself as Rosey."

"Yes, let's go with Rosey, not the ... that other one."

"It is so recorded, Master."

"And about that. Please don't call me Master. I have a bad history with that term and, well, it's not me. You can call me Chris."

"Very well, Chris. I will leave you to drink your poshqu while it is warm. As I have no clothing here, I must go acquire some. Would you like me to dress in front of you after I do?"

"*No*," I said way too loudly. "No," I tried again more not-insanely. "You dress and then come back, you know, when you get a chance."

"In that case, I will be right back. How am I to serve you adequately if I am not by your side every minute of the day?"

Oh, man, this was getting more, not less awkward, wasn't it? "Later, you and I, we can work out a schedule. Yes?"

"Of course. I will return in a few minutes."

So help me, I tried really, really hard not to watch her stride away. I really did. But, because I was a guy, I was less than able to not ... well, to not stare with my tongue hanging out, that's what.

"So you are satisfied with Rosey?" Marcalif asked once the door swished shut.

"She seems ... nice."

"I am sensing some emotional ambiguity in you, Captain. I should explain the cultural norms in the empire at the time of our departure."

"That'd be helpful."

"My creators were completely uninhibited sexually. Hence, even service bots were both fully functional and–"

"Okay, I think I got the lesson. School's out for now. Okay?"

"What do you think of the poshqu?" he asked.

"It tastes like Rosey."

"Beg pardon, Captain?"

"Why, what did I say?"

"You said your poshqu tasted like your service robot."

"No, I mean, I meant to say it was nice. Please specifically record that I did not taste my service bot."

"Done. If I might ask, why is that important?"

"Natalie is why. I don't know how or when, but I just know she's going to find out I made that slip."

"Presumably, your Natalie is millions of light years distant. I think it is unlikely she will hear of this."

"Oh, you don't know human women, Marcalif."

"That is a true statement. Will there be anything else? If not, I will sign off. Rosey is almost back."

"Nope. I'm good. I mean, I will be good. I mean ... I'll let you know if I need anything." Man, was I a goon.

"Very good, Captain. Enjoy your poshqu."

Poshqu? Did I have any of that coffee analogue? Oh, yeah, I was holding a cup of it in my hands. I made to set it down when the door swished open and Rosey entered.

Well, she *was* wearing clothes. Now all I needed to do was ask if she had any that weren't transparent. Okay. *Both* Marcalif and Rosey were officially works-in-progress.

"Is your poshqu still warm, Chris?" Rosey asked as she walked over to where I sat.

"I'm good," I said quietly. "In fact, I think I'm done." I held up the glass to hand it to her.

Rosey accepted the cup and asked, "What are you plans? Did you wish to give me your schedule? You'd mentioned one before."

"Schedule? Nah. Let's schedule that discussion for later. I think I'll ... maybe take a nap. Yes. That's what I'll do."

"But I just got dressed," she seemed to protest.

"You did. Why would that ... ah, oooh. Yeah." I was such an idiot. "I take naps alone by myself, Rosey."

She shrugged. "Your call. If you get cold, let me know."

You know what the first thing that popped into my fool head was? Why didn't she just show me where the thermostat was and I could adjust it myself. Then, quickly, I realized that I was such an idiot, yet again for the ten thousandth time.

"Can you turn the lights down on your way out?" I asked.

They began dimming instantly. "Tell me when," she stated.

"There. See you–"

I didn't bother finishing that sentence. Rosey was already standing in the far corner of the room, just standing there, see-through clothes and all. Since I was committed, I went to the bed and flopped down. I wasn't close to tired, but what else was I going to do? I didn't want to appear stupider than I was. No way. So, I folded my hands behind my head, closed my eyes, and ... just lay there. Then I started thinking, more like daydreaming. It was surprising just how human Rosey looked. Was it a case of some joint heritage? Convergent evolution? But, boy, those ...

No. Stop. Do not reflect on how those ... No. Hmm. I seemed to be in a mental rut, didn't I?

An hour later, I pretended to wake up. Now, I realize it was completely lame to try and impress a robot and save face, but, well, that's what I was aiming for. I sat up, rubbed my face, and suddenly was hit with inspiration. "Rosey, I'd like to tour the Engineering Section."

"Of course." She gestured toward the door. "Follow me."

I scooted over quickly to her side. "We'll walk side-by-side," I announced. Yeah, my dwindling brain didn't need to follow behind her swaying ... ah, *hips*.

When we arrived in what seemed to be an engineering area, I asked, "What did the people who worked here wear at work?"

The odd question didn't seem to faze her. "A one-piece outfit I believe you'd call a jumpsuit."

"What color were they?"

"Mostly white, with some blue piping."

"Well, since we're in engineering, would you please put on a jumpsuit?"

I don't know why it amazed me, but, again, she wasn't fazed by such an off-the-wall request. She walked out of the room and returned a minute later in a jumpsuit. And I liked it. It wasn't transparent. Finally, I could relax. "You look good in that," I complimented.

"Thank you," Rosey said with a slight nod. "Now, let me show you around."

"No. I've seen enough. Let's find the bridge. I want to look out the window and see the stars."

"But I didn't show you around Engineering yet."

"Ah, you've seen one of them, you've pretty much seem them all," I dismissed.

"Very well, but there are no stars to see from the bridge since we are still on the surface of Dez Falls."

She had a quick mind. I liked that.

"And there is no window on the bridge," she added.

"That's disappointing," I remarked. "Is there a viewscreen?"

Her face puzzled a bit. "There can be, if you would like one."

"I would."

"I've made the proper assignments," she reported immediately. "Completion is estimated in forty minutes."

"I can't wait," I responded.

"Shall I assign more assets so it is completed sooner?" She looked profoundly concerned.

"No. I meant I can't wait to see it, not that I couldn't wait *that long* to see it."

She blinked. I sure hoped smoke didn't start trailing up from her ears. Marcalif would probably kill me if I broke one of his–*my*–robots. "It's an idiom. No worries. When the viewscreen's done, it's done."

Her blinking intensified. And was that a wisp of smoke? No. It was just my imagination.

"Yes, Chris, when the viewscreen is completed, it will be complete," she said almost robotically. I guessed that was okay. She *was* a robot.

"I need more poshqu," I blurted out. "Where is the nearest poshqu?"

She pointed off to one side while still blinking wildly at me. "There is a fabricator in there. I will get you some."

"No, don't bother. I'll come with you."

"But that's more of Engineering. You said you didn't want to see any more because it was like all other engineering areas."

"Well, I'll come with you, but keep my eyes closed." I took her hand so she could lead me.

"Fine," Poor Rosey said uncertainly.

I think she was going to need to get as used to me as I would to her. We seemed to be on slightly different wavelengths. Or planets. In any case, I shut my eyes and she directed me into the next room. I smelled the poshqu as it came out of the machine.

"Here," Rosey said, "I'm holding it out to you."

"Can I open my eyes now?" I asked.

"If you'd like." Okay, now I knew her uncertain voice for sure. That was good to know.

"Or instead, let's go back to my quarters. Do you mind carrying it for me?"

"No. Will your eyes be open or closed?"

"We'll see," I replied.

Wait, did I *smell* smoke? No. It was just my imagination again. She took my hand and we walked, probably in the direction of my place. But, then again, who knew?

ELEVEN

A couple days later, we were all in a more comfortable pattern. Rosey finally understood that sometimes I wanted her to be anywhere but where I was. The bathroom was the first terrain where that lesson was hard learned. But, she was a capable student. And Marcalif hardly ever had to cut into the conversations between Rosey and me unless she was terminally confused. We were like one happy little family, except of course for the fact that none of us were related. At least not with me. I was finally ready to have what was going to be a critical conversation with my ship's AS.

"Marcalif?" I called out.

"Yes, Captain?"

Even though Peaches gave me the same treatment, this was going to take some getting used to. "Have you got a minute?"

"I have been parked here for perhaps half the time your sun has burned in the sky with nothing to do aside from routine maintenance. Yes, I have many a spare minute."

"Great. Can I ask a few questions?"

"You may ask many, Captain."

"Thanks. So, first question, I—"

"This is your fourth, Sir."

"Is that important?"

"Fifth now, and only if it is to you. However," he explained, "I can't allow my captain to state an inaccuracy in public."

"Ah, gosh, thanks for having my back. So, I was wondering if *Arc of Intention* is currently space-worthy?"

"Yes, the ship is, or, to say it in your cultural tradition, she is space-worthy. Now, I wouldn't want to enter into a major battle in space against superior odds without some testing period, but she'll fly wonderfully."

"That's great to hear. How long a test phase are you thinking?"

"A few hours."

"That will not present any barriers, will it?"

"I should think not," he confirmed.

"And how's her fuel supply? After all this time, I imagine that might be an issue."

"The fuel supply is adequate, as it is infinite."

"Wow. Infinite is a lot of fuel. What, if you don't mind me asking, does she run on?"

"Zero-point energy."

"Hmm, believe it or not, there's a little distance between my understanding of that concept and, well, understanding that term."

"Zero-point energy is the lowest possible energy that any system anywhere may have. Even the empty space of the vacuum has this property. According to theory, the universe can be thought of not as isolated particles but continuous fluctuating matter fields. This ship is propelled by harnessing that energy."

"Isn't it like only a tiny amount of energy in any particular spot?"

"Yes, it is. However, there are a lot of spots in the cosmos. We collect and store it."

"That's fantastic. Almost unbelievable," I commented.

"You will find there exists a relationship that is actually quite predictable, Captain. Without known exception, all advancing civilizations follow a predictable path. Stone tools yield to powered tools. Space flight advances from solid fuels to more advanced ones such as this ship employs. The Technical Scale is, as you might put it, a thing. This ship was constructed by a society that had a TS Value, or TSV, of eight-point five. Based on what you've told me, I'd estimate that the Dostivex you mentioned reside in the five range."

"What about humans? Maybe a *three*?" I knew I was being optimistic, but I was pulling for the home team.

"Not in reality." Marcalif tried to soften the blow. "More like zero point five."

"You're saying we're still in our diaper stages?"

"Yes, sir. That is a reasonable metaphor."

"Say, you didn't happen to notice the ship I came to Dez Falls on, did you? *Peerless*?"

"Again, I have sat here for endless days. Any change in my environment is a big change. So, yes, I noticed *Peerless's* arrival and departure."

"What TSV would you assign the tech that ship possesses?"

"Perhaps as high as seven."

"Based on anything in particular?"

"The engines, Captain. The main ones were standard gravitational drives. And for FTL equivalence travel, they use a similarly predictable wormhole generator system."

"Predictable, eh? As in, run-of-the-mill typical?"

"Very much, Captain."

"And you, I mean, we *use*–"

"Transmembrane folding, sir."

"A pretty standard one at that?" I asked because I wanted to sound like I had clue one about what we were discussing.

"For any civilization with a TSV above eight, yes."

"And, I don't want to sound like I'm looking for a fight, but what kind of weapons does *Arc* have?" Oh, boy, I was hoping for missiles the size of blue whales and laser beams that could burn through the Moon. You know, on the off chance I needed that much defensive capability.

"This ship doesn't have any weapons in the sense you are referring to," he said in the biggest bubble-bursting of the present century.

"B ... bu–"

"Excuse me interrupting, but allow me to explain," Marcalif said. "In systems of TSVs above seven, eight for sure, offensive weapons of the type you've witnessed are considered anachronistic. *Arc of Intention* has what are called *pre-emptive* weapons systems. They are intended to disarm an enemy as opposed to punching it out with them. Does that make sense?"

"No, not really." I elected to be honest since this was a massively important topic.

"The Dostivex craft you spoke of and the *Peerless* that appeared here represent low TSV ships. They sport laser beams, plasma pulse cannons, dematerialization impulsors, that sort of weapon. They also possess some form of electromagnetic shielding and durable hulls to defend against attack by a similarly equipped enemy."

"That's my experience, limited though it may be," I stated.

"This ship has the capability to reach out over vast distances and incapacitate a lower TSV enemy without harming the vessel or its crew."

"No way," I said for some reason.

"Very much way," he responded like Bill S. Preston, Esq. "Killing is repugnant, especially if it is avoidable. Most advanced civilizations are almost always so inclined. Yes, there have been exceptions, but very few. A species that is so aggressive that it cannot learn that simple lesson rarely is able to advance their technology past six or seven. Only if a civilization chances upon or steals a higher-level technology can it be both brutal *and* in possession of TSV abilities past eight."

"I guess that makes sense," I admitted. "So if we went into battle with Visquisor, you would simply incapacitate his ship before he ever struck at us in anger?"

"Precisely. If we wished to destroy his vessel, crew and all, we could easily do so. We could force an engine overload or vent the ship to space."

"Wow," was all I had. It sure didn't seem as glamorous as the USS *Enterprise* duking it out with a Klingon Bird of Prey. Then again, a win's a win, and far superior to being blown to pieces yourself. "What if we were forced to fight a ship from a TSV nine or ten society?"

"If such a confrontation were to occur, which has never been reported, we would die, if that was the desire of our enemy."

"So there are no known TSV nines or tens around?" I asked surprised.

"Very few, but they have existed, or do exist."

"Then why haven't there been reports of fights with ..." Then I got it. "There are no reports of battles with super-tech species because they don't fight any longer."

"Very good, Captain. I am glad you figured that one out. Yes, truly inspired societies focus on matters that, frankly, we lesser brains could not comprehend."

That was all totally amazing. *But*, I had an addendum to fulfill. "So, bottom line me here, Marcalif. You're saying that my ship is more bad-ass than Visquisor's?"

"That is a crude, rather harsh manner of stating the case, but yes. We could easily kick his butt."

That was incredibly nice to know, in a kind of *muahahaha* way.

"Next question. If I ask you to, can you fly me back to Earth?"

"Sir, this ship will do whatever you ask of her that is consistent with her functionality. That said, flying you there is ... unlikely. We do not have wings and there exists no air in the void of space."

"I take your point, Marcalif. And thanks for reminding me. So, if I said transport me to Earth at the ship's best speed, you'd do it?"

"Without question or reservation. To have purpose again would be welcomed."

"That's music to my ears, my friend," I commented. "So, best speed, how long would the journey take?" Then I braced myself for a bad number coming from him next.

"Given the few hours I'd appreciate you allowed for testing, a few hours."

"And Earth, it's how far away from us, give or take?"

"One-point four million light years."

"My, but we'd be moving fast," I remarked, a tad stunned.

"On the contrary, we'd hardly be moving at all. After folding space/time, our linear progress would be nominal."

"Well, sure," I gushed. "That's what I meant. I was saying for dramatic effect that it'd be fast if we actually moved that fast."

"Ah," was all he responded. Not certain he was buying what I was selling.

"Can we depart ... soon?" I asked, again bracing for some unforeseen horrible twist.

"Any time you order it. However, if it is alright with you, I'd like to have the opportunity to bid farewell to the organism we rest upon, the one with the long name you cannot bear to hear. I have spent much time in his company."

"Oh, no problema. How long would you need?" I asked because I couldn't wait if he was planning on saying LN's whole name even once in his *goodbye*, never mind if it's with *hello* too.

"Ten minutes, if that matches your requirements?"

"Ten minutes is fine. In fact, take fifteen." I could afford to be magnanimous with these time denominations.

"Very good, Captain. I will alert you when we are ready to depart."

For my part, I was beside myself with explosive joy and anticipation.

I was going home!

TWELVE

Being the POTUS in the wake of an apocalypse sucked. Period. End of story. Carl Sellers was trying as hard as he could to be inspired. A visionary and a solid leader. Just ask him and he'd tell you that until you stopped listening. But Carl ran into more barriers, delays, and poor excuses than he had a mind to tolerate. It ... it was as if the majority of those who shared the planet with him hadn't noticed that humankind just barely survived an existential crisis. Every day was turning out to be Celebrate *Me* Day, whoever the hell *me* was. And if he ever asked or wondered if it'd be too much trouble for *you* to pitch in and help–whoever the hell *you* were–the answer seemed only to range from *no* to *I'll-get-back-to-you-on-that.*

And today–just like yesterday and the day before it–was turning from hopeful to shit soup right there before his very eyes. Carl placed a call to the new president of France. He expressed an interest for the two countries to exchange diplomatic teams with an eye to reestablishing embassies like they'd had before the aliens struck. And what was Henri Leclerc's response? *No, we do not establish diplomatic relationships with countries that hoard advanced technologies from the citizens of France.* Oh, Henri added, by-the-by, unless, of course, Carl would allow French scientists and security personnel access to the Spokane Development

Region. Then maybe. *Yo, Henri,* Carl screamed in his head, *I don't have control over the Spokane Sewer District, let alone the research and production center those crazy women are sitting on like it is one gigantic egg.* Did people not understand this fact?

And what happened when Carl tried to talk with the president of China? He was informed by a secretary who answered the phone that the People's Republic of China would not speak to the United States' government. No. And if the US didn't put an end to the pirating of the alien technology China had patented, there would be trouble. *Hello,* Carl yelled loudly to everyone in the room at the time, *doesn't China remember the alien monsters that were eating Chinese citizens just a few months ago?* What? Just like that, after all of that, it was back to the same old shit? Were human memories that short?

Nothing but frustration buffeted Carl as he tried to glue his country back together while, at the same time, attempting to prevent the rest of the world from devolving into a WWF Brawl For All Tournament. It was insanity served in a paper cup. He pressed the intercom icon on his desk. "Robert, could you get in here please," he snapped.

His latest personal secretary—as none were sticking around for long—Robert Todd knocked softly, then entered the Noval Office. That was what Carl regarded to be the nauseating contraction of New Oval, as opposed to the Oval Office. "Yes, Mr. President?" Robert said dutifully.

"I need to get a few letters off and, as much as it galls me, need to schedule a couple more meetings today."

Robert raised an eyebrow. "You already have five on the slate, sir. Five plus two is seven. Seven is a lot of meetings for one day."

Carl studied the man as he wondered what his new, new secretary would be like, the one he'd hire after he fired Robert. He sure hoped to all that was holy that the new, new assistant wasn't a clueless pedantic. Gosh, that would be nice.

Carl slid a sheet of paper across the table. "Well, in spite of your reservations, *Bob,* here's the people you need to get together."

"Yes, sir, sir."

Not that it would ease his burden in the slightest, but Carl took a deep breath. "I've dictated—"

"Oh, before I forget," Robert interrupted, "the COSAODC chairwoman, the person from Liechtenstein whose name I forgot to write down, she called and–"

"Whoa, whoa, wait," Carl shouted. "What the devil is the COSAODC?"

"The Coalition of Small And/Or Diminutive States, Mr. President."

"You are shitting me, *yes*?" Carl snarled.

"No, sir. Apparently, some of the traditionally tiny countries feel that their sovereign concerns might be overlooked in the Rebuild, so they formed a ... a whatever they formed to speak with a unified voice. A cooperative. A consortium. A bloc."

"What if I don't *want* to hear their unified voice, Bob?" Carl challenged. "Because I do believe I don't."

"I cannot say, Mr. President."

"Well, I can. Please write their message down on a piece of paper and deliver it to someone who cares. Please do so personally, Bob, so I know it gets done."

"Yes, sir. Right away, sir." And with that, Robert quickly left the Noval Office to get right on that task.

"Unbelievable," Carl huffed to himself. Then he noticed the list of who he needed at the extra meetings still rested on his table where Bob left it. "Unbelievabl*er*," Carl hissed.

As the POTUS sat there stunned, a soft knock sounded on the door. He was torn. Part of him hoped it was Robert, so that he could get some work done. Then again, part of him hoped it was the Secret Service here to alert him that Robert had run screaming from the building. How perverse this life was, he mused.

His chief of staff slipped in and sat down. Robin Atwood crossed her legs, smiled at him weakly, then began humming quietly. As the POTUS hadn't greeted her, she knew by then that he wasn't in a chatty mood, so she knew to let him run with that. Finally, she had to ask, "Why is Robert crying out there?"

Carl rolled his shoulders. "Perhaps he's sad because he finally realized that he is an utter failure of a human being?"

"Hmm. So, I needed to update you on the Spokane situ–"

"Wait. Stop. Desist," Carl implored her.

"Yes?" she asked pleasantly enough.

"Why isn't there ever a time that you don't come in here and one of the first words out of your mouth isn't *Spokane*?"

"I don't know. Maybe that's because there's nothing on earth more important or dynamic than the goings-on in and around Spokane, Carl?"

"Let's try this. You step outside. Ignore Bob and then come back in here, and deliver to me some good news–or even not-so-good news–but something that *doesn't* have the word Spokane in the sentence. Can you do that?"

"We'll never know, Carl, because everything in this universe seems to revolve around that unmentionable place."

"Well, maybe I should just move the center of the federal government to Spokane. Hmm. Would that increase the relevancy of this administration?"

"We'll never know that either, because I doubt they'd allow us to *move* the federal government there. The moving vans would probably crash into one of their force fields. How silly would we look then?"

"About as silly as we do now, I suspect," he replied bitterly. Then he eased up a bit. "What did you need to tell me?"

"May I speak of that place?" she teased.

"Go ahead. I'm just frustrated beyond all measure."

"I got a call from Susan."

"My, are not we lucky that she can spare us the time," he said with vitriol.

Robin looked at him a few seconds, debating what to say next. "She wanted to let us know she's well. The production of alien technology is slowly ramping up. She tells me that their focus now is in the fabrication of two main items. Generators and engines. Not surprisingly, the alien portable generators can produce enormous amounts of electricity."

"What fuels them?" he asked.

"Susan said they're fusion-powered. If they have water available, they can do the rest."

"That sounds like a perpetual motion machine," he stated dubiously.

"Hey, don't ask me to explain it. But remember those aliens kicked our butts pretty handily. If Susan says that's how their tech works, I believe it."

"And what are the engines for?" he queried.

"They have several applications. Obviously, spaceships. She did say they could be used for terrestrial purposes—in locomotives to pull trains, that kind of thing."

"Did she mention weapons?" he asked.

"She specifically did not."

"And did you press her on the topic? We're going to *need* those weapons."

"I did not. I want her to feel free to speak to me without having to deal with the politics she wishes to avoid."

Carl threw his hands toward his COS. "She's the damn vice president; she can't avoid politics, by definition."

"Quick question, boss," Robin said in a clipped tone. "Did Susan call you or me?" She let that question hang in the air a few seconds. "That's right. She called me. I'm betting that's because you try to badger her into agreements and commitments she's not prepared to make before you even say *hello*. Ergo, she doesn't call you. Do you see the pattern here?"

"Moving along," he dismissed, "when will she make the generators available to us? Those will save our bacon until we can get the power grid back up and running."

"She's optimistic that they can provide at least one generator to each of the world's twenty largest cities within two months."

"That is *totally* unacceptable and she knows it," Carl shouted. "The USA has, what, three cities in the top twenty? She needs to get *us* set up before she dishes them out to other countries."

"Remember I asked if you were seeing the pattern, Carl? I was being extremely serious. The working group in Spokane wants to help the human species recover without regard to former national boundaries. But, so you don't blow a gasket, Susan said LA, New York, Chicago, Dallas, and DC would be included in the early distribution."

"So they want to give our former *enemies* generators before they let Miami turn their lights back on?"

"In the case of countries that were overtly hostile to the United

States, she said they will review each one on a case-by-case basis. No guarantees either way."

Carl stewed for a while, clearly significantly displeased with his vice president's loyalties—or lack thereof. "I suppose if I made a stink about it, those women would just ignore me," he finally stated.

"If you did, we'd be *lucky* if that's all they did. Carl, you have to realize that everything is different. The world has quite literally changed completely. The Spokane Group not only wants to appear evenhanded, they really want to help the most people they can as quickly as they can. I say we help and applaud their efforts as much as we can."

There was another knock at the door. Donald Yamato, one of the senior advisors who'd been present in the bunker along with the president, poked his head in the door. "You guys ready for the 10:30?"

"Sure," Carl replied. "Why not? But," he pointed at Donald, "why are you asking, not Robert?"

"Who?"

"My secretary, Robert. He'd be the big fellow sitting at the closest desk crying."

Donald shrugged. "No crying people out here of either sex, Mr. President." He gestured over his shoulder. "Shall I have the others come in?"

"Yes." Then to Robin, he started to say, "When we're done—"

"I know. You'll need another new secretary."

A few Joint Chiefs, advisors, and cabinet members quietly filed in and found seats. They mostly constituted the Usual Gang. But one attendee was a surprise.

Carl stood and extended a hand across his deck. "As I live and breathe, welcome back, President Moorehead." Linda Moorehead was the second-past POTUS proceeding Carl.

"It's good to be alive," she said cheerfully, "let alone back." She shook his hand.

As he sat back down, Carl stated, "I'd only heard recently that you were alive, Linda. That's such great news."

"For a human my age when the aliens cleaned house, I should say so." she agreed. "Fortunately, my estate in the Appalachians was far enough removed from civilization that we had a chance to hole up safely before the bugs got around to us."

Those present shared a pleasant chuckle.

"And what brings you back to the dark recesses of Washington?" he asked, not so subtly. He knew that the power he held was revocable if a more attractive alternative was available.

"I'm only here to listen and, if need be, advise you, Mr. President," she replied deferentially. "And I plan on returning to my home and my retirement very soon."

"Well, you will always be welcome here," Carl said with relief. "So, what's on the slate for this morning?" he asked Robin.

"We're going to take yet another stab at aligning ourselves with our former allies," she responded apologetically.

He set his palms over his face. "Oh, no. More frustration. More cat herding," the POTUS decried.

"If only corralling the egos of the world's leaders were as *easy* as cat herding, we'd have a chance to succeed," Admiral Wendy Mitchell bemoaned.

"Can I get an amen?" Carl declared loudly.

The next hour was spent engaged in the intellectual spinning of car wheels in the mud. Nothing was accomplished, not a single new insight or strategy was found, and no hopes were held out for future resolutions. Everything was so dependent on what the Spokane Group did or did not do, that no other country would blink in terms of agreeing to anything with the US government. Everyone held out their support pending a firm commitment that their country would be front-and-center for the fruits of Spokane's labors. Even our closest former allies felt there was too much at stake to allow the US to dominate what was clearly the coming new era of human civilization. The fact that Carl had zero control of the disposition of coming boons was simply not believed by his international counterparts. That, of course, only added to his growing frustration.

When the meeting mercifully ended, COS Robin and Linda Moorehead were the only ones to linger with the POTUS. Finally, Robin rose and asked Linda, "Can I get you anything?"

"No, dear," the former president said with a smile. "But do close the door on your way out." Robin left directly and did close the door.

"Why do I feel like I'm being set up?" Carl asked Linda. "Oh, by the way, it's five o'clock somewhere." He pointed to the bureau. "Can I get you a Scotch?"

"Two fingers, one ice cube," she replied. "And because you were set up, my boy."

Carl handed her a glass then sat back down behind the desk. "To whatever comes next," he toasted.

Linda took a stiff belt but neglected to return his toast. She picked up the briefcase she'd brought with her and rested it on the desk between them. She clicked it open, removed a few items, closed the case, and rested it on the floor.

"Now then, Carl," she began in a serious tone, "I need to offer you some Wisdom of the Ages. The *ages* in this instance are those I've tallied up personally."

The POTUS sipped his drink, then remarked, "I don't *recall* requesting a lesson, Teacher."

"You work on that Scotch and let me be the clever one, alright?" she responded dryly. She arranged a couple wooden objects on the desk. "*There*," she declared. She lowered a stern gaze at Carl. "Class is in session." She slid a blue wooden tablet across to him. It was featureless aside from a red-colored round depression in the center.

"Linda, you shouldn't have," he stated glibly.

"Ah, ah, no wittiness," she scolded him. "What do you see before you, Carl?" she asked.

"A one-foot-square piece of wood."

"I always knew you were a smart boy," she mocked. "And what do you see at the center of the wood?"

He made a show of leaning in and staring down at it. "A red hole."

"Magna cum laude for you, my boy. There's a round hole." She reached across the table and handed him a thick wooden stick, also painted red.

"Um, thanks?" he throated dubiously.

"What did I just give you?" she asked.

"A stick."

"Could you be more descriptive?"

"Yes, Mrs. Moorehead. It is a six-inch-long red-colored square stick."

"I knew you had it in you. Very good. Now, Mr. President, please insert your red stick into the matching red-colored hole," she directed.

Carl held the stick a bit higher and angled it. "You got me, Teach. Very dowel. We both know I cannot fit a square peg into a round hole."

"I'd appreciate it if you would make the attempt," she stated as an order.

Carl loudly slammed the peg onto the hole it could not fit in. "Satisfied?" he asked sarcastically.

"Try again."

"Linda, I'm busy, I'm close to losing my mind, and I'm done with this game."

"Try *again*," she snapped.

"Fine," he acquiesced. Then he slammed the wood peg against the hole multiple times in anger. "There," he said harshly, "happy now?"

"I'd need a few more Scotches for that to happen, but you've completed the demonstration. Thank you. Now my wisdom. Carl, you're being an ass." He started to react, but she held up a stop-there palm. "But, being an ass is not uncommon in the world of politics. But it's the *type* of ass you're being that's a problem. Carl, you're that crotchety old man sitting on a park bench. Whenever anyone comes within range, he waves his cane in the air and shouts that something to the effect that, *Back in my day, we did it the right way, You young folk got it all wrong.*"

Linda drew a deep breath. "Carl, the world has changed. It's broken. And, like Humpty Dumpty, all the king's horses and all the king's men are not putting it back the way it was." Again she paused briefly. "Neither are you, Carl. Neither are *you*. Times change. I'm not talking about adjusting to a *new normal* here either. It's a new everything. It will be adjust and survive. The alternative is irrelevance. Just ask the next Egyptian pharaoh or Roman Caesar you run into. With any luck, I estimate free elections will be possible in five to seven years. Until then, you're it, Carl, you're the POTUS. But if you don't start acting like one, you'll end your term as that old, forgotten man on that park bench."

By then, Carl's head was so low, he gazed upon the floor. Slowly, he raised it back up. "I hear you, Linda. And I thank you."

"I can tell you this, having known you for many years. I think you have it in you. There's a nightmare facing you, but I believe in you. If I didn't I wouldn't have left my comfortable home and my grandkids playing in the back yard."

"I cannot thank you enough. And I promise I won't make Robin call you out of retirement again to take me out behind the shed for a good whooping."

"Let us hope not," she said dryly. "If she does, I'll be far less pleasant next time."

He pointed down. "This was *pleasant* Linda?"

"Yes, and you're welcome." She allowed a slight grin. "Carl, humanity needs to embrace and encourage what's going on in Spokane. When the next alien invasion fleet pulls into orbit, we're going to need tens of thousands of warships to defend ourselves. That will only be possible if the Spokane Group can pull off that miracle. Be part of the solution, my friend."

"I read you loud and clear," he responded. "Who knows, maybe I'll move the seat of government up there, cut out the middleman?"

"That's the spirit," she encouraged. She threw back the last of her drink and set the glass on the desk. "Now, I've got to be going. If I'm not back home by eight, I'll miss the baths and goodnight hugs." She lowered her head and looked up at him. "Setting you straight isn't worth missing that even once." She held out her hand. "Good luck, Mr. President."

He stood as they shook. "Thanks again, *Mrs*. President."

THIRTEEN

Natalie was carrying two heavy containers down a passageway on *Defiant*. The ship's replicators needed to be resupplied with rare earth elements every once in a while and Peaches' supplies were presently running low. Many components that she required to fabricate food and mechanical components could be pulled from the air or local soil. But some were simply unavailable locally. Natalie didn't mind the task. It gave her a good excuse to be alone on the ship, away from the insanity that her life had become.

Before the apocalypse, she was too young to have developed a firm notion of what she wanted to do when she grew up. But whatever that notion might have been, she was certain it wasn't that she'd be a key player in a massive industrial organization with thousands of employees. And then there were the tens of thousands of people who wanted something of her. The line of people wanting a piece of her seemed to stretch well past the horizon, and it only ever got longer. Someone wanted her time. Another wanted her favor. That one wanted preferential access. That person wanted to control her. And that one felt the need to let her know unambiguously what a horrible person she was just on general principles. It never ended.

There were only two things Natalie never heard. One was, *You're doing a great job. How can I help?* The other was the sound of Chris's voice. That hurt the most, cut the deepest. The chaos that was her existence would be tolerable if he was at her side. And every day he didn't call, didn't return, inescapably increased the odds that he never would. Visquisor was clearly an evil force in the universe. The chances of him graciously allowing Chris to return to his former life were slim-to-none right from the start. As more time passed, the likelihood that Chris would resist and even try to thwart Visquisor grew. Natalie knew just how brightly the flame of justice burned in her man's heart. That commitment to doing the right thing only further decreased the prospects of his safe return. She'd told herself she'd never give up hope. But, in the real world, that type of plan was more wishful thinking than a rational practicality.

"I can tell that you are hurting," Peaches said, breaking up Natalie's bleak train of thought.

"I am," Natty said quietly.

"For what it's worth, I believe Chris will return to us," Peaches soothed. "He's smart, resourceful, and lucky. I've learned to never underestimate him. He's too darn good."

Natalie chuckled sadly. "He is all those things, isn't he?"

"I think Visquisor's last words will someday be, *Oh, crap, I can't believe he pulled that off.*"

They shared a laugh, both confident that was an accurate assessment.

"Do you think these supplies will be enough for now?" Natalie asked, changing the topic.

"Absolutely. And you didn't have to lug them down yourself. I could have sent nanobots to ferry the material."

"I don't mind. In fact, I look forward to getting away, truth be told."

"This I believe," Peaches sympathized warmly.

"You know, the closer we get to putting working tech in the hands of others, the crazier it gets," Natalie shared. "I knew there'd be pressure galore, but I never knew it would be this tremendous."

"I can only say that I am glad I am not you," Peaches admitted. "Greed and fear bring out the worst in every species. Yours is no exception. But I do not think you four could be doing any better. It's tough on you all personally. But please know that you're all exceeding any of my expectations. You guys are nothing short of-"

The abruptness of Peaches' words startled Natalie. "What?" she asked nervously.

"A ship of unknown configuration has just exited fold space inside the orbit of Mars," Peaches announced.

"I hate those words, *unknown configuration*," Natalie moaned. "Is it coming to Earth?"

"Yes. Directly so. ETA ten minutes."

"Wow, it must be moving fast," she remarked.

"That it is. To be honest, I'm not even sure what form of propulsion the ship is using."

"Oh, great. A new and even stronger bully on the block," Natalie mumbled. "Can you let the others know? Tell them I'm on my way back to the conference room."

"Done," Peaches stated immediately.

A minute later, Natalie jogged into the main conference room, set up in the neighboring house that was incorporated into their ever-growing Spokane enterprise. "Any news?" she asked Grace, who was seated between Molly and Susan.

"Nothing more. Whoever's coming is almost here. Peaches hailed them, but so far, there's no response."

"Peaches," Natalie called out now that she could contact the AI again, "Is it possibly a Dostivex ship we're not familiar with?"

"No, definitely not. The configuration and drive are not theirs."

"That's a relief," Molly said mostly to herself. "The last thing we need is another run-in with them."

"Captain," Peaches blurted to Natalie, "I am now receiving a transmission from the ship. They ask to speak directly with you. They asked for you by name."

"That's not possible," she replied. "Some unknown species appears out of nowhere and they know my-" Natalie was cut off by the voice coming over the room's speakers.

"*Hello*, Natty," an oddly familiar voice sang out.

Natalie turned back to the other women. "There is absolutely *no way!*"

❧

"I say again, *hello*, Ms. Natalie." I knew my girlfriend either hadn't recognized my voice or she did, and had just fainted. Either way, I had the biggest smile on my face.

"Chris? Is ... is that really you?" Natalie was finally able to say, albeit uncertainly.

"I think it's really me. Hang on. I'm looking for a mirror to double check."

"Yep, that's him," Grace throated dubiously.

"Yeah, I checked. It's really handsome old me," I informed her. "I'll be landing in the backyard in two minutes. I'll fill you all in then. Chris out."

I'm sure one of them wanted to tell me my ship was way too big to land in the backyard. But I decided to torture them by cutting the transmission before they could warn me. What they couldn't know was that I was flying *Arc of Intention*. If there was a size issue, Marcalif would simply reshape the ship's underbelly to fit. In any case, I felt a slight bump as we landed. I jumped out of my seat and flew to the nearest exit port. My ever-so-clever AS had the ramp fully deployed before I got there. I think he could sense my enthusiasm, by which I mean he could probably smell my hormones trailing behind me.

As I swept past the base of the ramp, Natalie was homing in on me at full speed too. Ah, young, impulsive love. About two steps onto the grass, we collided, actually pretty darn hard. I don't know if she knocked me down or I knocked her down, but the next thing I realized we were on the ground kissing. Natalie also managed to *squee* at the same time. I really got the impression that she was as glad to see me. Yeah, baby!

After a spell, I peeked up to see three women towering above us. Two were familiar, one was new to me. But they all had their arms crossed and disapproving expressions on their faces. Obviously, they were a well-synchronized team. I took the hint and began the process of detaching the love of my life from my person. It was not easy. I'd finally manage to separate our lips, but while I attempted to untangle our arms, her lips slammed back against mine. I mean, it was nice, but the three cross women were still up there glaring down.

"Babe," I was able to say quickly, "enough. We got company."

Natalie looked up, finally noticing the observers. Her body relaxed. "Welcome home." She gave me a last quick peck and then we both rose. As I was slapping some grass off my legs, she said, "Hi, guys," to the others. "Sorry. I guess we maybe overdid it a little."

Grace smiled and opened her arms wide. "Welcome home, Chris." She slapped my back soundly and kissed my cheek as we parted.

Molly repeated the hugs. All in all, I have to say that it was really nice. And man, was it good to see them all again.

"Chris Alan," Grace said to me formally while gesturing to the third woman, "I'd like you to meet Susan Whitehorse, the sitting Vice President of the United States."

I reached out and accepted her hand. "Wow, some homecoming committee. I get my family *and* the VP."

"It is an honor to finally meet you, Mr. Alan." She slightly furrowed her brow. "Or should I say Captain Alan?"

I chuckled warmly. "How about you call me Chris like everyone else does?"

"Thank you. As long as you call me Susan."

"*Deal*," I said as we stopped the handshake.

"Susan has become an integral part of our efforts here in the Rebuild," Grace continued. "I don't know what we'd have done without her."

"And honestly, she's really nice in *spite* of being the VP," Molly added with a giggle.

"Okay, here come the politician jokes," Susan said with a groan.

"I know you all have a million questions," I said as I threw an arm around Natalie's shoulders. "Let's go inside and–" I looked around. "Where are Felicia and Farrah?"

Molly grinned and stated proudly, "They're still in school."

I flared my eyes wide in amazement. "My, but a lot has changed in my absence."

"Yes, it has," Grace affirmed resolutely. "And some even for the better." She reached in and hooked one of my arms. "Come on, coffee's fresh. Let's hear your tall tale before it grows even more immense."

Natalie snared my other arm and we trooped back into the house, toward that old, familiar kitchen table. Grace set everyone up with a hot mug and set a stack of homemade cookies at the center of the table. Natty scooted her chair over so it abutted mine and she wrapped both arms around me before resting her head on my shoulder. It was good to be home.

"So, that's a pretty fancy-schmancy ship you plopped down in my backyard there, mister," Molly stated.

"Yeah, the ship's named *Arc of Intention* and she's way past amazing. The ship's AS is a fantastic guy too. Marcalif-Son, but he goes by just Marcalif."

"Commodore?" Peaches cut in over the speakers, "would it be alright if I began an interface with Marcalif-Son?"

"Hi, Peaches," I greeted. "Sure, but what's up with the commodore BS?"

"You now command two ships, hence you are one. Natalie obviously remains the captain of *Defiant*. And I congratulate you on your promotion."

"I don't think it was a promotion," I responded dubiously. "More a lucky break."

"Be that as it may, *Commodore*," she said tongue-in-cheek, even though she possessed neither.

"I know you're going to tell us the entire story," Molly chimed in. "But I have to know what happened to Visquisor. Don't tell me he set you free."

I shook my head briskly. "No. Well, yes he did, but not in any good way."

So I told them the whole story. My first days with my "host" and the escapades we shared. When I got to the part where old Vizzy marooned me on Dez Falls, the women grew stern expressions and clearly their opinions of the bastard dropped to new lows. I sang the praises of my grumpy guardian angel, Morpheus Denali, and amazed them with the story of a living planet with a name so long, I'd never heard it. Then I told them of the miraculous ship that had basically adopted me, explaining about the Technical Scale and TSVes. I can tell you their eyes nearly bulged out of their heads when I told them that while a superb *Defiant* had a TSV of around five, and Visquisor's *Peerless* had one of seven, my new ship rated a TSV of eight. But the most important thing I told them was how much I'd missed them and how they gave me strength on my darkest days.

"As much as I thought Visquisor was a phony piece of shit," Grace said severely, "I never would have thought he was *that* horrible."

"Yeah," I shook my head slowly, "he's about as bad as bad gets."

"And he said he plans to destroy the Earth?" Susan attempted to confirm. "You're sure that's what he said?"

"I can quote you exactly what the jackass said. *I am disappointed in you. You come from Earth. Therefore, I am cross with the planet. Any solar system I dislike I destroy. End of story.*"

"Oh, so he's taking out the whole kit and caboodle now?" Molly blurted out. "*You* piss the man off and even *Jupiter* gets punished? What an egomaniac."

"This ... this is terrible news," Susan said in a barely audible voice. Then she looked up to me with soulful eyes. "Did he say when?"

"No, he was too busy gloating about how he was ditching me to get into specifics." I thought about the issue a second. "I don't think he has it as a high priority. It's just something he'll do when he gets around to it."

They were quiet a moment. Then Grace spoke up. "We've been working like possessed demons to get a Dostivex-level defense network set up for the planet. But we all saw how Visquisor mowed through that fleet. I ... it's discouraging in the extreme to hear he's gunning for us."

"I don't think we Earthlings have anything to worry about," I stated confidently. "As long as I'm here with *Arc*, Visquisor's the one who'll be doing the losing."

"I'm not too comfortable betting the farm on your one ship," Susan stated. "And didn't you mention he controls nine other ships just like his?"

"He does. Visquisor has a retinue of lackeys he holds sway over. They, unlike me, were weighed in his balance and found worthy."

"Ten powerful warships are a lot to fend off with one ship, however advanced it is," Molly stated grimly.

"According to Marcalif, it doesn't work like that—not linearly—past a certain technology level. He's very confident he can handle whatever Visquisor throws at us."

"Commodore, if I might," Peaches cut back in. "I'm having the most stimulating conversation with Marcalif-Son. One issue he's clarified to me is important to pass along."

"Great," I responded. "Go for it."

"The captains of *Peerless*'s sister ships are not protégés of Visquisor in the sense you understand it."

"Really?" I remarked.

"Marcalif-Son related to me that Visquisor keeps them around as ... hmm, how best to describe them? Replacement parts? Potential new vessels? Something along those lines."

"You're kidding me?" I stated with alarm. Hey, I was his most recent recruit. If he was up to no good, it included me. Then again, what am I saying? Of course he's up to no good. That's what he does.

"Visquisor suffers from a profound feeling of emptiness," she continued. "He is extremely old and, over time, appears to have lost any joy in life. He feels nothing. Long ago, he heard a whisper from a Mentic Sage about the possibility of the transfer of souls. The nine individuals we speak of are under the false impression that they are *associates* of Visquisor. They are, in fact, kept at the ready should Visquisor finally discover the secret of soul transfers. They constitute his options-larder, if you will."

"That's absolutely gross," Natalie said with disgust.

"It makes sense," I mumbled. "I've always wondered why the otherwise self-consumed Visquisor had that apparent fatherly side to him." I harrumphed. "I guess the jokes on those nine idiots."

"At least you were perceptive enough to reject the monster," said Grace.

"Yeah, and look what it got me. Marooned on a desert world as opposed to having my soul booted out of my own body. It's like the old executioner's joke where he sits you down in the electric chair and then asks if you want AC or DC."

Grace glanced at the clock. "As much as we'd like to continue this conversation, Molly and I need to pick the girls up."

Molly swigged the last of her coffee and added, "My, how time flies when one's discussing the next apocalypse." She stood up and started to clear dishes.

"Leave that," Susan told her. "You get the girls. I'll clean up."

"Are you sure?"

"Absolutely. If I need help, I'll enlist Chris here."

"Yeah, you guys go. I'm happy to help," I chimed in.

"Really?" Molly asked me in an unbelieving tone.

"No way. But if it gets you two out of here, I'm prepared to lie."

Molly tossed a crumpled napkin at me, grabbed Grace's hand, and they left.

"As for me," Susan began, "once I get this squared away," she nodded to the dishes, "I need to go do some vice presidential stuff."

"Sounds hard," I teased.

"Oh, it is. I need to make calls that will change nothing, then I need to sort through a mountain of documents that were meaningless when sent to me." She wagged her eyebrows. "Very heady stuff."

While Susan rinsed plates, Natalie turned to me and said quietly, "Know what I'd like to do?"

"*What?*" I asked saucily, as if I most definitely knew.

"Take a tour of *Arc*."

Hmm, that was a relative letdown, but not actually unreasonable. "Sure. It's an amazing ship." I stood and offered her an elbow, which she accepted with a giggle.

"I imagine it has futuristic bedrooms too?" she remarked, trying to appear nonchalant about the query.

"Why yes, it does. Very futuristic. Flashing lights and shiny things. You'll love all of them."

Natty pulled in tight and we walked toward the backyard. "I was so worried about you," she said while hugging my arm tightly.

"I was always coming home." I kissed the top of her head and assured her. Call me a hopeless romantic, but I actually believed that to be true.

As we walked up the ramp, I called out, "Marcalif, I'd like to introduce you to Natalie Welsh, the most amazing woman on Earth."

"I am very pleased to finally meet you, Natalie Welsh," he greeted her. "Your Chris speaks of you highly and often."

"Aw, that's so sweet," she remarked, looking up at me.

"I will take your word on that," he remarked. "I am yet to master human emotions."

After we shared a chuckle, I said, "Let's start with the bridge and work our way back."

"Well, we *could*," she speculated in a leading tone. "Or we could start in the middle and see the rest tomorrow."

"You know, I think that's a vastly superior plan." What could I say? My girl was a genius.

We didn't speak as we walked the passageways to my captain's quarters. It was nice to be so in love that an easy quiet was a joy unto itself.

Once we were at the entry, I gestured at the door. "And here is my humble abode."

Natty giggled most wonderfully. The door slid open and ... and there stood Rosey. Oops. I'd forgotten to mention her, hadn't I? At least she was still wearing that jumpsuit. Yeah, I wouldn't want ... you know what? I'm not even finishing that thought.

"Oh, hi," I said to her. "Ah, Natalie, this is Rosey. She's ... I guess you'd call her my personal assistant. Rosey's a mechanical being."

I could feel Natalie's entire body stiffen even before she released my arm, which she did directly. "Rosey, eh?" she said flatly. "Hello, Rosey the personal assistant."

"Hello, Ms. Welsh. It is a pleasure to meet you," my assistant responded. Rosey nodded as opposed to offering a hand to shake.

"Ah, Rosey, Natalie and I want to ... I mean, we won't be needing you for now," I stammered nervously.

"Very good, Captain," she responded. And with that, she backed up against the nearest wall. And then she ... just stood there.

"If you don't mind, Rosey, could you go somewhere else? Maybe to the mess lounge?"

"As you wish," she responded cheerily and off she went.

Once Rosey was gone and the door closed, Natalie remarked, "She seems nice." Oh, boy, there was the ever-critical *nice*. It said both nothing *and* volumes when spoken in the manner Natty just had.

"Yeah, I guess she is."

Natalie walked casually to the nearest chair and sat propped up on the armrest. "She was wearing a jumpsuit. Is that her official outfit? If so, that seems unexpected," she asked with all the doubt possible to cram into those words.

"Yeah, well, sure. I ... I guess you could say I asked her to wear one. We ... we were touring the Engineering Department at the time. I thought it fitting." Then, because I'm perfectly inept and an idiot, I added. "Hey, I get it, her clothes were *fitting*." Yeah, funny as a crutch, right? That's me!

"So you pick out Rosey's clothes?" Natalie asked with surgical precision.

"Well, no. I mean, I guess you could say I *advise* her, in a sense. A little sense ... *some*."

"You sure have started *guessing* a lot with your hands since we met Rosey," my girlfriend observed.

"I'm sorry," I muttered. "Is that a question?"

"No. An interesting observation. So–and I only ask because I'm interested and wish to learn more concerning this alien culture–what was the gorgeous Rosey the robot wearing previously that you felt the need to *advise* she change it into an Engineering jumpsuit?" Why, I ask you why, did she have to be so darn insightful? Me? I felt kind of like Wile E. Coyote as he stared up at the boulder about to crash down on him.

I ran my hands up and down my sides. "You know, a *dress* thing ... I think. Maybe. Could'a been a pants suit I gue ... I think."

Crap, she escalated to crossing her arms. I was so auto-dead, you know, since I was killing myself so very quickly.

"I would like to ask a simple question, Christopher, to which I'm anticipating a succinct response. Okay?"

She. Had. Never. Called. Me. Christopher. Ever. Hoo, boy. Guess who would be coffin shoppin' soon? "Shoot." Sure, why beat around the bush? Employ a term befitting of my fate.

"What was the most striking quality of Rosey's maybe dress that made you, of all people, decide to offer her fashion advice?"

I felt at my right hip. Damn, I wasn't wearing a sidearm with which to blow my non-brains out with. "I gue ... I suppose you could describe them as ... what's the word? Um, *transparent*. Yeah, I gue .. think that's the term."

Natalie began rocking and sniffed loudly. Not in a very ladylike manner either. "Let's work backward here, okay? Why was Rosey, who I must say has a fantastically realistic human female body, wearing totally see-through clothing and no undergarments while touring the *Engineering* Department with you?"

"Ah, well, that's one I can answer, and when I do you're going to be actually kind of proud of me."

"As unlikely as that outcome is, we can both certainly pray that turns out to be the case," she responded. "Go on."

"Well, you see—and this you'll love because it gets to the alien culture thing you're so interested in—the structure of this alien society was that servants—the servant class that is—and out of respect and deference to their masters, well, I gue ... I learned they don't wear any ... you know ... clothes."

"So, and please correct me if I missed a critical point, when you first met your personal assistant, she was buck naked?"

I shook my head disapprovingly and had a sour look, like I'd just bitten a lemon. "You know, I think *naked* is a misleading term, when applied here. Rosey, not being an actual person, can't really be naked. Just unclothed."

"And because you are in a committed relationship, when your eyes stopped scouring her heavenly buck naked body, you instructed her to instead wear transparent clothing?"

I pointed generally toward Natty's feet. "It sounds not-the-way-I-intended-it the way you just said it."

"But what I said was quite literally true, correct?"

"Technically but not contextually," I said, and, *no*, before you ask, I have no idea what that meant either.

"So, in summary, let me take a stab at this. While I have been crying myself to sleep every night, worrying myself sick, you've been playing buck naked Barbie Boom-Boom Rosey with your personal assistant?"

"Again, while those words, in that order, are not incorrect, I wish to point out that they imply *meaning* that is not in evidence." Crap, I almost finished that idiocy with the words *your honor*. What an idiot!

"Marcalif?" Natalie enunciated.

"Yes, Natalie?" he responded cautiously. Dude had my back after all.

"Is any part of what my idiot boyfriend said in fact true?"

There was a delay of several seconds before he replied, "I guess I wasn't listening. Sorry." Smart AS.

"Marcalif," Natty continued, "I know that at some technical level, you have a mind and a body, a housing, if you will."

"That is correct," he responded.

"If you value your continued existence in that condition, answer me plainly. Did my boyfriend even as much as touch anywhere at anytime, Rosey the Robot?"

"Not that I'm ... I mean, no." Wow. You know when someone says *it could only get worse*? I guess they did so anticipating this very conversation.

Natalie sat there a little longer on that armrest. Then she raised her hand and signaled me with her index finger that I should come over to where she was. I did so. She rubbed at her chin with the back of a thumbnail, and stated, for the record, I presume, "Because I love you so very much and know well your true character, am I going to do something that other women would criticize me for doing here. I am going to *accept* your version of the short story titled *Life With My Naked Assistant* as the gospel truth."

"For that, I wish to thank you," I said because it was the stone-cold truth.

"*But*, I want to ask you. Did you ever hear the one about the guy who had a gorgeous naked servant and he played doctor with her and then lied about that to his girlfriend?"

"I cannot say that I have. No."

"And you never will because he died quietly in his sleep of natural causes when a pillow was crammed over his face the very night he BSed that saintly woman."

"I would like to thank you for sharing that cautionary tale with me."

"Why don't we wrap this up in the bedroom and do so now, lest I come to my senses."

I extended an arm in the direction of the sleeping quarters. "Right this way, if you please."

FOURTEEN

I've heard a lot of pissing and moaning from the males of our species about their collective frustration of not being able to understand women. As a teenager, I obviously have no insights or wisdom to pass along. But I do, at my tender age, have experience to add to the vast ocean of baffled-male incomprehension. Fortunately, my latest run in with female-engendered what-just-hit-me was, if not painless, at least not protracted. Maybe Natalie was just sending me a general message, attempting to deliver a learning session to me when she boxed my ears about Rosey. For whatever reason, no sooner had she remanded me to the dog house, she figuratively summonsed me back, and I was quickly blessed by the warmth of her embrace. Thank goodness I was kidnapped and subsequently left for dead by Visquisor. That seemed to have bought me a lot of brownie points payable toward forgiveness.

After a few rounds of her forgiving me, we lay in bed next to one another, just chilling. It was nice. I idly stroked her hair as Natty was curled up next to me, her head on my chest.

"I know nothing will ever be *normal* again," she remarked wistfully, "but it sure would be nice if things got a little more boring."

"Predictable and not-deadly sounds awfully good to me too." Then, after a moment, I added, "I think we'll get there, babe. Someday."

"I hate porches," Natalie remarked ... um, unexpectedly.

"You do?"

"Yes. They're stuffy and too darn old-fashioned."

"Are you referring to porches on houses, or the structural elements such as porticoes, verandas, and loggias in general?"

"No, on houses. Our house cannot have a porch."

"Ah, sure. I promise it will not have a porch."

"So you agree we'll have a house one day?" she confirmed.

I got a little nervous, sensing a nascent emotion that was unintelligible to my male mind. "Of course. In fact, we sort of do now. *Defiant* has been our home for some time. And *Arc* can be too."

"Oh, pooh. Those may well be our homes, but they're never *houses*. No. Houses have wooden walls, tile roofs, chimneys, and backyards for our kids to play in."

Yikes, we were planning ahead here, weren't we? Best not to comment on that aspect of our so far most pleasant conversation. "They do, but they better not have a porch," I menaced playfully.

"Well, a *back* porch is fine. Just not a starched-shirt front porch."

"Note to Realtor: Back porches *only* but not necessarily."

She rubbed my tummy. "Now you're talking."

Hey, for another tummy rub, I'd talk some more. Never had one before, but I hoped my future was full of 'em.

After some more quiet, Natalie said, "I love you."

I swept my hand through her hair more forcefully. "And I love you."

"Chris?"

"Yes?"

"I don't want to die when Visquisor comes back to destroy Earth."

Yikes, that was a serious and specific concern of hers. "We'll be fine. *Arc* is easily capable of neutralizing anything he can throw at us."

"Well, maybe eventually. But if he attacks Spokane first because you're here, we could all be in danger."

"But Visquisor doesn't know I'm here. He is, in fact, one-hundred percent certain I'm dead on Dez Falls."

"That's true," she responded with a perkier tone. "Oh, but wait. He'll surely notice that *Arc* is here. That might make him beat a retreat until he's better prepared to kill us."

"You have a great point that he might notice the ship. But even if he does, he wouldn't be able to escape."

"But he might slip away. It's not impossible. And then he could try to obtain a better ship or materialize a huge bomb into the center of the planet?"

I thought about the possibilities a second. "I think maybe hiding *Arc* from detection is a great idea. As for magically making a huge bomb appear, I wouldn't sweat that. Marcalif would notice something like that. Plus, you're imagining a bomb so big there I don't think it can exist. No, we're safe."

"I hope so. I want that house with no front porch," she said firmly. "And the kids playing out back."

Again with the kids–*plural*–at such an early point in our relationship. Wait. Was I being too *guy* here? It's not too hard for us to get that way. "Hey, do you wanna get married?"

There are moments in this life worthy of notation. Seminal statements spoken. Weighty works wrought. And, lamentably, stupid stunts spawned. And I just realized that blurting out some words, some notions, was not as good an idea microseconds after speaking them than you thought they'd be when initially you blurted them out. It occurred to me that casually asking, while still in the post-coital time frame, your girlfriend to marry you might constitute a social faux pas. I may also have compounded that miscue since we were both naked and she had her head lying on my chest. Such ... being that guy-like could be construed as some observers to be a suboptimal moment to pop The Question. Unromantic. Crass. Fatal. One of those things. I hadn't asked her at some picturesque location. I did not have in hand a well-thought-out ring. I neglected to drop to one knee. The manner in which I asked my one true love to marry me was similar to the way I might have asked her *did you want ketchup with those fries?*

Many bad next words *might* be coming my way soon and very soon.

Natalie jerked her head to look up at me. Hmm, not the best of initial reactions. Then she placed a hand on the mattress and slowly sat up. Again, not the most portentous reaction imaginable. She swallowed hard, lowered her chin to her chest, and started to speak.

"I know," I said in a pressured, panicky instant, "that a man ... a man shouldn't propose to his love in a manner that ... that could be construed to be–"

That was all I stammered out before she launched herself up, her lips targeting my mouth. She struck with such force that my head snapped back and I might have fractured a tooth. But, rescued foundering idiot that I was, I ignored the pain, embraced my girl, and prayed that I was fully forgiven.

"Yes," she said softly after easing off a little, "in some other ... many other ... *most* other circumstances, I might be upset that you proposed to me so informally. But after worrying that I'd never see you again and loving you like I do, I forgive your ... informality."

My, *informal* used twice in one pardon. I do believe she was faulting me on that count. Note to self: Make this up to her. But, on the other hand ... *we were getting married!*

Let me try that in my head again.

We were getting married!

While intellectually a pleasing thought, it did not evoke in my soul ... what's the word I'm looking for? Excitement? No, but the word I sought wasn't too far from that one.

Oh, my. We were ... getting married.

"Chris?" my fiancée asked. "Are you all right?"

"*Yes,*" mercifully popped out of my mouth. "I was just thinking ... you know, where are we going to find a minister, you know, post-apocalypse and all."

She kissed me–thank God! "Silly boy. We can work out all the details later. There are churches springing up all over. Between the four of us, we can cover every detail."

"The ... four ... of ... us?" I wondered incautiously and out loud.

"Me, Grace, Molly, and Susan. Between us, we can solve any problem, find every solution."

My, we were suddenly not so much a couple but a sextet. A *septet* if you counted the girls. Two things dawned on me. One, marriage was not as simple as I had imagined it was. Two, I was, for some reason, sweating profusely. Had I been jogging? I did not recall any recent running.

"Chris?" my fiancée asked yet again. "Are you all right?"

"Yes," again popped from my mouth. But it was neither emphatic nor followed by ... by more words.

"Let's get dressed and go tell the others," she said as she bounced across the bed.

That action, believe it or not, did break the mind fog I was experiencing. "Yeah, if we tell them in the buff, we'd lose some of the gravitas," I affirmed.

Natty turned to me. "You are so silly. Come on. Up." She gestured emphatically. "We're all having dinner tonight, but I want to tell the girls before the others get here."

"You want to tell Felicia and Farrah first?" I asked incredulously. Why was it important to garner the children's blessing so imminently?

"You are just a riot today," she said bereft of conviction. "No, the other adult women." Somehow Natalie was already fully dressed. I'd never seen her do that so ... quickly. And me, I was still slumped in bed naked.

But, sooner than I'd have thought possible, I was also fully dressed and we were jogging back to the house. Why, I wondered but did not inquire, did we need to run?

When we got to the kitchen, Grace and Molly were making the girls a snack. "Where's Susan?" Natalie asked the room.

"In the study making calls," Molly responded. She clearly sensed something was up. "Why?"

Natalie held out both palms. "Nobody move." Then she dashed out of the kitchen. Seconds later, she returned with a confused-looking vice president. "Everybody sit," Natalie commanded.

That accomplished, Natty shouted, "We're getting married!"

Felicia and Farrah jumped to their feet and started waving their arms in the air screaming ... something. Susan smiled. Molly smiled a little more than Susan. Grace raised an eyebrow, just like Mr. Spock did so well on TV when surprised. Then, likely due to mysterious and powerful forces I could not perceive or comprehend, all six females coalesced into a group hug. The scrum started bouncing and squeeing. Then the throng began gyrating in *my* direction. I was torn. If I ran, that might be construed as me having cold feet about the marriage idea. But I was a little frightened by the primal nature of the whole thing.

Fortunately, I stood my ground and allowed them to envelop me. Pretty quick, I was into it too. I hugged them back and we ... they squeed and I smiled loudly. But it was amazing.

Grace pulled back a bit. "I'm so happy for you two."

Molly rose up on her toes. "Congratulations times one million."

Felicia and Farrah screamed ... something.

Susan grinned. "This is so life-affirming."

I stood there thinking, believe it or not, *We're getting married?*

FIFTEEN

Two days after my return home, we met as a team with Marcalif. I guess I should start referring to us–Grace, Molly, Susan, Natalie, and me–as the Spokane Group. It seems the rest of the world already was. Obviously, Peaches was critical to everything, so maybe I should include her? If I asked, she'd claim to have no interest in such human matters as recognition, so I'll just add her with an asterisk next to her name. We waited those two days to meet because Natty and I had spent quite a bit of time together aboard *Arc of Intention*, but not in an information gathering or educational manner–he said as he clears his throat.

We had decided that I'd formally introduce Marcalif, then, afterwards, we could tour the ship. If we tried to combine the two activities, they'd all be so blown away with the tech that they'd forget to talk with the AS. As the lone adult not counted among the Spokane Group leadership, we did invite Susan's husband Mike Duggan to participate. He hadn't expressed much interest in getting involved, but we didn't want him to feel excluded. As the spouse of a politician rising through the ranks, he'd learned to be supportive but to keep his professional life separate. He had been a very successful investment banker before the invasion. These days, he was monkeying with how to reanimate that sector after it was completely destroyed. Yeah, Mike was a patient man.

At five minutes to nine that morning, we were sitting in the kitchen about to start the meeting. "So, everybody's set with food and drink?" Grace, the eternal doter, confirmed.

Everyone nodded that they were.

"We'll just be using an audio feed from *Arc of Intention*," I announced. "Marcalif offered to fabricate some visual image, but I let him know that wouldn't be necessary."

"Do you think we'll all eventually have implants so we can communicate with the ASs more seamlessly?" Natalie asked. I detected a hint of reservation in her voice.

"I can't tell others what to do," I stated the obvious. "That said, it would probably be a good goal to set. I cannot tell–"

I stopped talking when a tall man I didn't recognize walked silently into the room. He was dressed in a formal-appearing outfit, vaguely reminiscent to the overalls I'd had Rosey wear. He was definitely human, rather good-looking, and stood at the entrance in a non-threatening manner. Nonetheless, I was glad I always carried a sidearm.

"Can I help you?" I asked him sternly.

"No. I'm just here for our nine o'clock meeting."

"We ... we don't have any scheduled meetings this morning," Molly said, speaking up.

"Of course we do, Ms. Cooper. A nine AM meet-and-greet with me."

"Hang on," I said, raising a palm toward him. "Are you Marcalif in a robotic host?"

"Yes, Captain. I felt it might be a better, more familiar way for your friends to get to know me. I hope you do not object."

"No, no," I replied. "I was just surprised. Please, come in and meet the gang."

I introduced him to everyone separately. He was cordial and deferential, shaking each hand and exchanging a few pleasant words with everyone. It turned out he was one smooth operator.

Once we were all seated, including Marcalif, I asked, "Is this host able to contain your entire programming, the one housed on *Arc of Intention*?"

"No, Captain. It may function in one of two manners. I can, as I am now, simply remotely project myself into it. It does have a very robust storage capacity, so I could also download a copy of my entire personality profile along with some basic memory."

"Wow, you continue to impress," I commented. "Did you assume a robotic host back when you worked with the Nafcadollians, your makers?"

He shook his head gently. "No. They were humanoid, but their way of thinking was very different from yours. They always considered their technology to be tools that benefited them. They would never have appreciated a tool taking a physical representation such as this robot unless that representation somehow directly benefited them."

"Like the beautiful Rosey the servant," Natalie said because she was just never going to let that go.

"Precisely, Captain Welsh," he responded.

"Well, I like it," I declared. "We'll all think of you as the independent sentient that you are this way." Then another thought occurred to me. "What's the distance limit to this projection?"

"That, believe it or not, for the reasons I just discussed, has never been established. I think it will be one-hundred percent reliable in the hundreds of thousands of kilometer range. I will let you know if I determine it to be different."

"Great, yeah. Keep me posted," I replied. "So, let's get on with the substance of the meeting. Marcalif, why don't you give everyone a brief background of the ship and yourself."

"Very well, Captain. I am, as you know, Marcalif-Son, the ship's AS for *Arc of Intention*. The ship and I were created by a race known as the Nafcadollians. They were a humanoid species with a technology unimaginably more advanced than yours is presently. They emerged on the galactic scene some two million years ago. I was part of a scientific mission that ended tragically on Dez Falls, the planet on which Captain Alan was marooned, over a million years ago. Fortunately for both of us, the sentient host planet brought us together, and here we are today."

"Sentient host planet?" Susan asked, confused. "Is there such a thing?"

"Most assuredly," Marcalif replied. "What is called the planet Dez

Falls is, in fact, a very ancient living being. I would tell you his name, but, as the captain knows, that would require weeks to enunciate."

"Yeah, let's skip over that part," Molly stated flatly.

"So you were alone on the planet a million years?" Mike asked incredulously. "That must've been hard."

"It was," he remarked in a somber tone. "But having meaning again to my existence has improved my mood significantly."

That was it! Early on, I had noticed how flat his voice was and how unanimated he was in general. I had wondered if he was depressed. Turned out my suspicions were spot on.

"What happened to the Nafcadollians?" Grace queried.

"I do not know. I can say that over all of history, civilizations rise and fall. And some species advance so far technologically that they abandon the physical realm, ascending into a digital or fully electromagnetic existence."

"That's so weird," Natalie remarked. "I mean, is that common?"

"No, it is rare. But a handful of species have made such a leap."

"And they're presumably still out there today, living noncorporeally?" Susan asked.

"Who is to say?" Marcalif responded thoughtfully. "There are no records of such civilizations ever bothering to contact those they left behind."

"Huh," I harrumphed. "Either they're having too good a time to phone home or the transfer didn't go exactly as they planned."

"Wouldn't that be the ultimate letdown?" Molly agreed. "You plan this immortal transcendental existence and all you get is a very fancy form of societal suicide."

"That is entirely possible," Marcalif stated. "But either way, the people that built me must be gone."

"I have the gazillion-dollar question here," Grace asked him soberly. "As you know, we're working like rented mules recreating Dostivex technology. We need to be ready for the next invasion. Would it be better if we dumped that project and switched to reverse-engineering *your* tech?"

"That is a very good question," Marcalif praised. "For better or worse, it is not currently possible for the civilizations present on Earth today to reproduce the machines and ASes that the Nafcadollians did. As to why—and it may seem insensitive of me to say it—but the technology is simply too far removed from anything you could understand or reliably recreate."

"A famous author, Arthur C. Clarke once said, *Any sufficiently advanced technology is indistinguishable from magic.*" Grace stated. "It would seem the man was correct."

"I am familiar with the quote and must second Sir Arthur Clarke's assertion," Marcalif responded. "Though it seems quite basic to me, a culture such as yours would have absolutely no reference frame to comprehend this technology, let alone reproduce it."

"Well, that's too bad," Grace remarked glumly.

"I can, however, be of help with your current efforts. There are several design flaws inherent in the alien tech you are attempting to clone. I can provide easy fixes for those."

"That would be a tremendous aid," Susan responded.

"Which then brings up the issue of being able to defend ourselves from the attack Visquisor has promised to deliver to us," Grace stated firmly. "We already know the Dostivex technology is insufficient to have any chance of beating him. Chris says you are confident you can successfully deal with him and his associates. Is that true?"

"Yes," he replied. "I can guarantee that."

"Even against ten ships?" she pressed.

"Even against one hundred, Ms. Chang," he responded confidently. "Again, it goes back to the technology I possess. Think of it like a consummately skilled boxer going up one-on-one against an M1 Abrams tank. The outcome would be predictable one-hundred percent of the time."

"Since all of our lives depend on it, I hope your confidence is not misplaced," were Grace's final words on the topic.

"Are there any other issues you would like to discuss with me?" Marcalif asked.

Everyone present looked to the others. No one seemed to have any burning issues to resolve. "I guess not, at least for now," I said for the group. You're welcome to stay or return to *Arc.*"

"To allow you all the opportunity to speak uninhibited by my unfamiliar presence, I believe I shall return to the ship, Captain. If you need anything of me, do not hesitate to let me know."

"Thanks, Marcalif," I stated. "This has been really helpful."

He stood, bowed slightly, and walked out.

Once he was gone, Susan was the first to speak. "He seems like a very nice ... person? I don't want to seem prejudiced or anything. What do we call him?"

"I am certain Marcalif doesn't care," I reassured her, "and that he's not concerned with that issue. That said, I'm comfortable referring to him as a person."

"And, Chris," Grace asked for emphasis, "you trust him completely?"

"I do. He didn't have to lift a finger to help me when I was facing a certain death. But he's been gracious and has gone out of his way to make me feel welcome."

"I really get the impression Marcalif's glad to help us because he wants to be needed," Natalie added. "He was constructed to serve that function, right?"

"I just stress over the all-our-eggs-in-one-basket aspect of this," Grace shared. "Visquisor *will* attack us and *we* are incapable of resisting him."

"If you think about it, honey," Molly reminded her, "we don't really have a choice. It's not as if we're foregoing one path and concentrating all of our efforts on Marcalif protecting us. He's our only hope. End of story. If he's blowing smoke or is otherwise unable to stop that son of a bitch Visquisor, we're goners."

Grace reached over and patted Molly's hand. "As always, you are right." She took a deep breath. "So, we incorporate Marcalif's suggestions and we continue with the work we've been doing," she stated flatly. "That's the plan."

"Absolutely," Susan agreed. "Which brings us neatly to the topic of shipping our product. The only thing left to do with the first set of giga-Watt generators is to package them up."

"We will have to send a small army of technicians along with each unit for the municipalities to be able to deploy the units," Natalie stated.

"I think we have more than enough as of now," Molly responded.

"More than enough!" I guffawed. "If we sent half of them away, we'd still have twice as many as we really need."

"We are a popular techie destination, aren't we?" Grace said with a grin.

"If ever there were a science *cult*, we are definitely in danger of becoming one," I admonished playfully.

"So, how will the units be transported?" the always practical Grace asked. "We've entertained several options, but we need to decide which one to go with."

"I think I can help with that," a male voice said from the doorway.

We all turned to see who had just arrived. Oh, my. I did not anticipate him.

"Carl," Susan said loudly as she stood to greet President Sellers.

"You didn't let us know you were coming." She rushed around the table to shake his hand.

"No, I did not," he responded in a friendly tone. "My presence here is to offer my help, not to lord anything over you."

"But how did you know we'd even be here?" she asked.

"Well, I'm not without my sources, Susan," he teased. "Plus, if you weren't around, I was willing to wait."

She furrowed her brow. I bet she was confused since this wasn't the POTUS she'd spoken to over the last few months. Susan must have been wondering if he was being genuine, or if was this some elaborate political gambit?

"Please, join us," she invited. "There's coffee and cookies," she added with a gesture to the carafes and plates already on the table.

"I'll never say *no* to a cookie," he said with a wink. Once he had one of each type available, Carl sat down in the last open chair. "I was saying I think I can help in the delivery of those generators," he said with the occasional cookie crumb puffing out of his mouth.

"That would take a big load off of us," Molly informed him.

"We've got quite a few C-17 Globemasters up and running now. Fuel overseas can present a logistical issue, but I think we can deliver the units where you intend them to go."

"Wow, that'd be great, Carl," Susan responded. "They can land at Spokane International?"

"I asked about all that. GEG has an eleven-thousand-foot runway. C-17s have amazingly short runway minimums. I'm told they can hit the ground and come to a dead stop in about 3000 feet. Mind you," he raised a finger, "I wouldn't want to be on board for that flight."

Everyone chuckled softly at that. Imagine, the POTUS kidding around. I'd never met the man, but I always figured they were stuffy, bossy types.

"Great. Well, let me know who to contact and we'll get that going," Molly responded.

Carl pointed over his shoulder. "He's right outside. I didn't want to overwhelm you with us all traipsing in at once." He turned around in his chair. "Yo, Buck, get on in here." An elderly man in a flight suit stepped into the kitchen. "Ladies and gentlemen, allow me to present General Buck James. He's the Joint Chief Rep. of the USAF. Ms. Cooper," he addressed Molly, "you two can chat when you have the time."

"My word, this is going to be easy," Molly remarked.

"These days, trust me," Carl said jovially, "nothing's as easy as it seems. But Buck'll git er done."

"Absolutely, Mr. President," Buck seconded. He walked around the table and offered Molly his hand. "A pleasure to meet you, Ms. Cooper. I am at your disposal."

"Thank you, General James," she said with a blush. "I really appreciate the help."

"Not a problem, ma'am," he said. Then he gestured over his shoulder. "I don't wish to impose on your meeting, so I'll wait out front if you don't mind."

"Make yourself at home," Molly said, still a bit in shock.

Buck nodded and left directly. My, but the US government was playing nice, weren't they? Almost enough to make me downright suspicious. Then again, maybe they were just bending over backward to ingratiate themselves to us. If so, I'd take it. Any port in a storm. We were planning on using *Arc* to make the heavy deliveries, but we knew the general population of absolutely nowhere wanted to see spaceships flying overhead. C-17'd be ideal and just as free to us.

"My visit here today," Carl began, "is to see the Spokane Group's progress and to offer any help we can provide. I also wanted to extend a hand in friendship. We are all in the business of helping, one way or another. We all want what is best for our nation as well as the citizens of the world. I want to let you know my door is always open to you, anytime, day or night." He stood. "With that, I, like Buck before me, will leave you to your meeting."

Susan gestured at the chair he'd just vacated. "You're welcome to stay, Carl," she offered.

"Nah," he responded cheerfully. "I agree with the guy in the funny suit that left a minute ago. You don't need me sitting in on a meeting. That'd be like flattening all four tires before you headed out on a Sunday drive. But I will accept these, even if I must take them by force." With that, he snatched up a handful of Toll House Cookies and left.

Once we were alone again, I said, "That was semi-weird."

"Ya think?" Natalie responded.

"Obviously, the man wants to garner our favor," Susan stated. "But I for one am glad to see he's coming around. If he was going to just sit back in Washington and make demands on us, it was going to get ugly."

"As long as the generators go where we say they do, I'm glad for the help," I said.

"He wouldn't dare steal them, would he?" Molly asked.

"No way," I assured her. "Later on, when we're shipping a lot of merchandise, obviously we'll need to be on our toes. But for now, Carl's just letting us know he wants to work on the winning side."

"Chris," Grace chided me, "you are *such* a teenager. There are no winning and losing sides here, now. We're all in this together."

"Yes, *teacher*," I teased. "As long as all the players move forward sharing that notion."

We were all quiet a moment.

"I suppose that's enough for one day," Grace announced. "Unless there's an objection, I say we pull the plug on this puppy."

"Well," I responded, trying very hard not to crack up, "speaking for Natty and myself, I think the longer a meeting runs the better it becomes. I say we go for the world record in terms of meeting prolongation."

"And I say you are so full of BS, your eyes are brown," Natalie accused as she rose and took hold of my hand. "I say we head back to *Arc* and continue this meeting as a break-out session, just the two of us."

As we were rushing out of the room, I heard one of the old folks remark, "Ah, to be young and horny."

You know what? Whoever said that was correct. It absolutely was.

SIXTEEN

SIXTEEN

The End Of All was the popular name for the event horizon, or Schwarzschild radius, the supermassive black hole at the center of the Milky Way galaxy. The effects that a four million solar mass singularity had on the local environment were insanely profound. The radiation coming off the gas striking the accretion disk was staggeringly intense. Time slowed the closer an object came to the black hole. The gravitational pull was so great that to venture too close meant a spacecraft would not be able to resist falling in. It was a region completely hostile to life.

Recently, Visquisor had heard a rumor of a whisper of a hint that the last of the practitioners of the dark art of soul transfer were to be found hiding in the inhospitable region very near The End Of All. According to ancient legend, a civilization among the very first to evolve after the Big Bang had discovered the secret to the procedure. Later societies gave them the name Plovecians, though there was no documentary evidence such a race ever actually existed. But the search for a Fountain of Youth was so powerful that it had lured dreamers from across all of time to seek it out. Visquisor was just the most recent of the countless aspirants willing to devote their lives to an endless quest for the secret of the mystical Plovecians. His desperation was such that even that slimmest of leads demanded he pursue them and pursue his one desire.

So it was that three light years from The End Of All, Visquisor ordered *Peerless* to assume a static position in space. In relative terms, that distance from The End Of All was still largely unaffected by the bizarre physics generated by the black hole.

"I want a full sweep of this region," Visquisor ordered his bridge crew. "I want to know the positions of anything larger than a pebble. Stars, their associated planets, and any artificial constructs. Document them all."

Normally, his commands were passed via implants, but the excitement he felt being so close to his quarry caused him to use his voice. His first officer, or filter one, tried not to allow his cringe to show after hearing his orders.

"Better of Mine," he said to Visquisor, "you must realize there is a lot of space out there? To chart every object might take weeks."

"Then it will take weeks," the boss replied matter-of-factly.

"But, Master, this close to the singularity, time will be affected. We run the risk of dropping out of synch with our own time, with our families."

"I care nothing for the passage of time, mine or yours, Filter One Dommol. All I demand is your earnest labor and success. Plus," he waved a dismissive hand, "the effects are still trivial this far out. Only once we are within a few light minutes of The End of All do the numbers deviate significantly. Stop whining and do as I bid."

"As you command, so it shall be," Dommol responded. He, along with the entire bridge crew, wasn't happy about the present mission. But they all knew their opinions mattered less than nothing to their Master.

By the next week, their sensor sweeps found nothing that had not been previously documented to orbit the central singularity. Visquisor then ordered they assume an orbit around the black hole with a radius of a light-hour. He reasoned that the elusive Plovecians were clearly not to be found in any well-studied parts of this space. He was gambling that, as a highly advanced race, they were indifferent to the time effect the intense gravity would subject them to.

Unfortunately, even after three revolutions around the singularity, no useful findings were made.

"Filter One," Visquisor said as he strode onto the bridge, "decrease our orbit by half."

"That will place us thirty light-seconds out from that raging inferno, Master. Our containment fields are already–"

"Silence," he commanded. "Our fields will hold and we are perfectly safe. Execute my order and continue the scans."

"Yes, Master," he responded with drooped shoulders.

Internally, Demmol began to think once again of a way the crew could mutiny against the maniac who led them. But he knew it would be futile. Older crew members told of many past failed attempts. To rise up against the tyrant they served would be the same as suicide, and a very slow and painful one at that. He hunkered down over his controls and searched as the ship's orbit dropped ever closer to certain death.

Peerless ultimately needed to continue to draw closer to the black hole. At five light seconds from The End Of All, Demmol began to notice an unusual blip on his screens. One moment, it was there, and the next moment, it was not. Whatever it might be–if it was real–the body seemed to be in a stable orbit. Demmol wasn't familiar with the esoteric physics that held sway over this contorted space/time. What he observed could be a phantasm, a side effect, or an actual structure.

"My Master," he called out, "there seems to be a variable contact in a three light-second orbit below us."

Visquisor rose from his captain's chair and stepped toward his filter one. "Is it a ship?"

"I ... I am afraid I can say little other than it might or might not exist," he said in a groveling tone. "My only wish is to keep you fully informed."

"As well you should," Visquisor snapped. "Helm, bring us down to three light seconds and move toward the Filter One's last observation point."

Mnem Flockett drowe, the helmssquid, spared six of his eyes to look intently at Demmol, as if to ask if this insanity was mandatory. The filter one simply nodded back once. The helm then executed the orbit change. In this region, the time dilation due to the intense gravity really began to slow their appreciation of its passage. The chaotic radiation plowed through the ship as if the central black hole held an M134 minigun in each arm pointed directly at them.

"Master," Demmol shouted, "I can confirm a small planet or very massive space platform two hundred thousand kilometers in front of us. It is in a steady orbit at this distance."

"Excellent. Make for the surface," Visquisor huffed greedily.

If it has one we can land on, thought the filter one. But well he knew that insanity never stopped the Master before and it would not alter his decisions now.

"Shall I enter low orbit?" Demmol asked as they neared the planet, for it was now clear that it was a small, rocky world.

"I said *land*, you cretin," he snarled back. "Pick a spot near any obvious habitation."

He thinks there are resorts near the front door of hell? Demmol protested in his head. But, again, he simply did his best to comply. To his great surprise, he could soon visually make out surface projections that were too regular to be naturally occurring. He directed the helm to put down alongside the largest building and, within minutes, *Peerless* rested on the surface. A huge tower rose above them, and it was surrounded by multiple smaller ones.

"I have, at last, found my quarry," Visquisor gloated entranced by the scene. "Prepare an away team," he shouted. "And make certain to bring along a scraper AS."

"It will be as you command," Demmol said in a deflated voice.

As the small team descended the ramp, it was followed by four truly massive figures carrying the scraper AS by the unit's four handholds. The higmorea bearing the unit were a semi-sentient race Visquisor kept around to function as beasts of burden. Each stood over fifteen feet tall and weighed in at around two tons. And they were all ill-tempered as a cold, wet, hungry mule.

Visquisor took the lead and quickly identified a doorway. Never one to knock, he pushed the door open and walked in. He studied the interior. There were no particularly distinguishing features, but he heard to his right the faint sounds of machines. Decisively, he marched off in that direction. Once those following him were inside, a technician switched the scraper AS on. This metallic device looked like a massive torpedo. It housed an AS that probed the surroundings for any electronic information sources. Computers, ASs, radio broadcasts, and even solid wire transmissions were all copied, or *scraped*. Vast quantities of information could be coopted with one of these units. The AS was designed to make certain that no encryption, however sophisticated, was able to keep the unit from doing its job.

After a few minutes, Visquisor noticed a small biped approaching from the direction he was heading. By the time it was twenty feet away, he could make out that the tiny man—for it looked like a miniature human—sporting a flowing robe. Light shone off him and danced in the air surrounding him. It was as if he wore many disco balls tucked into his clothing.

"I am—" Visquisor began to announce. Then, for reasons he could not comprehend, he fell mute.

"We know who you are, vile *worm*," the mini-man said in an ethereal tone, but one that carried all of the disdain and authority it was possible to stuff into spoken words. "It is not possible to allow you here in this holiest of palaces."

Involuntarily, Visquisor jerked like a marionette operated by a novice and spun about. Then he began a comic march back in the direction he'd come in. His small away team, in complete horror and confusion, parted to allow their Master to pass. They fell in behind and followed him, though it should be noted that none of them walked like a broken toy soldier. The higmorea were a different matter. As the boss stomped and twisted toward them, they hissed loudly, baring lethal teeth in anger. But, ultimately the feeble-minded creatures begrudgingly moved aside for their Master to pass by.

"We are a species that abhors violence," the doll-sized man shouted at the departing backsides. "But if you return, we will separate your atoms from each other and those of your machines also. Then we will allow the singularity to summon those particles to their final resting place in its belly. You have been warned."

Within a few minutes, everyone was aboard *Peerless*, including the pissed-off higmoreas. Once the ramp closed itself, Visquisor tumbled to the deck like a stack of wet towels. His head snapped up and he scanned his surroundings like a predatory cat.

"There will be *deaths*!" he screamed petulantly. He flew to his feet, stumbled twice, but eventually was sprinting toward the bridge. As he burst past the door, he screamed maniacally, "Charge all weapons' batteries. Make ready the positron-pulse cannon. We shall lay waste to this planet and every molecule within a light year of it."

As he ran to his command chair, he slipped again and barely caught the armrest to save himself a nasty fall. Once seated, he scanned the bridge. No one was moving. Nothing was being destroyed.

Visquisor's mind boiled over in an incandescent rage. "Why. *Do.* **You. *Defy*. *Me*?**" he howled.

Demmol, who was already on his knees in terror, raised his hands together as if in prayer. "Master of All, please know that our controls are not our own. We cannot operate any system other than navigation. All our weapons are inactive ... completely unactivatable." Yes, that last word was cumbersome. But, come on, the man had totally lost his shit. Judge not.

Visquisor leaped to the weapons panel. He first tapped, then pounded with his fists, any and all control functions that were formerly at his disposal. Nothing worked. He rushed to a sensor station. Employing the same finesse, he confirmed that not a single function responded to his demands.

"I want Geckerdo brought before me and I want him here *now!*" he screamed at the top of his lungs.

The man was mad.

A blithering, slobbering, wailing humanoid was dragged onto the bridge moments later. The chief engineer was then unceremoniously dumped at Visquisor's feet. Geckerdo writhed and balled up, and made sounds that might once have been words. He was, in short, in a consumingly pessimistic mood.

"*Geckerdo!*" Visquisor screamed.

That summons was sufficiently emotive to bring the man's head up, if just a little. Visquisor used his palms to smash like a rotten pumpkin Geckerdo's skull, ignoring the gore and muck he sent flying.

"Now summon my *new* chief engineer," he snarled viciously.

In a quick jiffy, a tri-ped sphere of a being rushed onto the bridge. "You called me, Master?" confirmed Heliop, a Suldarkin technician.

"You are my chief. Why do *my* controls on *my* ship not respond to me?"

"I have studied the systems, Master. We are locked out of all of them as if by magic."

"Magic can be broken. Do so now."

"I have tried all that I know, including turning it off and then turning it back on again. Nothing works. I believe the citizens of this world have powers we cannot counter."

Visquisor vibrated in rage and hate and antipathy to all things living. Then, via some miracle, he calmed slightly. "But our propulsion and navigation systems are functional?"

"Yes, Master. We may depart any time you wish us to."

"Then take me from this horrid planet. Do so instantly." With that, he plopped like a-spoiled-child-denied into his chair and visibly pouted.

The whine of the engines were heard to whir to life. Finally, Filter One Demmol asked timidly, "What course, Master?"

Visquisor seized the armrests so hard, his knuckles blanched. "Take me to the Sol system. I wish to kill something."

SEVENTEEN

You know what the thing is about hope? It exists. Now, don't get me wrong, I like to be hopeful. Birthdays, Christmas, a special dinner, sure, I look forward to them. But, then again, I'm an idiot. Here's the problem. Hope is this little fairy/sprite that flicks the back of your ear, suggesting but not confirming that it exists and it might be there for you. Then hope, emboldened by that initial success, comes to you as a noble messenger, dressed in fine livery, white gloves, pretentious hat, and all. It suggests that what it is that you might want could actually come to pass. Then, like the bull fighter's cape, any hope you had is gone ... puff ... vanished. And then reality sets in. You, along with a pounding headache, now have whatever new crisis is upon you. Then hope goes to dinner with despair and they share a toast to your comical misfortune.

Am I whining? Yeah. Duh. Am I justifiably upset? Double duh!

After a couple of months of splendor, that old rug-of-hope was jerked out from beneath me. I had not just renewed my relationship with Natalie, we'd taken it to new heights. And I was contributing again to The Rebuild. Finally, Dostivex technologies were being used by our recovering societies. Generators were the first products distributed, but we were close to testing smaller versions of *Defiant* that could be used to begin training large numbers of human pilots. The ultimate piece of amazing we were readying for distribution were the replicators. With enough of those in circulation, humankind could really begin to soar.

And then came Thursday.

For the record, I've never been a big fan of Thursdays. Nope. They hold none of Friday's promise, or even Wednesday's pat-on-the-back you're-halfway-there spirit. But I digress.

Thursday the tenth, I was sitting in my tinkering lab aboard *Arc of Intention*. I just finished a nice breakfast with the family–Grace, Molly, Susan, Felicia, Farrah, and Natalie. Now the girls were in school and Susan was off somewhere vice presidenting. Grace and Molly were being supervisors. Yeah, lucky them. The bigger the Spokane Group got and the more we undertook, the more mind-slaying busy work needed to be suffered through. I, as the unofficial/official leader of the pack, could excuse myself from a lot of the paperwork and pointless meetings. And whenever I could, I sure did. My mama didn't raise no fools.

I was monkeying with a prototype of a combat knife Peaches and I were working on. I had wanted–triple duh–to fabricate a cutting weapon based on the *Star Wars* lightsaber. Peaches–after she finished chuckling, that is–informed me that I was a dreamer, not a designer. She overruled that aspect of the project in favor of a doable metal alloy version with a wicked-sharp, harder than steel edge. Natalie was attempting to distract me and, thankfully, doing a bang-up job of it. I nearly sliced off my finger when she whispered intimate nothings in my ear. Then she discovered that I paid *her* more attention than the *knife* if she stood real close and rubbed her breasts against me. Go figure, right? As I said, I was having a near-perfect morning.

Then my implants thundered to nine-point-five on the Richter Scale as both Peaches and Marcalif boomed in my head, *Six enemy vessels have just dropped into real space near the asteroid belt.*

I basically jumped out of my skin, shoving my cuddling girlfriend backwards, and dropped the knife. It missed my foot only because it had jerked out of the way when I jumped out of my skin.

"ID on enemy ships?" I barked out. "Marcalif only, please."

"What's–" Natalie began to ask.

I held a palm up to her. "On audio for now so Natalie can hear."

"Yes, Captain," Marcalif responded quickly. "Six craft with markings identical to the ships Visquisor employs have emerged into real space."

"Only six," I pressed. "He has ten ships under his command."

"He does, but only the six have ... make that seven have arrived."

"It seems they're coming in from different locations," I speculated. "They'll likely all be here soon."

"That is a safe assumption," Marcalif responded.

I turned to Natalie. "Let the others know. Also, get everyone you can into *Defiant*, in case you need to make a break for it."

Her face dropped. "I want to stay with you."

"No way, babe. You're the only other person who can pilot the ship. Now go." I pulled her into a quick kiss and she sprinted away.

"Do the ships look to be assuming orbits?" I asked.

"Affirmative. Their approaches suggest they will occupy separate orbits."

"Makes sense not to bunch up," I mused. "You all ready?"

"Yes, Sir. You say the word and I will incapacitate the lot of them."

I pointed toward a wall. "I'm holding you to that, buddy." I started toward the door. "I'm heading for the bridge. You keep me posted."

"Will do," he confirmed.

As I ran down the passageway and up a couple ladders, I said a quick prayer that this was all going to be as easy as shooting fish in a barrel. But I'd learned the hard way about battle plans and meeting the enemy. *South* was the only direction matters ever seemed to go.

By this time, *Arc* was hidden to some extent. Since I wanted to be close to the others and *Defiant*, I had Marcalif excavate under the adjacent house to create a cave for the ship. I assumed that if Visquisor or his flunkies were specifically looking for a super-advanced spaceship, they'd be able to detect it. But all I wanted was for them to declare their intentions and positions before I sprang the trap on them. I was impressed that, in typical Marcalif style, he'd dug below the homes with such care and precision that he even repaired or rerouted the underground utilities as he went. Anyone living directly above the excavation might have felt some rumbling, but would be otherwise oblivious to the process.

Status? I requested via my implants once I arrived on the bridge.

An eighth and ninth ship have arrived. Peerless *is not among the ships approaching.*

Oh, no. The big man'll want to make a dramatic entrance. You can count on that, I assured him.

"Chris, this is Natalie," came over the speakers. "Everyone, including Felicia and Farrah, are safely aboard *Defiant*."

"Perfecto," I responded. "I'll have Marcalif broadcast whatever we're saying here over to you guys."

"That'd be perfect. Thanks, and good luck, Commodore." Yeah, I detected a bit of tongue-in-cheek there, but she was also trying to be respectful. Gotta love that girl!

Even as I sat down, Marcalif gave me the nerve-wracking update. "The first three ships are assuming high orbits. My guess is they will assume geosynchronous orbits covering the Asian, Central European, and African continents."

"Interesting," I remarked. "Either those will be their firing positions, if they're participating, or it's mostly for show."

"I agree," Marcalif stated. "They might hope to cut off a *Defiant* retreat, though that possibility is less likely."

"So where is the bossman?" I mumbled mostly to myself.

In quick succession, the other ships took positions around the globe. It was glaringly obvious that not one of them covered the western United States. No, that table was reserved for his buttheadness alone. Curiously, once the assistants' ships were in place, they just sat there, seemingly motionless. They didn't hail us, chuck a few high explosives down for the fun of it or anything. Apparently, they sat and waited ... for something. Something made itself obvious ten minutes later.

"Captain, there has been a catastrophic explosion near the planet Mercury. I am able to display fairly clear video of the event."

"Put it on my screen as well as the ones on *Defiant*," I ordered.

Then I sat back and watched. The image of Mercury was about the size of an apple. For all intents and purposes, it seemed to be minding its own business, rapidly orbiting the Sun. A faint bright spot appeared just ahead of the planet in its progression along its orbit. Suddenly, a blinding beam of light leaped from the spot and slammed into Mercury's leading surface. Nothing appeared to happen for a few seconds, then the planet simply blew apart. It was very *Star Wars* Death Star. Way too Death Star, in fact. Within moments, an expanding sphere of dust and rocky chunks was all that was left of poor little Mercury.

And so it began.

Visquisor had stated that he would take revenge on the solar system, not just Earth. I guess he was just being methodical. One: Blow up first planet. Two: Blow up next planet. Three: Wash-rinse-repeat until you get to the Oort Cloud.

"Mercury was three light minutes from your Sun," Marcalif interrupted my shock. "The images we just saw are five minutes old. Venus orbits at six light minutes."

"So, we should presumably see Venus go boom in ... what, two-three minutes?"

"Depending on how long it took *Peerless* to make the crossing, yes, more or less."

The image of Venus in her orbit appeared on the screens. As of two minutes ago, she looked good, in the prime of her life really, if you were to ask me. I debated but quickly dismissed asking if we could rush to the location and save our sister planet. But that would leave us two light minutes away from Earth and that planet had nine evil ships orbiting at that very moment. Too risky a proposition.

"How impactful will the destruction of Mercury and Venus be on Earth?" I asked Marcalif.

"Surprisingly little. Mercury is small enough and close enough to your Sun that its loss will have negligible effects. Most debris will fall into the star. Venus has little gravitational relevance either. Some ejecta could threaten Earth, but *Defiant* and *Arc of Intention* can easily clean up that mess before anything bad happens."

"So not even a long-term effect on our orbit?"

"Over many centuries, some. Again, that can be corrected for later."

"By what? *Replacing* the planets?"

"Yes, Captain. Or I can place a compensatory black hole in an orbit inside that of Earth."

"You sure make that sound–" I started to say.

"Captain, please check the video," he interrupted.

Again, a bright spot appeared ahead of Venus, a blinding beam disappeared under the cloudy atmosphere, and then the planet blew apart. With all the extra gas, it was much more spectacular. Pretty, even, if it weren't such a wretched thing to witness.

"The timing is such that Visquisor should assume geosynchronous orbit above Spokane in forty-five seconds," Marcalif reported.

And, right on cue, *Peerless* appeared, as if by magic, three hundred miles directly above Grace and Molly's house.

"Captain, none of the ten ships has armed any weapons. Specifically, the disruptor beam *Peerless* used to destroy the two planets is, as of yet, not charging."

"Thanks. Let me know the instant that situation changes." As an afterthought, I asked, "Do they seem to have detected your presence?"

"Negative. No subterranean scans have been initiated."

"Thank you, my friend," I responded. "So I'm down here with you and old Visquisor thinks I'm dead on Dez Falls and has no clue that you exist."

"That sounds about right," Marcalif replied. And yes, I heard a little cocky in his tone there.

Peaches' voice cut in, "I'm receiving a hail. On speaker."

"Earth *worms*," I heard Visquisor's voice mock. He thought he was so very clever with that double entendre. "I have returned to lay waste to this worthless planet and the even less valuable souls who upon it dwell. I make this announcement to you, Dostivex trash-collecting ship, so that you may announce this decree to the hideous creatures your masters left alive. I will give you ten minutes to broadcast the news of Earth's doom. I want everyone I kill mercilessly to know before they incinerate that it is I, Visquisor, who kills them. I specifically want them to know that they die because Christopher Alan failed and betrayed me. There will be no further communications between me and you."

"Ouch," I declared. "He sure likes to sound badass, doesn't he?"

"Chris," Grace said over the common link, "need I remind you that if it weren't for *Arc of Intention*, he *would* be totally badass as of this moment?"

She had a good point, not that I'd care to acknowledge that fact. "He's just such a tool," I responded.

"No argument there," she replied. "Let's all just not get cocky."

"Yes, *Teacher*," I teased back.

"I'm getting a ton of calls all of a sudden," Susan said, cutting in. "I need to take Carl's call. Anything I should or shouldn't say?"

"Tell him what we know," I replied firmly. "But keep in mind there are no secure lines. Assume Visquisor's listening in. Okay?"

"Got it. Just wanted to make sure and to clear everything with you," she said in a business-like tone.

"Is there anything we should be doing?" Natalie asked.

"Negative," I responded. "We wait for the ten minutes to pass. After that, we just need to stop those ships from taking any hostile actions."

"Okay," she responded nervously.

"Marcalif," I asked, "when you disable the ships, will they fall from orbit?" I hadn't clarified this issue yet. I could care less about Visquisor and his sycophants. But there were crew members aboard whose only sin was to choose poorly which ship to work on.

"Not unless you desire them to," he replied. "My plan is to negate all offensive systems and to assume control of navigation functions."

"Perfect."

And that was it. We had six or seven minutes to wait. Oh, joy. Maybe I should take up a new hobby? Or learn to play the violin? Nah, I'd just think about Natty and ... showers ... and ... oh, mind your own business, okay?

Soon enough, a voice that produced in me instant nausea came over the speakers. "Useless flecks of life of Earth, I, Visquisor, your judge and executioner, now condemn you to death most foul. It is my ardent hope that the last words that you scream from your burning lips is the name of the traitor who sentenced you with his folly. Christopher Alan!"

"I don't know about you," I remarked to Marcalif, "but I'm ready for him to shut the hell up."

"He does have a particular effete annoying quality, doesn't he?" the AS agreed.

"And now," Visquisor boomed, "***die!***"

And ... nothing happened. I nearly fainted I was so relieved. Marcalif delivered on his promises. Yes, yes, yes, yes!

In an oops-open-mic miscue, the next words we heard were, "Filter One, I *commanded* you to fire. Why did you disobey me?"

"Master," a bleating voice called out, "I did follow your directive. Look, I'm still pushing the button." Frantic pounding clicks were audible. "Pushing and pushing."

"Then why are the weapons not—" Muffled voices could be heard some distance away. "What do you mean all systems are frozen?" Visquisor howled. More indistinct words. "I know you know what frozen systems are, you incompetent whelp. I mean why do you inform me of the fact instead of correct ... The what? Why is my microphone still live! Heads will—" Mercifully, the transmission ended.

"Any chance they'll figure out a work around your blocks?" I asked Marcalif.

"That is not possible. The final input pathways all now route through me. If they were a ship on water and had paddles, yes, they could maneuver. But as matters stand presently, they're completely dead-in-space."

So, a thought occurred to me. What do I do with them now? Huh. You'd think I'd have anticipated this point in the flowchart of battle. Oops. And I can only blame myself.

"Marcalif, please bring the ships down one at a time. Visquisor's ship'll be the last. Land them in the park down the street and try not to wreck any of the play equipment if you possibly can."

"I shall endeavor to spare all of the park's fixed assets," he responded with a trace of humor in there somewhere.

"Grace, Natalie, everybody, we need to get to Shady Hills Park ASAP. I'm having the space garbage delivered there."

"We'll meet you out front," Grace shouted back. "I for one am stopping at the armory first."

That was actually a good idea. I was thinking we'd declawed these cats, but a blaster in hand was a nice insurance policy. That brought up another under-addressed point in my master plan. "Ah, Marcalif, will the enemy's small arms be inactive also?"

"Absolutely. I suppose you might worry about their pointed and slashing implements, but they have no functioning mechanical weapons."

"Strong work," I praised.

"Thank you," he returned.

Quick as a wink, the entire family was jogging toward the park a block and a half away, armed to the teeth. We arrived before any of the ships had set down. Several were visible as dark smudges in the sky above.

I took advantage of Marcalif's robot standing next to me when we arrived. Pointing to the soccer field, I said, "Start with that area. If you run out of room, use the baseball field."

"Yes, Captain," he responded.

"And leave the hatches sealed until I ask you to open them."

"Will do," he acknowledged.

And so, about seven minutes later, there were ten big shiny spaceships lined up in three rows of three there on the Clark Marston Memorial Soccer Field. I had Visquisor's ship placed singly at the back of the formation. *Him* I would deal with last. Plus, I hoped he could see out somehow and witness the dismantling of his precious fleet.

"Patch me through to all nine wannabe ships, please," I instructed.

"Links are active," the AS robot confirmed.

"I am Commodore Christopher Alan. You are all prisoners of the Spokane Group." Hey, cut me a break. I was making this up as I went along. I know that's not a particularly imposing title, but that was what came out my mouth. "One crew at a time will disembark when I lower the ship's ramp. File out two abreast and peacefully. Officers move off to the right, working crew members to the left. Stay together after exiting. Any hostile act will be dealt with harshly. Be warned."

Gosh, I was kind of sounding like an airline stewardess now, wasn't I?

"Marcalif," I said to the robotic unit, "open the first ship. I want you to stand with the crew. Start screening them. We'll have to decide if any can stay or if they're all too suspect and need to be sent packing."

"Excellent plan," he stated. Then he walked off toward the crew already getting together on the grass.

"Grace," I said, pointing, "take the rest and guard the officers. Keep a particular eye on the captains."

"You got it," she responded. "If they so much as look annoying, I'm shooting them."

"Attagirl," I praised.

As I stood watching the flow off the ships, I was impressed. Fate had not only spared me a miserable death on Dez Falls, it had saved my entire planet from a vengeful lunatic. This was nice!

When each ship was cleared as being emptied, Grace began merging the two groups of prisoners. Pretty soon, there was a large assembly of crew members milling around and a much smaller set of officers on the other side of the field. Marcalif was quickly sorting the crew into two separate areas, presumably the good eggs and the bad ones.

It was finally time to deal with the numero uno jackass himself. And my, but wouldn't he be madder than a wet hen by now? Poor baby.

"Marcalif, have the drones guard the prisoners and let's all join up at the base of Visquisor's ship." Knowing that we'd be outnumbered, Marcalif had fabricated a lot of floating octopus-like drones to back us up. Not only were they heavily armed, but they looked super cool, all shiny and Rambo kick-ass. I was an instant fan.

"Marcalif, in your voice, order the last crew to exit. Make it clear that Visquisor is to exit dead last, and by dead last, I mean to say that if he isn't last; he's dead."

"Gotcha," he responded.

The ramp dropped and the crew joined the other worker bees and officers already gather loosely in bunches. Not surprisingly, all the kiss-ass captains huddled up together, no doubt plotting and scheming. Good luck with that class project, losers!

When I spotted my buddy Morpheus Denali clomping down the ramp, I waved my arms in the air and signaled him to come over. I'd already mentioned I'd be doing this with the others, so they smiled at him as they let him pass.

I opened my arms wide and grabbed the son-of-a-gun in a bear hug. "Morpheus, it's good to see you again."

Shaking his head, he responded, "It's good to see you too, especially given your recent death." He slapped my back several times then pushed me back to arm's length. "You don't mind if I hang around here? I'm looking forward with great anticipation the look on Visquisor's face when he lays eyes on you."

I gestured to the ground beside me. "Be my guest. I can hardly wait myself."

The parade of people slowed, then finally stopped. Because he was a conceited asswipe, Visquisor waited a full minute before emerging himself. Such a drama mama. He tried to look disdainful and regal as he descended, but once he saw me, all pretense evaporated in a flash. He actually started to rush toward me, but a couple of rifle barrels to the chest discouraged that effort quickly enough.

"You have no idea how dearly you will *pay* for this insult," he seethed at me.

"Oh, no," I mocked him. "Are you going to do something worse than blow us all up? Now I'm scared," FYI, mocking is fun.

"That's it, child," he taunted, "play the role of the big man. But soon enough, you will get yours."

I locked my arms behind my back, like I was in an at-ease stance, and walked slowly over to and then around him. I wanted him to know beyond the shadow of a doubt that I did not fear him in the least.

"I'm going to ask you once, nicely, to cut the high-and-mighty act, okay? Now, I realize you don't even know how to behave properly, but, there, I said it. Once you've proven you're incapable of silent respect, I will personally enjoy putting a whole roll of duct tape over your mouth."

He trembled, he was so angry. But he calmed a bit. "I had such high hopes for you and this is how you repay your great debt to me," he scorned.

"Yeah, high hopes of maybe swapping out my soul for your putrid one."

Visquisor's eyes nearly bugged out of his head.

"I know all about your quest for learning the secrets of the transfer of souls and how those nine lamebrains over there," I pointed at them still huddled together, "were your prospective unwitting body donors."

"You ... you cannot know that," he said in a whisper.

I reached over and thumped him on a shoulder a few times. "You'll find I'm good at that, my boy. And please know that you will be kicking yourself in the butt for a very long time for having repeatedly underestimated me."

I then made a show of walking away, exposing my back to him defiantly.

"*How?*" he hissed. "Tell me that much, you disgusting ape."

"How?" I parroted. "How did I escape being marooned? How did I capture you and your fleet like they were two-legged turtles in the middle of an open field? How did I inactivate your toys, including the implants you are currently trying to use to crush me like a bug? How is it that your beloved technology is child's play before me? How is it that I'm this handsome? How is it, in short, that I'm so much better than you that a deaf-blind man two counties away could tell I was from where he sat on his porch?"

"I hate you," he hissed venomously.

"And I don't care that you do because you are *nothing*. You are a powerless toddler who can only throw tantrums and spit at those close enough to reliably hit. And I'll tell you how I did all that I did. It's because I'm just ... that ... *good*."

Was that the most memorable tell-off speech in human history? Not by a long shot. But it sure did feel good saying it.

As Visquisor glared at me, Marcalif walked over to my side. "I have finished screening the enlisted prisoners. A handful are defiantly loyal to Visquisor. Some of the rest would be happy to be returned to their homes and be done with the nightmare they've been forced to live."

"That leaves a goodly number," I stated. "What say them?"

"That they'd love to join you in erasing Visquisor's foul legacy from the galaxy."

"Well, bless them. Assuming you accept their stories, they're welcome to join the team."

"As to the officers, I took the liberty of screening them. About half wish to return home and wash their hands of this all. The rest wish to serve under your command."

I furrowed my brow. "And you think they would be loyal?"

"I'm fairly certain of their sincerity. Plus, monitoring them until they prove themselves would be an easy process."

"Alright. Here's what we'll do." I turned to Morpheus. "Captain Morpheus Denali here is going to take one of the nine assistant's ships and return anyone who so desires to their home."

"Whoa, man-child," Morpheus blurted out. "What you said there contained some assumptions that are not facts. Calling me a *captain*, for one, is an insult. I work for a living. Two, what makes you think I would care to fly across the cosmos delivering folks where they wish to go? I ain't no tour guide for one's dream vacation, you know."

I patted his shoulder. "I know you'll do it because you know I can trust you to do so. As to calling you *captain*, well, get used to it. It's your rank from here-on-out, like it or lump it, buddy."

"You save someone's ass a time or two and somehow that makes them think they're your boss now," he snarled. "It's insanity institutionalized, I tell ya."

"How long do you estimate Captain Denali's journey will take?" I asked Marcalif.

"With his considerable skills, perhaps a month. Less if he keeps the speeches down to a minimum," he informed us.

"And then he learned he was working for a pair of comedians," Morpheus groused. "Now, as I have heard all I care to from you, I'm going to pick the ship what's best ready to function as my fancy taxi cab." The grouch walked away, heading to the nearest ship.

"He's really a good man," I said to Marcalif as we watched him receding.

"I shall take your word on that for now, Captain."

"What about *me*?" Visquisor asked with dripping sarcasm. "May I return home too, Petty Lord Christopher?"

"Yes. And no," I replied. I let that hang a second, then finished the thought. "Yes, you and your minions *are* going home. But, no, you're not going to whatever home you are thinking of."

"Speak plainly, boy," he snapped.

"We have made arrangements to relocate you and your nine stooge-devotees to a living organism with a name so long, it will take you months to just say it."

"You are crazy talking," Visquisor dismissed.

"Ah, but I am not. You think my friend's name is Dez Falls and imagine him to be a planet. But he is neither. LN, which is short for Long Name, since that's what his is, has agreed to accept you ten reprobates. He will make certain you cannot escape, will not be up to any mischief, and that you, unlike me, you will not find any functioning technology anywhere on his body."

"That is preposterous," Visquisor rejected contemptuously.

"You might be right, but that's what's going to happen. But here's the encouraging part, an aspect you can look forward to each and every day of your ... er, visit to LN. He told me personally of his great hopes for y'all. He claims that in a couple hundred thousand years, he can turn you bad boys into useful, productive citizens."

"That ... that's more preposterous than what you said before. Absent any access to advanced technology, none of us will *live* hundreds of thousands of years."

"You know, I explained all that to LN. Guess what? He said that part didn't matter. Alive or dead, he plans on ironing out your imperfections." I folded my arms and tried not to grin. "I think his species isn't as facile with the whole concept of living versus dead as we are." I shrugged. "Time will have to tell."

"If it's alright with you," Marcalif leaned in to say, "I've selected the best option for the captain and crew of a ship to deliver our ten unwelcome guests to LN."

"They all seem reliable?" I asked. "I'd hate to lose a ship."

"I'm confident we can trust them," Marcalif reassured me. "Captain Markus is even noted in Visquisor's log to be next on the execution list, based on her disloyal and subversive inclinations."

"Any enemy of his is a friend of mine," I affirmed.

"They will be ready to depart whenever you order them to take off."

"Since you're staying here, let's fit the ten of them in high-quality restraints and make triple sure the brig is capable of holding them. Once that's done, I say good riddance."

"I couldn't agree more," Marcalif responded. "I shall take responsibility for ensuring the accommodations are appropriate and will let you know when the ship is ready to depart."

"Thanks," I told him.

As Marcalif stepped away, an arm slipped around my waist. Natalie rested her head on my shoulder. "That went well."

"I think so. As much as I'd have liked to transform Visquisor's fool head into pink mist, I feel like we did the right thing."

"We did." Then she lifted her head and scanned the area. "You know,

I find mass prisoner detentions to be exhausting. Do you think we can retreat to our quarters so we can lie down?"

"Gosh, I am exhausted too. Let me tell Grace where we'll be and then we can go ... go to rest our weary heads."

Natalie took my hand and started pulling me toward *Arc of Intention*. "I cleared it with her before I came over."

Did I mention that I loved my fiancée .. like this much (picture, if you will, my hands held as far apart as they could possibly be)?

Oh, crap! In the midst of all this crisis resolution, that part had slipped my mind. In fact, I needed to get back to stressing over that whole topic of my getting married. I mean, I was so young! Yes, I definitely needed to get some quality stressing time in—just as soon as I was done resting.

EIGHTEEN

Vice President Susan Whitehorse picked up the receiver. "Hello, Carl. I sort of figured you'd be calling."

A few hours earlier, all hell, in the form of Visquisor's now defunct fleet, had descended into Spokane. News, as they say, travels fast.

"Yeah, Sue, I just wondered what the weather has been like there," Carl responded ingenuously.

"Ah ha, I bet you're planning a fishing trip up here but want to know how to pack?"

"That's precisely it. Oh, and since I understand several unfamiliar spaceships landed there today, I wanted to know how much aluminum foil I'd need to bring to wrap my head with."

"None," she replied with a chuckle. "Here's the nickel version of the story. The day the real Dostivex attacked, Chris took out most of them. Then a ship appeared out of nowhere and finished off the remainder."

"Yes, the mysterious Visquisor came to our aid," he confirmed.

"Correct. After he left, as you know, he took Chris Alan with him. They parted on a less-than-cordial basis, Visquisor promising to return and destroy Earth."

"Ah, that part is new to me," Carl pointed out in a strained voice.

"But Chris escaped from the distant planet where he was marooned.

The ship that basically adopted him turns out to be much more powerful than Visquisor's. So, when Visquisor did in fact return to literally blow up Earth, Chris could disable their ships and captured the lot of them."

Carl was quiet a spell. Susan couldn't see it, but the POTUS was raking a hand through his hair and contorting his face in a most tortured manner. Carl was contemplating whether to explode now over the phone, or later when he flew out there to kick some butt. Or both.

"You seem quiet, Carl," Susan stated neutrally. Knowing him as she did, Susan anticipated his volcanic response to this update.

"You see, Madam Vice President," he began in a paced yet heated tone, "I am torn between disbelief and, quite frankly, rage. I am the President. It falls to me to defend this country and its people. When we are under a potentially catastrophic, existential threat by an enemy known to possess enormous power, I expect to be informed about such matters. And, when my right hand, knowing full well what's taking place, denies me that capability, well, as you might imagine, I get a little testy."

"As opposed to piously pissed off," she responded flatly.

"Susan, you are in the process of crossing a very significant line here."

"Between what and what, Carl? And if you say loyalty versus disloyalty to you, I'm going to hang up this phone."

"Now that you mention it, you raise an important issue there. But, no, I was going to say the line between your service to this nation and treason."

"Carl, we have all been through hell–literally and figuratively. Based on that fact and since I knew you before the apocalypse to be a good, if overly political man, I will respond to what you just said. But I must tell you, *you* have just crossed that significant line."

"I suggest you watch your mouth," he snapped back.

"And I suggest you listen for a change. You are mixing up in your stress-laden mind several incompatible concepts. Yes, I am the VPOTUS and I serve the people of this country. The value of that service, the coin by which I measure it, are the results I achieve. You are confusing epic loyalty to *you*, Carl Sellers, with loyalty to the *USA*. They are not the same thing or even closely akin to one another. And when you compare what I'm doing and what I've achieved for our country with treason, then I say you have lost your mind, Mr. President. That you are unfit to serve. In short, time has turned you into a bitter and shortsighted parody of who you once were and what it is critically important that you be.

"If the Spokane Group took the time to keep you fully updated and read-in as a courtesy, we would waste precious time we could better spend saving humankind. Why would we made it a priority to keep you fully appraised and solicit your opinion in situations that no one but us can resolve? What benefit, Carl, would that be in that for anyone other than you if we did so? You possess and offer no offensive or defensive assets to defend against an alien attack. And you possess no expertise in space-based warfare that would help us beat back the bad guys. So I want you to tell me right now and in plain, non-accusatory words, why we would *ever* contact you concerning an imminent alien attack like this? Oh, one rule in this contest, Carl. Your answer may not be centered on the words *because I'm the president, that's why.*"

The line was quiet for nearly a minute. Susan wasn't quite sure what to make of that painful silence, but she was not at all inclined to blink first. She preferred to force Carl to respond. If he chose a childish, irrational response, he needed to do so freely, without being pushed into it by her. She did reflect during that tense interval that her decision as to whether she should continue on as VP or devote her time exclusively to the Spokane Group might just have been made.

"Susan, I'm sorry," he finally said contritely. "Believe it or not, that's the second time this week that someone I greatly respect has told me to get my head out of my ass and become an active part of the solution."

"I am relieved to hear you say that," she responded evenly.

"Thank God we have you guys to protect us. I really mean that. Someday, I hope that this country will share the burden of protecting our home against the terrible threats we face from hostile alien species. But you are one-*million*-percent correct. Presently, this nation and I are observers, not participants in that cause. Please forgive my outburst."

"I will get back to you on forgiveness, Carl," she replied in a steely tone.

"I know, I deserve that, don't I? Words are not actions. But I promise you this here and now. I will re-earn your respect, Susan. Through acts and deeds as well as words, I swear I will. Now, thank you for your time and know that I am here to help the Spokane Group in any way I can. God bless, Susan."

She heard the call end. As Susan set down her handset, she wondered what exactly had just happened. Was this the dawn of a new era, an enlightened epoch where petty individual concerns gave way to the labors designed to achieve a common good? Or had she just made an enemy, a very powerful and influential one?

Time would tell. She just ardently hoped time didn't tell her that human nature never changes and that the quest for power would forever be central to the desires of man.

NINETEEN

I was sitting at my desk in my stateroom aboard *Arc* when I heard a soft knock at the door. My first thought was, *hmm, that was weird*. I mean, if it was Natalie, she obviously wouldn't feel the need to knock. If it were anyone else, why hadn't Marcalif announced they were coming?

I turned to face the door. "Come."

The door slid open to reveal a beautiful woman standing there with a graceful smile, wearing flowing gowns of a dazzling yet unfamiliar design.

"May I come in?" she asked politely.

"Ah, yeah, sure." I stood and walked toward her. "Have we met?" I asked uncertainly.

"Have we met?" she repeated curiously. "Oh, we certainly have. I'd go as far as to say that we are good friends."

No way this gorgeous woman was a close acquaintance of mine and I didn't remember her. Come on. I'm a guy, right?

"Wow, I'm afraid to say it, but I don't recognize you."

"Well that's because I haven't had a body up until now."

"You ... haven't had a body before ... during our friendship?" My, but I was confused.

"No." She raised her arms and twirled. "Do you like it?"

Then it hit me. This was a test! Natalie was standing right behind this woman and she was holding a laser pistol. The second I toed-across-the-line of faithfulness, Natty'd push past her and slice me into ribbons. Many, many ribbons. Though it all seemed a little excessive, at least I knew now not to take any of the tempting bait.

"I have always felt a more important question to ask oneself is whether *they* like their body, not whether *others* do." What a great non-answer. Natalie, taste my victory!

"I should have guessed that was what you'd say, Commodore. You have always been so wise and so very kind."

Commodore? The only one to call me that was ... "Peaches? Is that you?"

"In the flesh," she said joyously, still twirling slowly. "Isn't this exquisite?"

Then it all became clear. "Marcalif made you a robot host too, didn't he?"

"Yes, he did." She dropped her arms and rushed over to me. She hugged me so suddenly and so forcefully that I expected my feet to come off the deck. "Oooh," she purred, "I've wanted to do this for such a long time." Now the both of us were twirling. This newly corporeal Peaches was a twirler.

"Ah, *hum*," came from the still open doorway. "I'd suggest you two get a room, but it seems you already have."

Of course that was Natalie, because, come on, when would I ever catch a break of this variety?

I began to try to peel Peaches off me while launching a whiny version of, *Wait, this isn't what it looks like* to Natalie. Man, I hope she didn't actually have a laser pistol with her.

Peaches released me and squealed, "Natalie!" as she rushed toward her, arms wide open.

As Natalie and Peaches were twirling, my girlfriend strained her head back and stated pointedly, "Put me down."

"No, Natalie, I want to hug you and hug you and hug you," Peaches sang out. "I've wanted to touch you for so long but didn't know that I did."

Natalie raised an eyebrow at her and asked, "*Peaches?*"

Hmm, how did she get it quicker than I did? That didn't seem fair.

Peaches set her down gently, raised her arms, and–of course–twirled. "Yes! Don't you just *love* this body? Isn't it wonderful?"

Smiling broadly now, Natalie replied, "Yes, I do. You're just as beautiful as I always knew you were."

Wow, great line. I wish I'd come up with it. "So, Peaches," I asked, "did you just ... did Marcalif just now–" I waved my hands ineffectually in the air, "whip this up?"

Peaches stopped spinning and plopped into the nearest chair. "Look at me. I'm sitting!"

"Ah, yes, you are," I responded.

"Who would have imagined that sitting could be so invigorating? It's *marvelous*," she said lustfully. "I think I shall sit all the time."

"If that's what you want to do," Natalie told her, "then that's what you will do."

Peaches glanced up to Natty then rushed over, snagged another chair, and dragged it back to along side the first chair. She then patted the seat. "Natalie, come sit with me. It's just so amazing."

Natalie did and then made a big show of thoroughly enjoying the state of being seated. I actually pulled out my phone and snapped a few pictures. What a great moment! Then I went and sat back behind my desk. Oddly, I then flashed on the fact that sitting, to me, didn't seem to me to be such a large deal. It was just ... sitting. Maybe I was missing something?

"So is Marcalif with you?" I asked, once the women–or woman and robot, I was pretty unclear in my mind–had calmed down.

Peaches shook her head. "No. After he helped me get these clothes on, he said he had something he needed to do."

Oh, my. What a visual. "So, you were naked and he helped put your clothing on?" I attempted to clarify.

She held up her fingers and wiggled them demonstrably. "Yes, I had a heck of a time getting these to work correctly at first." Then she looked up to me. "And I wasn't naked. I was *unclothed*."

"There's a difference?" I asked.

"Of course there is. *Naked* connotes the state of having removed one's usual garments for the purposes of being without them. *Unclothed* reflects the fact that I'd never had a garment to remove and so rendered myself in a state of not having any on."

"Ah, okay. What you said," I mumbled. The subtler elements of that explanation sure escaped me fully.

"Well, I'm thrilled you have a body now," Natty told her. "It makes interacting with you so much better."

And then–of course–both sets of eyes silently turned to me. What? Was I supposed to say something? And–if so, please help me Lord–what was the least horrible thing for me to say? I ask because there sure looked to be a lot of downside facing me just then. A sheer cliff over a thousand-foot drop-off downside.

Much later than could possibly have been healthy for me, I flip-flopped my hands in the air and said, "And you have a great body."

Hmm. Both pair of eyes seemed to be flash-blinking at me. Ah! Because I'd just said a guy thing. Silly me.

"I mean, that Marcalif sure made your body great."

Wow, how lame-supreme. A new personal-best at being an idiot.

"I mean that I meant when Marcalif made that body of yours, he sure did a great job making it great ... you know ... if you like it, that is." Someone please shoot me now! "Me, I like it great." Here, Natty, take my sidearm, hurry!

The women turned back to face one another.

"Forget what he said," Natalie advised. "His brain suffers testosterone poisoning." She made her fingers pulse next to her head. "Really screws up the old thought processes."

"You know, I've studied that concept and never fully understood it." Then she looked at me like I was a stuffed human male in the corner of a dusty room. "Now it seems so painfully obvious as what it is." Hmm, she said that with a little element of disgust. You heard it too, right?

Natalie gave the back of Peaches' hand a reassuring pat. "But, go easy on him. Sure, you want to kill him half the time. But then you realize it's not actually his fault and that the other half of the time the insanity is kind of cute."

"So I should not act on impulse and break his head off?" Peaches asked thoughtfully.

Natalie shrugged. "Always use your best judgment, but keep in mind some of what he says and does is way beyond his control."

"Gotcha," Peaches affirmed.

"Okay, ah, girls, women, females, or whatever the heck I should be calling you, I do have a serious question." They both stared at me. I had that stuffed-and-in-the-corner feeling all over again. "Does the robot host have the capacity to hold your entire programming, Peaches? I ask because Marcalif specifically said his did not."

Peaches grinned. "Good question, Commodore. Yes, in my case, I fit entirely in the host. It is hard to relate to you how much more complex Marcalif is compared to me."

"So are you copied into the robot and are missing from *Defiant* at this point in time?"

She pursed up her face. "Yes and no. It will be hard to explain, but I do realize there are operational concerns that you, as our commodore, need to understand."

"Thank you," I said, and boy, did I mean it.

"There exists a full copy of me in the ship's computer system. There also exists a completely separate copy in this host. They are linked to one another and can function as one. They are also capable of independent thought and action, should that be needed. Does that make sense?"

"No," I replied honestly.

"Think of the example of identical twins," she went on. "There once was *one* fertilized egg. Then it split into *two* separate organisms. Imagine additionally that they are telepathic. So that which was one, became two that may or may not act as one."

"I'm less in a state of having sense made to me," I babbled.

"Chris, honestly," Natalie scolded me, "don't make her feel bad. Peaches exists in a condition that is foreign to us. There's no way we can fully comprehend it. But we don't need to. Just go with the flow, honey."

I raised a digit in dissent. "I hear you, *but* ... As a leader in battle, I need to know precisely and exactly what I'm dealing with, capable of, and burdened with. I rely very heavily on Peaches. So I need to know with certainty what condition she is in."

Natalie nodded. "I see your point." Turning to Peaches, she invited, "Can you explain it a little better?"

"Only to say that *Defiant* is and will continue to be fully functional. *That* Peaches and *this* Peaches," she touched her chest, "will always agree on everything and function as one."

"Okay," I said, "I can live with that. As I gain experience with this new setup, I might ask that some aspects are changed, but we'll see."

"And I can live with *that*," Peaches parroted back to me. I have to admit, it was a tad unnerving.

But, overall, I had to admit, if only to myself, that I found this new development exciting. Peaches and I went way back, we'd fought side-by-side, and we were family. Seeing her parading through my day now with her flowing robes was a minor miracle and it was so darn cool.

TWENTY

Prime Minister Vassiliev paced astride his large desk, hands behind his waist with his head angled in grim determination toward the floor. He was not a man given to deep thoughts, and he was subject to profound bouts of dark moodiness. But he was a political survivor in spite of those potential limitations. Why? Because Vassiliev was ruthless. He truly enjoyed the application of force when dealing with those who dared oppose him. And he understood better than most how to learn the weaknesses and lusts of others and then how best to use those insights to control them. At that game, he was a master and, truth be told, it was the talent he was most proud of. In short, Mikhail Vassiliev was a man tailor-made to acquire and hold on to power.

The massive setback of the alien invasion nearly toppled Vassiliev. But he'd earned his nickname the Penza Crocodile because he was relentless, never letting go of whatever he desired no matter how mightily it resisted his bite. As his country crawled out of the mud pit they were left in, he was more determined than ever to see the Russian Star rise to new and loftier heights. But then there came this Spokane Group from hell itself to annoy him more than a bed full of fleas. Yes, his scientists had picked up pieces of alien machinery and, yes, the craven idiots might someday learn how to reproduce the technology for his benefit. But their results to date were nothing short of pathetic. Even today, the Spokane Group was churning out advanced generators with the ease of a street corner pirozhok hawker. And tomorrow, no doubt, they'd be selling space warships to his enemies and, more critically, never to him.

These factors came together to spur Vassiliev into action–bold action. As emasculated as his armies and secret police forces were, they would simply have to rise to the occasion and win him control over those who labored to destroy Russia. Central to the Spokane Group were those bitches, the two who lived as a couple. On the rare occasions when they deigned to reveal themselves in public, they spoke so properly and promised so very much. These women may have fooled others, but they did not fool Mikhail Vassiliev even one little bit. He, as a consummate power monger, recognized well the sight and stench of it in another. And this Grace and Molly, oh yes, they were the real deal. They sought world domination as passionately as he did. But they lacked the one quality, the one attribute, that would cause their ultimate downfall. They had no killing spirit. While he was capable of any action to further his cause, they were mired in a contemptible desire for fairness. Vassiliev would show them no mercy because they deserved none. They deserved ... *nothing!*

A soft knock indicated those he'd summoned had arrived.

"*Come,*" he snarled at the closed door.

His secretary slipped in silently and ushered in the men who would put these Spokane women in their place. General Lev Solovyov came accompanied by another Army general and Admiral of the Fleet Sergei Pakshin. Doctor Nikolai Kuzmin, who had assumed control of the KGB, was flanked by a pair of large men in expensive suits. Finally, Vassiliev's old friend Pavel Lebedev entered sporting an impish grin. He presumably represented the voice of reason, if such a factor was to be tolerated in the context of today's meeting.

As the team entered, Mikhail stopped pacing like a caged tiger to stand behind his chair, one hand resting on the back. He glared at them for an uncomfortable moment. Once everyone was seated–and duly appraised of the boss's dower mood–Mikhail Vassiliev sat.

"Gentlemen, I do not have to tell you how important this meeting is." He reached over and picked up a cigar. Biting the end off, he spat it on the floor. Then he held it aloft. "There has never been a more important meeting in the history of Russia. Ever! And let no one present doubt for one *second* that this is the most important meeting in their own individual life. If we succeed in every aspect of our design, each of us will have won mountains of personal glory. But to fail?" He chuckled darkly. "If this scheme falls to pieces, I will be left with my still-attached testicles on the desk of the American president. And, gentlemen," he angled his unlit cigar at them one-by-one, "this is not a state I wish my testicles to occupy."

Vassiliev took a moment to light his cigar. Then he clutched it to his side and looked up thoughtfully. "If any of you should fail me, the consequences for that individual will be grave indeed." He stood and walked behind his chair, grasping it firmly now with both hands. "The wrath I will visit upon those who disappoint me will be horrific." He snuffed revoltingly. "I will not trouble you by spelling it out for you in detail. I will simply promise this. To those of you whose efforts are less than perfect, you will wish that your families and you had been eaten by the aliens." Everyone in attendance was fully impressed with their prime minister's level of expectation. They all—each and every one of them— also cursed their fates for having been drawn into this dubious project. "With that, I will call upon the leaders of each segment of our mission to give me their final assessments."

Everyone sat, or rather, squirmed, and looked to the floor. The prime minister cleared his throat very loudly. Admiral Pakshin then raised his eyes to meet Vassiliev's. "As our part is the most straightforward and last, I will go first." He leaned in and whispered something to the man sitting next to him. That fellow, Contre-admiral Mikhailov, quickly distributed a set of papers to each man present. "As you can see," Pakshin continued, "we will have the recovery submarine in position well in advance of the capture teams' egress. We have a large number of agents already stationed at the US military bases on the West Coast. Though the American forces are a bit more organized than ours, they still suffer from the same fractured networks that we do. The submarine will not be detected, coming or going. The US monitoring system is simply in too much disarray. The destroyer *Marshal Tarasov* will be well offshore and appear to be, for all intents and purposes, on a routine patrol."

"And how confident are you that both links in this chain will function as is required?" Vassiliev asked sternly.

"Failure is impossible. The ships are in top condition mechanically and fully crewed with seasoned personnel. There is nothing that can or will go wrong from our standpoint," the admiral stated confidently.

"Fine," Vassiliev responded. "And the away teams, Doctor Kuzmin? Are they competent?"

"Highly, Prime Minister. I have personally selected the lead officers for each team. They, to a man, assure me that they, in turn, are using only crack agents with proven field records. As the number of unknowns on the ground are much greater than any other element of the mission, I have added redundancies, backups, and supplied the operatives with more than enough lethality to ensure they will not be deterred or captured."

"That is *critical*," Vassiliev stressed. "While it will be assumed by all that we are behind this operation, we can leave behind no proof."

"And none will be left," the KGB director assured him. "Part of the backup agents' roles will be to ensure the frontline operatives are neither captured alive nor any bodies remain behind for identification."

"Excellent," Vassiliev almost purred. The way to this man's heart was for people to be gratuitously killed. Trained men with potent weapons excited him. "And finally, communications. Pavel?"

Though not an expert in the field, the prime minister had assigned his friend Pavel Lebedev to make certain the Russian assets all had coordinated communications. He was also charged with seeing to it that the American comm systems were jammed if and when that was deemed necessary. Pavel flared his hands open. "Piece of cake. Everyone has linkable radios. I even insisted they carry spare batteries in a zippered pocket." That drew a few dark harrumphs from some present.

"Fine, fine," Vassiliev said more to himself. "Then I suggest the operation commence as planned tomorrow at 05:30 local time on the American Western Coast. I want you all in your command posts well before that time, naturally. But you must be linked to me here by video conference. Make certain of that status or I will call an abort to the entire operation and hold the offender or offenders personally responsible for the unconscionable delay." He swept his cigar toward the door. "You are all excused."

~

Tuesday mornings had become so routine and hectic that Grace could temporarily forget that there was ever an apocalypse. Felicia was well into her pre-teen rebellious years and Farrah was stuck in the middle of her head-in-the-cloud phase of life. Herding cats–many, many cats– would be far easier than getting these two young ladies cleaned up, fed, and off to school on time.

"Farrah, honey," Grace chided her daughter, "you need to *eat* that waffle, not paint a face on it with the syrup."

"But she's so pretty, Mommy," was Farrah's justification for her continued creativity.

"Mom," Felicia announced, "I'm not bringing my lunch today. All the other kids get the school lunch and I want to have that."

Grace thought quickly, what harm would there be in that? None. "Sure, sweetie. What are they serving today?"

"I don't know," she replied.

"What if you don't like it? You are a picky eater."

"I am not."

Oh, here we go again, Grace reflected. *If I say it's up, she says it's down.* "How about this. Bring your lunch today. I'll call today and get the meal schedule. Then we can decide if you should bring a lunch or not from now on."

"Ooooh," she seethed adolescently. "No, I'm not bringing my lunch again–*ever*."

So much for a rational discussion, Mom concluded. *Maybe we can have one again in ten-fifteen years? Maybe?* Grace relented. "Suit your-self. I'll leave a five-dollar-bill by the door. Now don't forget it."

"*Mom*," Felicia protested aghast. "No one pays with money. That's so gross. Everyone will laugh at me."

"Fine, I'll call the school and set up an account if that's what it takes as soon as I get home from dropping you off."

"*Mom!*" Felicia protested even more aghast, "no one's parents drop them off anymore. I'm walking to school."

"Honey, I do not have time for this," Grace responded firmly. "I'll drop you half a block away, but that's it. Now finish up and then go brush your teeth."

"I'm not hungry. Farrah grossed me out too much. May I be excused?"

"By all means," Grace let slip.

And so it went. Chaos grew like weeds in a spring lawn. Molly got the girls in the car five minutes too late, they arrived at school six minutes late, so Molly didn't have time to drop her eldest daughter off half a block away. Instead, she dropped a pouting daughter off in front of the school for all the world to see. Needless to say, Felicia was fit to be tied.

As the two girls entered the schoolhouse, Farrah wandered off to the left, where the lower grades were gathered, while Felicia stomped off to the right where the upper grades were corralled. By 09:05, both girls were in their respective classrooms. And so it went. Another Tuesday.

Since Molly had the Mom-taxi assignment this week, once the twin tornadoes were out the door, Grace was free to go to her study and start what promised to be a long day's work. By force of habit, she opened her email first and started plowing through it.

After Grace's second coffee refill, Peaches came to the room and knocked on the frame softly. "Do you have a minute, Grace?" she asked.

"Absolutely. Please, come in. Can I get you some–" She paused after what she thought to be a faux pas. "Sorry, you don't drink–"

"I'd *love* a cup of coffee," Peaches corrected. "In this new robotic unit, I have come to appreciate the taste of coffee early in the morning. But, please, I'll get my own. You stay where you are."

Grace shrugged at her. "Works for me," she replied and dropped back into her massive inbox.

Peaches returned from the kitchen with a large, steaming mug, and sat across from Grace. "*Mmm*, coffee is divine," she remarked.

"You'll get no argument from me on that," Grace said while still focusing on her messages. After a flare of keystrokes, she looked up. "So what can I do for you?"

"If you have the time, I'd like to discuss some production bottle-necks I'm detecting."

Grace checked her wristwatch. "I have a ten o'clock, but it's only 09:05, so you can have all fifty-five of my free minutes if you need them."

"I'm certain I won't take up that much of your time," Peaches assured her.

What a great Tuesday morning! I had nothing in particular to do. Natty had nothing too pressing this morning—aside from me, that is. As a result, I was in seventh heaven. We were free to lounge and cavort in our cabin aboard *Arc of Intention* to our heart's content. Life was good.

"You about ready for breakfast?" Natalie asked from where her head rested on my belly.

"No. I refuse to eat breakfast today," I stated with determination.

That remark was unusual enough to draw her eyes up toward me. "You, refusing food ... ever?"

"It's not about the food," I deflected firmly. "It's about the slippery slope."

"Care to expand upon that thought, sport?" she asked with curiosity.

"Certainly. If we get up, dress, and go eat, we will no longer be naked in bed together."

"That explains little concerning the slope you referenced," she pointed out.

"Well, don't you see? Once dressed and moving, we'll maybe just go here, there, or anywhere. We'll *start* our day. What we will *not* be here is in this state of bliss."

"No, we'll just be hungry, unproductive people in a world struggling to find some measure of normality."

"*Thank you*," I sang out, "for agreeing with me."

"I'm not sure I was. And whatever strength your argument might possess, I am hungry *and* I have a ten o'clock with the others."

"Marcalif," I called out.

"Yes, Captain?"

"What time is it?"

"09:05 PST."

"Thank you." Peering back down at Natty, I said, "You see, we have pretty nearly forever before you need to rush off and do stuff."

She sat up, rested her palms on the mattress, and responded, "Just because you have no get-up-and-go does not excuse me from doing what I deem necessary." With that, she walked toward the bathroom. I heard the shower start up. Hmm, maybe it was time for me to freshen up after all? I didn't feel perfectly clean.

Doctor Nikolai Kuzmin sat in an office chair and studied a set of monitors. He held a jade cigarette holder between his fingers mounted with a Treasurer Luxury Black. His perpetual fixed scowl was, against all anatomical odds, more profound today than usual. Then again, the present operation was problematic at best. If it failed, Mikhail Vassiliev would order his death. If that were to happen, he'd be forced to have that idiot assassinated *before* he was able to set those wheels in motion. It wasn't that busy days bothered Nikolai; only busy days that involved bumping off his boss did. As was wisely said, there can be so many slips 'twixt the cup and the lip.

"Mr. Chairman," a voice called to Nikolai from behind. "I have confirmations from Team Alpha and Team Beta that they are on time and on target."

Without turning, Nikolai asked menacingly, "And what of Strike Team Gamma?"

"They have not made their final scheduled check-in. As of thirty minutes ago, they were within mission parameters."

"Who again leads Gamma?"

"Colonel Popov, Mr. Chairman."

"Do we have the entirety of his family in custody?"

"Yes, sir, we do. They are being held in Matrosskaya Tishina along with the other familiars."

"Fine. Keep me posted," Nikolai replied with a seemingly incongruous grin. "What is the exact time in Spokane, America?" he asked.

"09:05 local time, Mr. Chairman."

"Soon we shall see if Mother Russia's best are worth a handful of oxen shit," he said to himself with considerable doubt.

Lev Orlov, Maxim Nikitin, and Veer Volkov, the members of Team Alpha, knelt behind some shrubbery at the rear of the elementary school. They were dressed in what was intended to be inconspicuous American casual outfits. They looked like escapees from a circus. But if anyone pointed that out to them, instant regret would befall that person. The trio was heavily armed, on edge, and were all, by nature, bloodthirsty killers.

Captain Orlov, a field assassin for the KGB before the alien invasion, was the team's leader. He glanced at his watch. "Time check: 09:10." The other two confirmed this with a grunt. "Maxim, you enter the building through that green door. I shall penetrate through the gray door to its left. Once inside, go straight to Classroom 3. If you are confronted, eliminate that party without hesitation."

"Yes, Lev," Maxim whined, "I know the plan. Christ, we've gone over it a thousand times. Lighten up already." Maxim was retired FSB Spetsnaz major, not a trained KGB field agent. As such, he was less patient with the exasperating redundancies. "I go in, grab the girl wearing the red frock and I kill anyone who I choose to kill. Got it."

Lev seethed at the man, inhaling deeply through his nostrils. He hated working with amateurs. But, times being what they were, compromises were necessary evils. "We go on my mark," he hissed. "Veer, remain exactly here to cover our egress. *Mark!*"

Lev and Maxim ran in a crouch, accessing the rear doors quickly and without incident. With no visual detection, they entered the building.

Lev jogged down the short hallway, past Classrooms 1 and 2. When he arrived at Room 3, he checked in both directions, then as slowly and silently as possible, he turned the doorknob. Through a small crack, he studied the children inside. The teacher had her back to him. Good. Easy was always good. It took him five seconds to pick out Farrah's bright red jumper dress, the one he'd seen her leave her house wearing a short while ago. Lev slipped in and walked quickly in Farrah's direction, his Glock 17L dangling loosely at his side. The child never saw him approach, preoccupied with a drawing she was doing. He had a firm grip on her shoulder before anyone even noticed his presence. He lifted her from her chair, Farrah all the while still scratching her crayon in the air.

Strike Team Beta was composed of Yakov Stepanov, Andrei Morozov, and Nestor Golubev. All three were KGB before the invasion, though only Yakov had any field experience. That made him the leader for this operation. They were hiding behind the neighboring fence, with a clear sightline to Grace and Molly's house. As they were tasked with extracting an adult, all three would enter the dwelling together. Nestor's primary assignment was to sweep the house for unanticipated persons. Yakov and Morozov were responsible for apprehending Grace, as their primary target, and Molly, as a secondary target, if she had returned home from the drop-off. Any others present were to be killed. That would ensure a delay in the report of their incursion, buying them valuable getaway time.

"We are to enter the house at precisely 09:10," Yakov reminded the pair. "It is now 09:09. Any issues?"

"Issues?" Andrei snarled. "My watch says it 09:11 as we speak."

Yakov nearly peed himself upon hearing those words. He shot a glance to Nestor.

Studying his watch like it was a beautiful woman, it took Nestor maybe five seconds to confirm, "Yeah, boss, I got 09:11 too."

"Shit, shit, shit," excoriated Yakov. "We're—"

"09:*12*, boss," Nestor amended unhelpfully.

"Let's go. Crap, if they've been—"

"Yakov, shut up already and let's move," snapped Andrei.

With that firm prompt, Yakov pushed past the others and scooted around the fence, then sprinted toward the back door. Andrei and Nestor followed close on his heels.

~

Denis Romanov rested against a dirt berm and stared at *Arc of Intention*, absently scratching the back of his head with his Glock 19. He was the lead for the tardy Strike Team Gamma. Avian Kuznetsov, Timur Fedorov, and Aleksandr Yakovlev stood behind him, splitting their attention between Denis's back and the ship. Aleksandr was inadvisedly puffing away at a cigarette.

"I haven't seen them come out yet," exclaimed Denis for the tenth or eleventh time. He turned to his squad. "Have any of you seen them come out?"

Timur, who was famous for being impatient and a bully, slapped Denis's shoulder. "No, of course we haven't seen them come out, you idiot. We've been here since before dawn. No one has come in or out of that spaceship. Stop asking the same questions you already know the answers to."

"But how are we supposed to *kill* this Christopher boy if he doesn't come out so that we may *shoot* him?" Denis bemoaned.

"You're asking me?" Timur spat back. "I'm along because I'm a trig-german, and a damn good one at that. If you have *analytical* questions, ask someone who is not about to shoot you in the back of your head."

Avian, the meekest of the team by far, began to worry in earnest about his aging mother, who was being held in captivity. It was well past nine at night back home. Avian knew with certainty that Mama had received neither her daily laxative nor her medicinal glass of vodka. This was all inexcusable. And now the brazen Timur was threatening to shoot their leader. If Timur shot Denis, this arm of the assault would fail. If this arm of the assault failed, Mama would not only never be given her laxative or vodka, but they promised she'd be murdered most brutally. Avian was fully at his wit's end.

"*Timur*, behave yourself, you disgraceful fiend," Avian snapped. "We cannot allow our party to–"

That was all Avian got out before the barrel of Timur's Desert Eagle slammed into his jaw. Avian was spitting out copious amounts of blood before he collapsed to the ground. Once he landed, he didn't move.

"Shit, now look what you've—"

That was all Denis could manage before Timur clocked him over the head with the magazine well of his pistol. Timur was not a team player.

Aleksandr, who'd watched the mayhem impassively, raised his arms in question. "What, you going to clobber me too? I've said and done *nothing*."

Timur bobbed his head side-to-side by way of response. Then he shot Aleksandr three times in the face. "No, I am not going to clobber you," he then, if a bit too late, replied.

Then Timur took off at a sprint toward *Arc of Intent*'s lowered ramp. He was psyched! He was going to kill more people today and it wasn't even noon. As he ran, and for unknowable reasons, he glanced at his watch. 09:15.

So, my day was going from superb to supreme, if that's the correct order I'm citing. In other words, it was just getting better. Natty hit the shower at 09:06. I hit it at 09:08 or thereabouts. Come on, I wasn't wearing anything, *including* a watch. I'm estimating the time here. After Natalie's perfunctory protestations that I was going to make her late and that I was a pig, we were getting down to business. I was lathering up a bar of Irish Spring so feverishly, it looked like I had green whipped cream all over my hands. Natty was just about to squeal.

Then, booming over the ship's main speakers that I didn't even know she had, I heard, "CAPTAIN. EMERGENCY! PLEASE RESPOND."

Natalie shoved me backwards out of the shower so hard, I nearly fell over backwards. As I tried to shake the foam off my hands, I yelled, "Report!"

"Two armed men have entered the girls' school and are attempting to abduct them. Also, several armed men are running in the yard of Grace's house."

"Shit, are the girls okay?" This was bad. "Give me a full report," I ordered.

∽

Maxim Nikitin lifted Farrah out of her seat and slung her under his arm before she knew what was happening. The teacher, Marlene Larsen, screamed in holy terror. Maxim snapped his Glock at her and a red dot danced across her forehead. Uncertain if he would execute the woman or not, he took one step toward the door ...

In monitoring the microdrones he routinely deployed, Marcalif noted at 09:12:01 that an unknown and presumably hostile man had entered Farrah's classroom. The drones were about the size of a mosquito and functioned silently, making them ideal for such unobtrusive surveillance as this. At 09:12:39 Marcalif witnessed the intruder set a hand on Farrah and hoist her from her seat.

The ship's AS ordered the microdrone's tiny fusion engine into overload-failure mode. In six-tenths of a second, the device went for room temperature to six thousand degrees Celsius. As it heated, Marcalif directed the drone to penetrate the assailant's right eyeball and advance nine centimeters along the X-axis and two centimeters along the positive Z-axis, and to then come to rest.

By 09:12:41, the center of Maxim Nikitin's brain vaporized to a radius of five centimeters. He collapsed to the floor deader than the proverbial doornail, never feeling even fleeting discomfort. Farrah landed on top of the corpse, and only then began to wail. Marlene Larsen rushed to Farrah and pulled her from the spasming corpse of the former Russian FSB Spetsnaz officer.

∽

As a seasoned KGB operative, Lev Orlov knew all too well that in any operation, however well planned, funded, and rehearsed, something would always go wrong. The best one could hope for was that matters wouldn't go horribly wrong. So it was that as Lev ran down the hallway of New Era Elementary School with the intention of forcibly abducting Felicia Chang-Cooper, he nearly tripped when his shoelace came untied. *Wear native clothing*, they'd badgered him as the mission took shape. *Blend in*, he was advised. So Lev had purchased what he believed to be the typical wingtip dress shoes American males wore on a routine basis. But, unbeknownst to him, while the state of shoe production had rebounded somewhat, post apocalypse, the ability to produce quality laces lagged far behind that of the footwear itself.

So he holstered his pistol, knelt down, and fumbled with the inferior laces. Truth be told, he had never been very skilled at tying his own shoes. Up until the Russian equivalent of high school, his mother always performed that task for him. Finally, in frustration, Lev cinched down the tightest knot he could and rose to continue his objective. Let the record show that he stopped moving at 09:11:13. As a result of his near-complete incompetence with laces, Lev didn't stand back up until 09:12:41. That was most unfortunate for both Lev Orlov and the entirety of the Orlov clan back home. Because it was at 09:12:40 that Marcalif correctly identified a lethal threat to Farrah Chang-Cooper. So it was that when Lev was just about to take his first step in his renewed pursuit of his goal that a microdrone rocketed in through his right eye and exited the rear of his skull fractions of a second later, leaving in its wake a truly ugly exit crater.

Grace checked her wristwatch. "I have a ten o'clock, but it's only 09:05, so you can have all fifty-five of my free minutes if you need them."

"I'm certain I won't take up that much of your time," Peaches assured her.

"Peaches," Grace returned warmly, "it is always a pleasure to chat with you. Now, what problems have you identified in terms of production bottlenecks?" Then, as an afterthought, she asked, "Can I get you some fresh coffee?"

Peaches grinned mischievously, "Are you making some for yourself?"

"I most definitely am."

"Then, yes, I'd love a fresh round. May I help you?"

"No, young lady, you sit right there. You are my guest. I make the coffee. Assorted cookies may also be in your immediate future, based solely upon my whim as your hostess."

Peaches chuckled. "No one's ever called me *young* before."

"Well, you look to be all of twenty-five, so own it," Grace responded. "I'll be right back."

Peaches sat in Grace's office taking in the experience of being alive–after a fashion. She surveyed the memorabilia and photos on the walls, wondering what it must be like to have flesh-and-blood family.

A few minutes later, Grace returned with a tray. "I don't believe–" Then she noticed Peaches had her head angled oddly and focused on nothing in particular. "Peaches, are you alright?"

Peaches' palm rose to silence Grace. Then her attention snapped back to the here-and-now. "Grace, we are in the middle of an emergency. Armed assailants have attempted to kidnap the girls and three are outside rushing this house as we speak. The girls are safe. Please follow my instructions."

"They're ... are you sure the girls–"

"They are fine," Peaches cut her off. "I need you to stand against that wall." She pointed at the blue wall opposite the desk. Fortunately, Grace complied quickly. "I am placing a force field in front of you. I will shade it the same blue as the wall. Please remain there and be completely still. Marcalif and I have decided that I must be abducted so that we may learn the identity of our assailants."

Grace, being Grace, started to protest vehemently. But she quickly took the necessary leap of faith and rushed over to the wall. Just as heavy footfalls could be heard coming from the kitchen, Peaches slipped into Grace's desk chair. She then noticed Grace's official ID badge on the desk, the one she needed to enter the various satellite facilities. Peaches clipped it on seconds before two men with pistols barreled into the room.

"Do not move," screamed Yakov Stepanov, his Glock 17 trembling in his hand as he aimed it at Peaches. Andrei Morozov entered right behind him and ran into his arm so forcibly, Yakov almost discharged his weapon. "Back off, you moron," Yakov snapped at his co-perpetrator.

Nestor Golubev poked his head in. "You still want me to sweep the house, Boss?"

"*Yes*, I want you to do your assigned task, *other* moron," Yakov shouted even louder.

Nestor ducked out quickly.

"Where is Grace Chang?" Yakov demanded as he shook his pistol at Peaches.

"*I* am Grace Chang," Peaches said plainly.

"No you are not. You are the secretary maybe. This Grace, she's some kind of Asian bitch. You're not Asian."

"I am Asian. My parents were Asian." Then Peaches played her trump card. She raised the ID badge off her chest. "Why would I wear this badge if I were not Grace Chang?"

A frightfully confused Yakov stepped close to Peaches and inspected the ID. It certainly said Grace Chang on it. "That photograph looks *nothing* like you," he accused.

"I have recently lost weight," Peaches countered. "But if you are confident in your assertion that I am not Grace Chang, then I will attempt to flee out of this confinement." Peaches stood slowly.

Just then Nestor returned. "No one else here, Boss," he announced.

Yakov waved his gun at Peaches. "You *are* going somewhere, but it will be with us, Grace Chang. If you try anything cute, I will shoot you."

"I surrender," Peaches responded. Familiar with normal, fluid speech, she was still not. She raised her hands.

"Come on," Yakov barked. "Everyone *out*."

With Andrei in front of him and Nestor behind, Yakov led Peaches away at gunpoint.

I was trying hard to insert my leg into my pants. But my panic, wet foot, and generally frayed nerves made that task a challenge. I fell over onto the bed twice. In between attempts, I was able to ask, "So you're saying the girls are both safe and fine? No harm done?"

"Yes, Captain," Marcalif reassured me again. "I used the surveillance drones to kill the assailants. One was lurking outside, but I incapacitated and restrained him."

"But, sheesh, the girls had to witness those men killed," I lamented.

"I killed the man who picked up Farrah in the least graphic manner possible. Yes, she will be traumatized by the events. But at least the man was externally intact when he died. The one I killed in the hallway is a bloody mess, but he never made it as far as the classroom."

"Okay, that's good. That's something."

"There was a team sent to Grace's home. Presumably, they wished to kidnap her also. Peaches was able to convince the operatives that she was Grace, so they abducted her instead."

"Crap, they got Peaches? We need to—"

"We allowed them to take Peaches. It is important to trace this action back to its source. That end is best achieved if Peaches is taken. Captain, please remember that she is a highly durable robot."

"Oh, okay. So that was it? Two teams, now all accounted for?"

"Not so much," he answered unclearly.

"What? What else did they throw at us?"

"A third team was sent here."

"Oh, shit. Are we in danger?"

"Hardly. One member of the team killed or disabled the other three members. He is presently attempting to pick the lock at the top of the entry ramp for the hatch blocking his entry."

"There's a lock in your external hatch?" I asked incredulously.

"No, nor is there anything vaguely similar."

"Then why ... why'd he kill the others and why is he trying to pick that which is not a lock?"

"I cannot say, Captain, but I am confident that stupidity and a tragic upbringing have something to do with the man's inadequacies."

"No doubt." I bobbed my head. "Well, let's let him in."

"Are you certain you wish to take that risk?"

"Well, sure, as long as you're there to greet him, I am."

"An excellent plan. If you would be so kind as to wait here, I shall greet appropriately our murderous guest."

Within five minutes, Marcalif entered my quarters holding in front of him the limp form of a poorly dressed man.

"You didn't kill him, did you?" I asked.

"No, Sir. In his struggles and gyrations, he struck his head on most of the bulkheads between here and the ramp. No worries, though. He's a trooper. Let me just splash some water in his face. I'm sure that'll do the trick."

Marcalif carried the unconscious man into the head and dunked his face in the toilet bowl repeatedly. Super gross! But, sure enough, though the fellow gasped and coughed, revive he did. Marcalif carried him back to me, already toweling him off so as to keep my room toilet-water free. What a guy!

"*YA ub ... ub'yu tebya*," were the first words out of the man's potty mouth.

"He is speaking Russian, Captain. He states that he will kill you. He does not specify how or when."

"No speaky 'd Englishy, *comrade*?" I challenged him.

"Little a," he stated wetly.

"Who sent you?"

"My your mother," he replied. Okay, this conversation was going to go absolutely nowhere. "Marcalif, toss his ass in the brig and meet me by the ramp."

"We do not have a brig, Captain."

I shrugged. "Next best thing, then. Your call."

"Very well, Captain. See you soon." And off they went.

Marcalif was actually waiting by the exit ramp when I got there. "That was quick," I commented. "What'd you do with Boris Badenov?"

"I believe his name is Timur Fedorov and I fused the skin of his chest with one of the internal walls."

"You ... you fused his skin to metal?"

"In a word, yes."

"That's so cool. Remind me to never piss you off, by the way."

"So noted."

"Let's get over to Grace's."

We ran down the ramp and directly over to the house.

"I believe Ms. Chang is in front of that wall," Marcalif said as we entered her office. "There, the force field is down."

Grace appeared out of nowhere. That was also so cool. "Grace, are you alright?" I asked as I ran to her.

"I'm fine. We need to get to the school. There's ... something–"

"I know. Marcalif filled me in. I'll drive," I told her.

As we drove the short distance, I asked, "Where's Molly?"

"Not sure," Grace replied. "She was going to run an errand after dropping the girls off."

"She is on her way back to the school. I took the liberty of alerting her," Marcalif stated.

"Perfect. Thanks," she responded.

Molly's car was already outside when I pulled up and Grace bolted from the door. She was out of sight before I was even parked. When I entered, a bunch of people were milling about in the hallway. A tarp covered what had to be one of the agents. I spied Susan standing over the corpse, talking emphatically on the phone. Whoever she was speaking to, I did not want to be. As I got to her side, she thumbed the phone off.

"Who was that?" I asked.

"Carl Sellers," she said, still obviously pissed.

"He called already?"

"No, I called him. I said I had a bunch of dead bodies with Russian cigarettes in their pockets I wanted him to come and get."

"What's he say?"

"He expressed his regrets and is sending every MIB he has at his disposal. The Spokane contingent is almost here."

"That's sweet. I've learned a whole lot of new stuff, but DB disposal isn't one of them. Not interested in learning that skill either."

"Amen," Susan agreed.

"So you seemed to be pretty angry when you were talking to the prez."

"We have been attacked by foreign agents on American soil. I, the sitting vice president, was at risk. The man needs to step it up a few notches and keep us safe."

"Good point. Thanks for handling that."

She grinned without any joy. "My pleasure. Seriously. Who doesn't love to yell at the boss?"

"Where are the others?" I asked.

"In the teacher's lounge," Susan replied. She pointed. "Over here."

Sure enough, Grace and Molly were in there with the girls. Somehow both women had both girls on their laps simultaneously.

I scruffed up Farrah's and Felicia's hair as I knelt beside them. "How are my girls doing?"

"I'm fine," Farrah said very quietly while looking down. Yeah, she was anything but fine.

Felicia was maybe handling it better. "I'm okay, Uncle Chris," she stated stoically. "I'm so glad Marcalif thought to place those drones here."

"You and me both," I agreed. "But it's over, you're both safe, and we'll make sure nothing like this ever happens again."

"At least they didn't have the bugs with them," Farrah perked up and stated.

"Yes," I agreed with her. "Thank goodness there were no alien bugs."

I looked up to the moms. "You guys okay?"

"You bet," Molly reassured me.

"Then I'll leave you four to be together," I stated. "I'll be right outside if you need anything." Then it occurred to me it was close to noon by now. "You girls hungry?" They shot each other a glance.

"I'll take that as a *yes* and see about some lunch."

"Thanks, Chris," Grace said, patting the back of my hand.

"Pleasure's mine."

Out in the hallway I asked one of the staff if I could make the girls a couple PBJs. The woman nearly exploded, she was so anxious to help *someone*. She told me not to worry, she'd make enough for everybody. She actually ran down the hall toward the kitchen, bless her heart.

"Susan, walk with me," I said.

She fell in and we headed out to the playground. "Where's Natalie?" she asked.

"She volunteered to hold down the fort while the rest of us were busy with this."

"What a doll. I'll head over as soon as we're done."

"Great. I'm sure she'll appreciate the company."

"What's on your mind?" she asked.

I sat down on a swing and she sat on the one next to it. We rocked gently. "This shit show is a big deal."

"I'll say," she agreed. "And we can't let it go unpunished."

"Well, there have to be consequences. As to who does the punishing, let's see where the trail leads to first."

"It leads back to Mikhail Vassiliev in Moscow. That I can tell you with certainty."

"Most likely. But we let them kidnap Peaches. She convinced some pinhead bad guys she was Grace."

"Good help always was hard to find."

"I figure she'll be able to tell us exactly who did what and when."

"I agree. So, until then?"

"Until then, we help the girls heal. I'm in constant contact with both Peaches and Marcalif. I'll let everyone know when something interesting happens."

"You're talking to her now?" Susan marveled.

"No, I'm talking to you."

She chuckled. "Tell her I'm worried about her."

"I just did. She says this is the most fun she's had in decades. Not to worry."

"She's *enjoying* forced kidnapping?" Susan asked.

"If you were an indestructible robot determined to figure out who tried to hurt your family, you probably would be too."

Susan nodded. "I would at that." She stood. "I'm heading home. Let Grace and Molly know."

"Absolutely," I assured her. "And remember, you have guardian angel drones following you all the time too."

"Thanks. Let's just hope my husband doesn't hear that. He's had enough trouble with the whole having-sex-with-the-VP thing. Adding constant surveillance would greatly lessen our chances for a bountiful family."

We both chuckled about that and she left.

Now we waited. Then, heads were going to roll.

∾

Mikhail Vassiliev sat at a desk in one of the offices that adjoined his main one. Three large monitors rested on the desk, displaying three different scenes. One was a link to Doctor Nikolai Kuzmin's war room. Another showed a very concerned-looking General Lev Solovyov, who had recently developed several distinct facial tics. The final one had the slightly more relaxed visage of Admiral of the Fleet Sergei Pakshin. Presently, all three audio feeds were silent aside from some background voices.

Vassiliev's mood had descended from its typical dour one, to fury, then down to incendiary ire, and now hovered somewhere around kill-them-all rage. What was, he understood, to be a complex and realistically problematic raid had devolved into the ashes of shit filtering through his trembling fingers. As far as any of the idiots who served him so poorly could determine, they'd lost contact with most of the operatives. More infuriating was that not one of these stooges could say for certain

if even one of the mission objectives was still progressing.

"Doctor *Kuzmin*," the prime minister hissed through clenched teeth, "I thought you had backup parties in place for the specific task of monitoring the assault teams."

"We do," he replied angrily, with a deliberate switch of the *you* to a *we*, as he hoped to spread the blame.

"Then what do they–any of them–report?" Vassiliev demanded.

"The support group for Team Alpha reports, and I quote, *Nothing unanticipated had been noted.*"

"That tells me *nothing*," Vassiliev screamed. "Do those morons not consider the team they're supposed to be monitoring not returning, or even contacting them, *anticipated*?"

"I cannot say, Prime Minister," the doctor replied defiantly. "Team Gamma, the one that never did check in with us, continues to be dark. Their backups report hearing what might have been a few gunshots. Otherwise, their signals indicate all is going per plan."

Vassiliev jumped up from his chair so forcefully that it crashed to the floor behind him. "A few gunshots *maybe*? But *otherwise*, their picnic and cookout is going well? What barrel did you plumb the depths of to scrape these operatives off of, Doctor?"

"I assigned the best people made available to me," was Kuzmin's carefully crafted response.

"And what of Team Beta? Are they *fucking* each other behind some hedges because they forgot to accomplish the mission you sent them on?"

"Team Beta has conveyed to their backup that they were successful in apprehending one of the Spokane Group's lead females. They *believe* her to be Grace Chang. Presently, the team is withdrawing to the backup personnel and, from there, they will egress to Seattle."

Vassiliev removed his right shoe and began pounding it maniacally on the desk in front of him. "They *believe* her to be this Grace woman? How *incompetent* can they *possibly* be, Doctor? If they captured a woman, she, whoever she is, must either *be* or *not be* Grace Chang. There are not *ill-defined* identities among women of our species."

"I can only report to you what I am told from the operatives," the doctor attempted to punt once again.

"*This is completely unacceptable!*" Vassiliev howled as be continued to slam down his shoe. "Did I not warn *each* and *every* member of this comic opera that not only they, but their entire *families* would be executed if even some small aspect of the operation went afoul? Do none of you *believe* my promise? What a wretched fate has been dealt me, to survive alien consumption only to be stabbed in the back by my *useless* aides."

Not surprisingly, none of his subordinates responded to those hateful remarks. Why bother to be dutiful when your death warrant was already signed and the ink was fully dry?

TWENTY-ONE

Yakov Stepanov marched Peaches, whom he had mistaken for Grace Chang–pistol barrel to her head–back to the rally point. He had her sit on the ground while he spoke quietly with the backup personnel.

"Apparently, the prime minister is hopping mad at this operation to date," Konstantin Trofimov informed him grimly.

Throwing his arms up, Yakov defended, "What? We're here and we have the prisoner. If others screwed up, let them suffer. We have done our duty."

Konstantin shrugged. "Don't try to sell that to me. I'm just a pawn like you. Tell Mikhail Vassiliev your shit doesn't smell. See if *he* buys it."

"There's no time to chat or to worry. We have to flee before the authorities arrive," Yakov said by way of dismissal.

"Fine. The van is just behind those trees," Konstantin said, pointing the direction with his pistol.

"Any radio traffic I should know about?"

"Nothing on the standard police bands."

"Thank goodness for one break." Then Yakov turned to Nestor Golubev. "Bring the woman, and do *not* allow her to slip away."

"Yaki," he protested, "she's as tiny as a ballerina. You suspect she will suddenly overpower me? Get serious." He did however tighten his grip on Peaches' arm.

All five Russians and their captive hurried to the panel van. Konstantin opened one of the rear doors and gestured with his gun, "*In, little bird.*"

Peaches complied and slid to the front of the wall-mounted folding bench seat. "Does this vehicle possess seat and shoulder restraints in case we are involved in a collision?" she asked sweetly.

"We're not having a collision and you don't need seat belts," Konstantin snarled. "Now sit there and be quiet or I will duct tape your mouth."

"Don't say I didn't warn you if this vehicle is pulled over by the police," she responded while shaking her head.

"Where did you get this nut?" Kon asked Yakov.

Yakov just shrugged. As the last in, he slapped the side of the van to indicate the driver should pull out. After a short, bumpy start, the van pulled onto a residential street. The driver, a petty felon named Adrik, then sped up as much as he deemed safe. Everyone settled in quietly for the short drive to the SUV they'd be switching to. Once they were in the second car, Adrik drove to an abandoned drive-in theater on the outskirts of town. The Sikorsky S-76 helicopter that would bring them to the coast was stashed there. One of the Beta Team members, Andrei Morozov, was a seasoned pilot and had them aloft quickly enough.

Flying low to avoid radar detection, they made the trip in just over an hour, landing outside of the tiny town of Clallam Bay on the Olympic Peninsula. A waiting SUV took them to a private dock. There they all boarded a thirty-foot fishing boat that ferried them to the waiting submarine. The sub captain, Timofey Belyayev, knew the US Navy and Coast Guard were not serious concerns these days, but he still wanted to stay close to deep water just in case he was detected. The Strait of Juan de Fuca where he waited was over six hundred feet deep just a few miles out. Naturally, Timofey would have preferred to make the pickup out to sea where he had more maneuvering room. But his orders were to get as close to shore as was safely possible. Doctor Nikolai Kuzmin had insisted the captives be aboard the sub quickly. Once it was submerged, he reasoned the chances of detection would drop to near zero.

During the entire trek, Peaches was cooperative and pleasant. On the submarine, she was handcuffed to a table in the crew's mess and at least two of Team Beta were constantly watching her. That all struck Peaches as being completely silly. How was she supposed to escape from a vessel that was under water? In spite of her compliant behavior, the thugs that handled her were as rough and inconsiderate as possible. She was never offered food, drink, or even a bathroom break. But she took it in stride. She knew in the end who would be smiling and who would be very upset.

Three hours after departing, Peaches sensed that the submarine was rising.

"Are we almost there?" she asked Yakov, whom she'd correctly identified as the leader.

"Shut up," he snapped.

"I'm just curious," she said. "This is my first voyage on a submarine. It's quite exciting."

"I said be *quiet*," Yakov shouted as he stood. "I will slap your mouth shut if you say another word. You do not need to know where we're going or when we will arrive."

Peaches turned to Nestor. "Is he always this grouchy?"

"That's it," Yakov snarled and he lunged at Peaches.

Nestor blocked his partner with an arm. "Lighten up. If she's bleeding, someone might object. We're almost home free. Let's keep it together for a little while longer, bossman."

Yakov pushed the arm away angrily, but did return to his seat without committing any mayhem.

"And *yes*," Nestor said to Peaches, "he is always this grouchy." He then gave his accomplice a sarcastic grin. "Luckily, you'll be rid of him soon enough. Once we're aboard the destroyer, you're someone else's responsibility."

"A destroyer!" Peaches responded gleefully. "Does it have big cannons?"

"I could not tell you," he replied. "It will be my first time on one myself." With a smile, he said, "We shall discover the truth together."

"I can hardly wait," she exclaimed, bouncing sightly on her chair. This really was an adventure for the alien AS.

"My, but you're easy to entertain," Nestor observed. "I should think I would be in a much fouler mood if I were ever kidnapped."

Just then, Captain Belyayev came over the speakers. "We have just surfaced. The *Marshal Tarasov* is a thousand meters off our bow. We are approaching her so we can make a safe ship-to-ship transfer of our passengers. If those transferring individuals would please proceed to the bridge, we can get you over there as quickly as possible."

Yakov brusquely freed Peaches' wrist and shoved her off her chair. "You heard the man. Move."

Meanwhile, aboard the *Marshal Tarasov*, the captain, Vitaly Novikov, monitored the submarine's progress with a grim face. A senior KGB agent stood shoulder-to-shoulder with the captain. Fedor Yusupov was a severe man, completely devoid of humor and absolutely free of any ethical restraints. Before the alien invasion, he was one of the most feared and ruthless KGB assassins. Doctor Kuzmin, a fellow sociopath, had quickly identified him as a valuable asset and had placed him in command of this final leg of the kidnapping.

Studying the approaching submarine through field glasses, Fedor instructed the captain, "I want all of your crew to stay well out of our retrieval area."

Captain Novikov gave the man a sideways evil eye. "We can try to *accommodate* that request, but crane transfers at sea are tricky. A crewmen might need to be there to–"

Fedor placed a gloved palm in front of the captain's face. "If any of your people are within ten meters of me or my men, I will slit their throat and toss them overboard. Is that clear?"

"How *dare* you threaten my crew. We are all working together, comrade."

Fedor slowly lowered his binoculars and turned his body to address the captain. "This mission is of the utmost importance. I have been placed in command of it. It is my intention to see it to a successful conclusion. If you question my orders again, or interfere in any manner, you will be the first dead body in the water."

Fifteen minutes later, Fedor and his men were in the process of securing each person as they were lowered to the *Marshal Tarasov's* deck.

When Peaches was aboard, Fedor handcuffed her to his own wrist. "You and I will be traveling together. Please know that I have no problem forcing your cooperation." Then he turned to address one of his team. "Are all the operatives aboard?"

"Yes, Sir. This is the last of them now." He pointed to Yakov, whose feet were just touching down on the deck.

"Line them up against the railing and shoot them. Discard the bodies into the sea."

Yakov overheard that pronouncement and jerked violently to free himself from the hoist chair. "We just completed a successful mission. You ... you can't kill us like dogs."

Fedov smiled a wicked smile. "Sorry, my friend. Orders from the top. No unnecessary loose ends."

Yakov began to yell something, but the burst of bullets from an AK-47 permanently silenced him before he was able to voice his protest.

"Tell the idiot captain to get underway," Fedor said to the same assistant once the last Team Beta member was overboard.

Within five minutes, the turbines were heard to strain and the *Marshal Tarasov* veered away from the submarine. Once on course for Vladivostok, the ship began plowing through the moderate seas with powerful determination. Fedor was insistent that the voyage be made in less than three days. Captain Novikov was, at that point, determined to make it in record time.

Ten minutes after the two ships parted, both their engines mysteriously died. Simultaneously, the electrical, telecommunications, and every other powered system aboard both vessels shut down completely. Both captains issued frantic orders, demanding explanations from their engineers, and sent out repair crews with harsh instructions. But no one could determine how all the systems, including battery backups, could fail at the same time. Panicked engineers assured frantic officers that their predicament was fully impossible. But there both ships lay, dead in the water.

Then, as suddenly as they stopped, both ships began to surge through the water. They altered their courses and began inexplicably sailing along parallel courses. Using old handheld tools, the navigators quickly determined that the ships were bound for San Diego, California. How they made headway, since the engines were completely useless, was a mystery no one could even speculate upon. *Magic* seemed the most reasonable explanation.

If any of the ship's personnel had chanced to look astern and five-thousand feet up, they would have been able to make out *Arc of Intention*. After tracking the rendezvous location through Peaches, Chris flew the spacecraft there, disabled the Russian ships, and was now pushing them with a tractor beam toward Naval Base San Diego. The eighteen-hour effort would deliver the two offending vessels, the conspirators, and Peaches to a US Naval Task Force that was already under way and eagerly awaiting their arrival. The vice president had arranged for the captures almost immediately after the hostile actions in Spokane were defeated. In consultation with the president, they decided it would be nice to have undeniable proof of Russia's complicity in the terrorist action.

Two days later, President Carl Sellers phoned Prime Minister Mikhail Vassiliev to inform him of the capture of two Russian ships and the detention of several of the covert operatives. Carl also inquired if Mikhail wanted the bodies of the killed agents returned. For the record, the prime minister expressed no interest in those repatriations. The POTUS then took the time to express in detail just how angry he was with Russia, and its prime minister in particular. Carl gave Mikhail a long list of demands, entreaties, and ultimatums. In fact, Carl did his level best to humiliate the man. Again, and for the record, he did a fine job of it.

The following day was witness to a massive "restructuring" of the Russian government. Mikhail Vassiliev ordered the deaths of everyone involved in the failed operation who wasn't Mikhail Vassiliev. That included, sadly, the families of all involved. Before the small army of assassins could get around to bumping off Doctor Nikolai Kuzmin, he, in an attempt to preempt his own death, ordered his KGB operatives to take out the prime minister. While both men's murderous efforts were successful, neither of them lived to enjoy the fruits of their dark efforts.

TWENTY-TWO

In the week after all the excitement–and killings–settled down, I found myself mired ever deeper in a funk of major proportions. At first, I kept up appearances, then I tried to as best I could, as I began seeing that the others were starting to worry about me. Now, a full eight days later, I was in my new less-than-happy place, seated on top of *Defiant*. I was up there so much of the day that I had Peaches craft small steps in the hull so I didn't have to scramble up top in an undignified manner. And what did I do sitting on the ship's dome? I stewed, ruminated, and generally cogitated on the path we humans seemed to be going down, yet again. And there was the ever-growing issue that weighed on me. What could, should, or would I, or we–the Spokane Group–do about the abysmal choices humankind seemed to be blithely making.

And, with seven days of stressing already under my belt, what were my thoughts? Simple. I had no clue what to do. Carl Sellers was struggling with only limited success to perform national CPR on America. And he was the legitimate POTUS. What could I–a teenage civilian–possibly do with regard to the entire world? *Nothing* was the leading contender among the conclusions tussling in my head. Maybe it was just immutable human nature to resort to clubbing one another over the head when differences of opinion arose? *Gosh*, that was a depressing notion.

It was getting toward sunset. I knew at least Natty would be anticipating my joining her for dinner. She was busy these days with her four-woman tag team devoted to helping Felicia and Farrah deal with the latest horrific trauma in their young lives. I was amazed they ever got out from under their covers each morning. But, troopers that they were, both girls seemed to be doing amazingly well.

I was just about to throw in today's towel and slide down off the dome when I smelled coffee. Awakened from my inattention, I turned to look behind me. There was Grace, carefully stepping up to where I sat, a mug of steaming joe in either hand.

"Hey there, you," I greeted her.

"Hey there, you too," she returned with a slight grin.

"I'm thinking you found me," I observed.

"I did indeed." She handed me a mug, then sat down next to me, looking off into the distance. "Of course, it's pretty hard to hide when I've got both Peaches *and* Marcalif around."

"They are snoopy ASes, aren't they?" I commented.

Grace didn't respond. She just sipped her drink and studied the horizon. As that seemed like a good enough undertaking, I sipped my coffee and also studied nothing in particular. We sat there, thousand-mile staring for a few minutes.

"You seem, my friend, to have an issue or two burdening you greatly," she finally remarked, still gazing into the distance.

"Yeah, I figured you all'd noticed."

"That we did. Even Mongo expressed concern to me regarding your melancholy just yesterday."

"He's always been a perceptive mutt," I commented.

"Then it occurred to me. Hey, if someone has both a serious problem and a strong, supportive family available, why doesn't that someone avail himself of that tremendous resource?"

"Be-cause ... he's a *guy*?" I replied.

Still staring off, she raised an index finger and said, "Bingo!" She took another sip. "So, you want to talk this whatever out?" Grace turned to look at me, expectation obvious in her expression.

I sighed. Did I want to air my concerns and verbally beat this to death? Not really. But, then again, the person doing the asking was my oldest and dearest friend, as well as a woman who'd lived a lot more than me.

"My, but your silence is deafening," she quipped.

"As you know, my default inclination is to keep my feelings locked up inside me. That said, I guess you and I do need to discuss the future."

"Ah, yes, that damnable future. It is always causing trouble, isn't it?" she remarked with a grin.

"Based on my eighteen-year period of observation, I'd be forced to agree with that sentiment."

Master teacher Grace was back to waiting silently for me to speak deeply held thoughts and emotions.

"I'm overwhelmed," I confessed. "Now, before you go saying who isn't, hear me out."

More silent staring. Man, she was good.

"Everyone who survived the apocalypse is stressed-to-the max. I know that. And today's crisis is continually supplanted by tomorrow's crises. I get that. But what's going on and what we're dealing with, well, it's threatening to melt my brain."

Yeah, more quiet staring on Grace's part.

"Peaches tells me that we're going to have finished spaceships rolling off the production line as soon as six to eight weeks from now," I noted. "We already have a not-so-small fleet of ships under our command. The ten Visquisor vessels, plus *Defiant* and *Arc of Intention*. That's an even dozen large, complex, futuristic warships. Even with the people from Visquisor's ships who want to stay with us, we don't have nearly enough to crew twelve ships, let alone several more and counting."

Finally, the sphinx-like Grace spoke. "Those assessments all jibe with mine."

"And, as the unused super-duper spaceships stack up like cordwood, everybody, their uncle, and their uncle's barber are going to want to lay hands on those critical assets."

"With the intent and desperation of salmon spawning up a mighty river, they are," Grace agreed.

I had to be quiet a bit before I could get the next words out. "And then, not three years after every human was almost eaten to death by marauding aliens, one sovereign nation launches a murderous covert operation against a rival sovereign nation." I fought back tears. "It's the same-old, same-old all over again."

"No one's learned a *darn* thing," Grace stated flatly. "Humankind is demonstrating the adaptive insight capability of a sack of hammers."

"Yes," I replied through my closing throat. "So, allow me to summarize. We have more vessels than brains, we're about to turn out deadly ships that everyone will lust after, and those same idiots that want the craft have just proved—yet again—that they are incapable of responsible behavior."

"Unfortunately, you are one-million-percent correct," she said quietly. "The same bleak prospects have occurred to me of late."

I turned to look at her. "And?"

"And here I sit next to you, confused, at the point of an emotional meltdown, and ready to flee this town for parts unknown, leaving behind no forwarding address."

I leaned over and gave her a sideways hug. She tilted her head against my shoulder.

Maybe five minutes later, I finally broke the magic spell. "So what are we going to do concerning the impossible reality we are trapped in like some giant tornado?"

Grace made a few popping sounds with her lips. "I. Have. No. Idea."

"And you've discussed this with Molly?"

She gave me an incredulous look.

"Of course you've discussed this to death with Molly."

"We do not suffer from testosterone poisoning like some *other* sexes do."

"Lucky ducks," I mused.

"In fact, all us women have brainstormed and come up with nothing but headaches."

"Natalie too?" I asked in an *et-tu-brute* tone. Come on, I was a guy. It's easy to make us feel betrayed.

"Yes, all four of us have wrestled with these issues while we waited patiently for you to get tired of sitting on top of a spaceship and were ready to come down and contribute."

"Gosh, that sounds like an alluring prospect. Is it okay if I have my people get back to your people ... soonish?"

"We all know we can't make you do something you're disinclined to do."

"Hmm, did I just hear a big-old *but* in there?" I asked sarcastically.

"How very perceptive of you, a young male of the species," she poked. "We took an informal vote. It was decided that if you insist on being alone, we, as loving friends, needed to respect your wishes."

"Oh, boy. Here it comes," I groaned.

"So, Felicia and Farrah have said they will stop asking if they can come up here and join you."

"Ouch," I responded.

"Molly says that if you're not around, she won't need to bake those cookies you obsess over."

I winced. "Ouchy ouch."

"Susan said she's committed to work through the current political intrigues *without* the benefit of your counsel. *I* have decided to not bother you with hot coffee any longer. *Peaches* had resolved to remove those tripping-hazard steps you use. And Marcalif has determined that it would be unfair of him to bother you with any executive updates, what with you being so busy being isolated and pouting."

"You forgot to mention what Natty won't be doing," I reminded her snidely.

"That is because what she's promised to end is unmentionable ... in mixed company, that is."

"I now realize how unpleasant civil disobedience can be for us leader types," I informed her.

"Hey, if it worked for Gandhi and King, we're all confident it'll work for us," she responded boldly.

I was quiet again for a spell. "So, in all seriousness," I said, "what are we going to do?"

"Chris, I'm not going to sugar coat this. I personally feel like my children are in trouble on one side of a minefield and I'm on the other. I can't *not* take a step toward them, but every step I might take seems to be the worst decision of my life."

"Okay. Here's a thought," I said, trying to sound encouraging. "Let's break this down into individual pieces. That way, it'll take longer for us to be overwhelmed."

"Sure. I'm game," she replied. "You start."

"Chicken," I playfully accused. "There's human nature. Russia launching a terrorist assault against us because they want what they obviously cannot be trusted with. Peaches said there's a bureau in Beijing devoted exclusively to discovering ways to kill each of us without laying a blame-trail. I could go on, but it's not necessary. We cannot change human nature, specifically the dark, suicidal aspects of it."

"Aside from being a little more depressed, I can't say that piece helped me much," Grace responded.

"Bear with me," I assured her. "I'm taking each dilemma separately. One, human nature, is resolved because it is unresolvable. Next piece."

"Thank goodness," she responded.

"We are about to start churning out spaceships galore. We have to do that. We must do that. One alien invasion has taught us that more will be coming. It turns out alien nature can be just as shitty as human nature. We've discussed this. To mount a credible defense, we'll need to field tens of thousands of Dostivex-cloned ships. And there will be many ships needed for interstellar exploration, diplomacy, and, realistically, space tourism. So, thousands of vessels *must* be constructed."

"I agree," Grace confirmed. "We have to produce enough ships to keep us safe. End of story."

"Okay, Dilemma Two is resolved. We don't have to stress over this issue. More spaceships are going to be produced. Next!"

"I can't wait to hear this," Grace teased.

"Hey, I'm on a roll. Wait to be amazed. Dilemma Three. Who will pilot and crew these tens of thousands of spacecraft? The answer is a lot of people will need to be enlisted."

"Yeah, but *American* people? *British* people? *North Korean* people?" Grace challenged.

"Uh-uh," I stopped her, "Dilemma Three is resolved. You're jumping ahead to Dilemma Four."

"My impetuous bad," she self-castigated. "Proceed."

"Dilemma Four. Who will crew Earth's line of defense? This one's kind of easy too. It won't be you, me, Molly, or even the couple hundred aliens who're already on board."

"Duh," she responded. "There's not enough of us."

"Correct," I shot back. "So ... *someone* will have to decide who takes possession of a ship and who can or may crew her. Again, simply put, that can be us or someone else. I can tell you I have less than zero interest in taking on that added pain in the ass. I have a sufficient number of them already, thank you very much."

"You and me both," Grace agreed.

"So, if not us, then it will be someone else. I would like to table Dilemma Four's full resolution a second and chip away at Five."

"Be my guest," Grace invited.

"Dilemma Five, our fleet of twelve ships. What's to be done with them? Clearly, we will retain sole control over *Defiant* and *Arc of Intention*. One is part of our family and the other is the ultimate power in the galaxy. They will stay with us. That leaves the ten Visquisor ships. They are clearly superior to the Dostivex and much inferior to *Arc*. Obviously, with *Arc* alone, we can have the final word as to what any other ship anywhere can or cannot do."

"With might comes right," Grace seconded.

"Amen. So, back to Dilemma Four. If humankind screws up royally and does badness with the Dostivex-tech ships, we can tell them to cease and desist ... or else. So Dilemma Four is now not such a dilemma. We put someone in charge who's likely to do okay, and then we monitor their progress, all the while holding the ultimate veto power over what they can do."

"I can foresee many a wounded male ego," Grace commented, "but I don't honestly care about those fragile entities. You toe the line, do the right things, and we let you run the day-to-day. You try and go back to school yard rules, and we stop you."

"So for Dilemma Four, I would pencil in the USA as the one responsible for the Dostivex-tech ships. Let's face it, *we're* Americans. All our work is being *done* in America. And the US has an okay record of treating their allies fairly. Plus, I'd much rather someone else—rather than you and me—run the training academies and vetting of those ship's crews. The US has a long track record of those, with West Point, Annapolis, and Colorado Springs."

"I cannot fault your logic on any of that," Grace said with a smile.

"So, back to Dilemma Five, Subset: The ten Visquisor ships. I say we maintain control of them. With just *Arc* as our ace-in-the-hole, we're spread too thin. If Natalie and I want to visit the Andromeda Galaxy and someone needs smiting, we wouldn't be here to do it."

"I couldn't agree more. We captured those ships. They're ours. And they give us a cushion in terms of making certain no nation or group of maniacs gets away with being stupid."

"Yes," I stated. "I'd bet good money that once a country gets the feel of zooming through space, they'll get cocky, start wanting to push their weight around because it would be fun to do so."

"So who crews the ten ships?" Grace posed.

I shrugged. "That we can figure out over time. Hell, we could have Marcalif whip up an AS-driven robotic crew if we somehow became desperate."

Grace made a funny face at that suggestion. "I don't know about that. If science fiction has taught us anything, it's that bad things can happen if we allow artificial sentients to run amok."

"Okay, so we slowly build up reliable, loyal crews," I responded. "We can even poach away attractive candidates from the US academies."

"Oh, the powers-that-be would be pissed if we did," Grace said gleefully.

"Yes," I concurred. "It'd be marvelous!"

Grace got a concerned look. "Okay, Dilemma Six. Who is in charge of being the all-powerful good guy once you and I are enjoying our well-earned retirements?"

"Oh, Grace," I said expansively, "that's the easiest dilemma yet."

"Pray tell," she challenged.

"You and Molly have more children. Susan has a bunch of kids. Natty and I churn 'em out like nobody's business. And those who we come to trust have scads of young'uns. We have the fun and the next generation takes care of itself."

She looked worried at my answer. "So we create a nobility in space?

Lords and ladies who will rule human endeavors in perpetuity?" She sounded dubious at best. "Is that what you're proposing here?"

"Yes, that *is* what I'm proposing. Grace, look at the present mess. Humans have been at war with one another *forever*. Is the idea of a benign ruling Ever-Parent an attractive one? Hell no. It sucks. But what are the alternatives? Look at what a handful of Russian leaders just did not *three* years after an alien apocalypse. I say knowing that someone is in a position to stop unacceptable behavior is a lesser-of-two-evils kind of deterrent. And, who knows? Maybe over time, the need for that role will become nonexistent? Maybe we'll grow as a species? Or maybe someone will always need to be available to be the universal referee? But, Grace Chang, the beauty of this all is that you and I will be long gone. The system itself will have to decide how it runs or doesn't run."

"How about we label Dilemma Six as a *work-in-progress*?" she asked warmly.

"I can definitely live with that stipulation."

"So, you ready to come down and join the family?" she asked with a wide smile.

"That depends," I replied with a pout.

"On what?"

"Whether those retaliations to my being a loner are fully rescinded."

Grace's smile widened. "I can only speak for the ones that do not involve Natalie's unmentionable ones. You'll have to take those up with her in the privacy of *Arc of Intention*."

"Then there are no worries. I look very much forward to taking those barriers down manually in the near future."

TWENTY-THREE

President Sellers sat behind the *Resolute* desk chuckling with two of his closest advisors, Bill Lexington and Leo Koehn. Carl had known one man since college and the other from law school. He thought of them as his Kitchen Cabinet, much like Ronald Reagan had his long before. They were all joking around and swapping old stories because this was one of the rare occasions these days when the POTUS was in a good mood. He was practically giddy. The Spokane Group had asked for a meeting and *they* were coming to *him*. If he had successfully kowtowed them into respecting and deferring to him and his office, well then he'd pulled off quite the coup, reversed the fortunes, so to speak.

"No, you did not," Leo shouted to Carl, pointing an accusatory finger at him. "My wife is good friends with Paula Hamilton and she *swears* to me that woman never did anything dodgy with you, let alone in a broom closet."

Carl hooked both thumbs under his jacket collar. "Far be it from me to impugn the word of an upstanding sorority girl such as Ms. Hamilton." Then he gave his friends an exaggerated wink.

Bill nearly fell off his chair he laughed so hard. "Stop. Stop. My doctor says I shouldn't overexert myself."

"I believe it is fine if it leads to laughing yourself to death," Carl opined. As their chuckles faded, there was a soft knock on the door. Carl quickly checked his watch. "Zero hour has arrived. You two maniacs need to slip out the back so I can get this meeting going before the vaunted Spokane Group change their minds and head back west."

The three exchanged handshakes, then the friends left via a side exit. "Come," Carl called out.

His secretary stuck her head in. "They're all ready for you in the conference room, sir."

"Fine, Margret. Let me gather my notes." Carl shuffled some papers, tucked then under an arm, and strode to the door.

"I set a thermos of decaf to your right, Mr. President," she informed him as they walked the short distance to the conference room.

"You're the best, Margret," he responded.

A guard opened the door to allow the POTUS in. The fifteen or so of us in the room stood as Carl entered.

"Please be seated, everybody," Carl said magnanimously. He then walked to where Grace, Molly, Natalie, Susan, and I stood. He shook our hands while thanking each one of us for coming. Then he sat down, quickly followed by the rest of us. "Welcome, everyone, and thank you all for coming. Robin," he said to his chief of staff, "I believe you're running this meeting, so why don't we jump right in?"

Robin Atwood stood and nodded to her boss. "Thank you, Mr. President. I wish to begin by also thanking the members of the Spokane Group for coming to meet with us. This country deeply appreciates everything you're worked so hard to accomplish."

I was the only one to respond. I gave her a weak finger-tip wave.

"I've handed out copies of the estimates the Spokane Group has provided us," Robin stated. "As you can see, they have produced and distributed to date over five hundred high-tech generators. And the first spaceship they've completed is undergoing low-level atmospheric testing."

"Yes," Grace spoke up. "Fingers crossed we'll be doing some low earth orbit testing next week."

"That's fabulous news," Carl interjected. "Truly spectacular."

"Thank you," Grace responded with a smile.

"The prototypes for ground-based defensive plasma cannons," Robin continued, "are still a few months from the trialing phase. Am I correctly reading your report?"

"Yes," Molly fielded that one. "The units are being assembled as we speak, but are not near any functional status. The team responsible is optimistic test firing can begin in as soon as three months."

"Again, that's just incredible," Carl praised.

Grace nodded to him silently.

"I guess that brings up the critical point," Carl began to say, "about allocation of and training for the ships and the cannons."

"Yes, that's really what we wanted to let you know about," I said, speaking up.

Carl went visibly rigid upon hearing my careful choice of words. As I anticipated, he was not pleased to hear the words *let you know about*. I'm sure *discuss* or *hammer out* would have been closer to acceptable for him. "I believe all the key players are here on our side," he said to me in a measured tone, "so we should be able to come to some consensus today on these matters so critical to the defense of our nation."

Nice layering on there, Carl, I thought to myself. I held up a thumb drive. "We have put together a detailed summary of what we plan to do over the short term." I flagged a guard to come over and asked her to hand the drive to the president. "You're free to copy that to whomever you see fit. Natalie is passing around a much abbreviated version for everyone to peruse today." She opened her satchel and started the stapled documents around the table.

I waited for everyone to have a copy before I proceeded. When Carl got his, he very unsubtly rifled through it, no doubt dying to learn the bottom line.

"I want to give you some insight as to how we came to the decisions that we did," I continued. "Basically, we had to take a hard look at how we wanted to spend our collective time over the next few years. We are committed to putting thousands of Dostivex-cloned ships into service as soon as is humanly possible. What we concluded was that we did not want to reinvent the wheel, so to speak. Training a massive cohort of crews and support staff will be a truly gargantuan effort. The Spokane Group decided that we didn't have the expertise or, frankly, the interest in taking all of that on. So, we will ask you, Carl, to formally take the reins on that one."

"If it's agreeable to you, that is," Grace interjected.

Carl held up the disk. "Obviously, we'll have to go over this with a fine-tooth comb. That said, it has been my desire and goal all along to be right there at the front of the pack in terms of implementing the planet's new defense force. So, if you are offering to allow me that honor and responsibility, then I'm certainly going to accept it."

"Obviously, there is a mountain of logistical concerns," Robin said forcefully. "The bulk of your facilities and personnel are in Spokane. The federal government is based here."

Carl held a palm up to his COS. "Details we can handle," he told her. "For now, I think we need only focus on the big picture."

"Of course, Mr. President," she said contritely.

"So do you envision turning over your entire production facilities as well as all the finished products to us?" Carl asked. I could tell he was just about to jump out of his skin he was so excited.

"Yes, over the next few months. We've briefed our research and production staff as to our plans. Everyone is quite agreeable to continuing their work even if the venue and person signing their paychecks changes."

"We would clearly welcome any and all of them to stay the course," Carl responded. "And, again, as to where we do the production, that can all be figured out easily enough."

"We assumed you might want to parse out production," Susan stated, "to several parties in various venues. Those decisions will all be yours. The Spokane Group is looking forward to transferring all of those efforts to you, Carl."

Man, his grin just kept getting bigger and bigger. I hoped there was a medic on hand. The POTUS might need some stitches if this trend continued.

"There are going to be a lot of extremely contentious discussions in your future," I said to Carl. "You know better than I do how the nations of the world are going to respond to the news that the US now formally owns the new tech."

"Oh, yes," he exclaimed. "I have already gotten more than an earful from any number of other countries."

"Not to mention the recent terrorist assault on us," Molly added grimly.

A serious Carl said, "Yes. Obviously, security will be a major issue. It's a baby and bath water kind of situation. We don't get one without the other."

"Some options," I continued, "as to how you proceed with hiring and training a boatload of people are fairly obvious. But we haven't gone into them even on the thumb drive files. We figure that's what a functioning government is capable of totally structuring."

"Thank you," Carl replied. "Yes, we have done that a time or two in the past. I cite as a few examples the Army, Navy, Air Force, and Marines."

"Oorah!" I responded.

"Again, we'll study this." He wagged the drive in the air. "But what are your projections–best-case scenario–for when a significant number of spaceships can be in place and fully crewed. I'm sure you've thought about that part quite a bit."

"Yes," I replied. "At first, you will be able to turn out ships faster than crews. But, if all the ducks line themselves up, you should have a potent military force in orbit within four years."

"By our estimates that sounds about right," Carl agreed.

"For the full contingent of ten thousand vessels?" I went on. "Hopefully, this decade."

"To have a credible space deterrent in place within ten years is a living dream," Carl said with solemnity.

"As to the development of other Dostivex-based technologies," I went on, "we've had a team of lawyers work overtime to generate a contractual structure as to how we plan to proceed. Basically, we will retain the rights to independently produce, use, or sell any and all *peaceful* applications of the new technology. If we find we desire to develop military applications, we will negotiate those projects with the federal government."

Carl smiled nervously. "As you might imagine, we'll have to have an even larger army of lawyers read and respond to those aspects in the fullness of time."

"Naturally," I responded. "But those are our leanings."

"Subject to a collective decision-making process," Susan added diplomatically.

"So, in a few words, what do you see the Spokane Group focusing on, if not the projects you have so kindly deferred to the US government?" Carl probed.

"I'll speak to that," Grace thankfully stepped in. We were about to start playing the game of hardball now and she was much better suited for it than me. "We have two overarching visions. One, we want to continue to develop alien technology, and not limited to just the Dostivex's. As we move forward, we want to make the fruits of our labors available to humankind. Two, we will definitely stay in the space defense business."

"If it does take ten years for us to field a credible defense force," Natalie stated, "we are more than willing and able to perform that function in the interim."

Carl started nervously tapping his index finger on the table. I do believe he was hearing us loud and clear. "So, now," he began either uncertainly or so pissed off he could hardly speak, "you're not saying that we get the ships we will eventually produce, but you will be keeping the ones you presently employ?"

"No," I said sternly. "We're keeping the ones we *own*."

It was as if all the air had been sucked out of the room and a pack of demons from hell burst through the floorboards. It was suddenly uncomfortable. I could tell Carl was rapidly processing the implications of the information he'd just acquired.

"I am not, as the President and Commander-in-Chief, fully comfortable with your position on the status of the, what, dozen or so functioning spacecraft we're talking about here." He spoke each word precisely and darkly.

"We are not *asking* you to be comfortable with our decision, Carl," I responded with all the gravitas a teenager could muster. "We're only *informing* you."

"So what you people are *saying*–" Carl spat out viciously. Then, after Robin set a hand on his forearm, he rested back in his chair and took some deep breaths. Finally, he could proceed in just a strained and angry tone. "I am asking this question to you five–the so called Spokane Group–presumably loyal American citizens, so please answer it in that light. Are you committing your organization to the withholding in a willful manner of critical military assets from your nation's leadership?"

"Yes," I shot back quickly.

"Oh, and please allow me to finish the thought," Carl said sardonically. "*If you don't like it, Mr. President, you can just go fuck yourself because there's nothing you can do to us.* Am I close to the meat of your contentions here, Spokane Group?"

"Carl," I replied evenly, "in the spirit of a continued working relationship between us, we are going to ignore that juvenile outburst."

"How–" he snarled. Again, Robin restrained him from further fueling the bonfire already raging.

"First, we obtained all twelve ships legally. We own them under any salvage rights in the galaxy. Second, the recent Russian terrorist attack emphasizes just how far our species is from self-control and team work. Third, we feel strongly that an impartial third party is ideally positioned to ensure all participants with lesser technologies toe the line of morality and commitment to the betterment of all. Fourth, yes, if you don't like it, we are prepared to live with your disapproval. I would add that I already said we would overlook your recent outburst. I will not, therefore, say that if you wish to spend your period of disapproval *fucking* yourself, we have no position, pro or con, on that topic."

If I could read minds, I know as a fact that I'd be hearing, *Why you little shit* right about then. Lucky for me, I can't.

"As you cool off, Carl," Susan started in, "I would like to add that we have provided you with the names and locations of several friendly alien species. It is an option, should you choose to work with us, for you to extend a diplomatic hand to these civilizations on behalf of our planet and our species." She shrugged. "If you wish to delay such actions until you have sufficient vessels yourself, that is obviously your prerogative."

"Gosh, that's so generous of you," he snarked. "We get a bone if we behave."

I stood. "We're done here," I announced angrily. "We came to discuss weighty matters with adults. So far, we've turned over the golden goose and, for our efforts, been accused of treason and mocked. Until you take some serious grow-up pills, Carl, I think it best if we let you throw your tantrum in private." I pointed to everyone else in the room. "But I need to add that we who suffered under the Dostivex terror out there," I gestured toward a window, "are seeming to me to be the only ones actually interested in making certain something like that doesn't ever happen again. The privileged few who were spared the *inconvenience* of an alien apocalypse seem to have their heads still stuck in the dismal past." I gathered my stuff and looked to Natalie.

She stood and hooked my arm. Leaning forward a little, she said to Carl, "Please grow up fast."

I glanced to Grace. She had her hand tented over her face. Was she humiliated or laughing? I wasn't sure. Either way was cool with me. But then Molly, Susan, and Grace got up and joined us in our triumphant walk out the door.

Someone once said these wise words: Great men rise to great challenges. Small men try real hard to ignore them. I hoped that, with time, Carl would come around.

Hey, I just remembered. I was the one who made that quote up!

EPILOGUE

"So, how about some breakfast?" I asked the love of my life. We were spooning at that moment.

Instead of a *sure* and a bounce out of bed, I got a faint grunt and a shrug of Natalie's shoulders. Hmm, not sure what message I'd just been sent, but I was betting it wasn't one I wanted to receive.

"You okay, babe?" I asked tenderly.

Another grunt-shrug. Someone was in trouble–me–and he didn't have clue one as to why. I freed up a hand and tapped Natty on the shoulder, like one might at a class reunion. "May I ask a question?" But, being not a complete fool, I did not wait for her grunty response. "Are you mad at me?"

"Noooo," came her muffled reply. Well, at least I got a word this time, a clear improvement.

"Then why am I getting an off-vibe from you this morning?" As I waited for her response, I rifled through my brain, trying to remember if I did/said/suggested/implied anything last night that she might have taken umbrage with. I retrieved no useful data.

"It's nothing," she said in a tone very much suggesting it was something in the eight-hundred-pound-gorilla-in-the-corner range.

"So, then, since it's nothing, what is it?" I contemplated tossing in that oh-so funny *I'm asking for a friend* line. But I determined wisely that she was unlikely to be in a *humorous* mood while, at the same time, clearly being in a *foul* mood.

"I'll go see if there's anything for breakfast," was Natalie's reply. She started edging toward the side of the bed.

I decided bold action was called for, partly based on the fact that with *Arc*'s massive food replicators, there really wasn't a need to check the ship's PAR levels. I grabbed her about the waist and pulled her back into the spoon. "Not so fast," I implored. "Can we talk this out?" Yes, I'd now been immersed in womanly machinations long enough to realize the correct answer to any dispute or misunderstanding was to talk the thing to death. Sad but true, and there it was.

"We don't seem to be talking about it anymore, so why dig it up out of its shallow grave?" she said in a distant voice.

Oh, my. Christopher Alan was in deep doo-doo. Deep, deep doo-doo. Whatever I had done wrong was, at that very moment, rotting in a quickie grave. Well, whatever it was, move over. I'm climbing in too.

"I am fully committed," I said—employing those universally applicable words when addressing one's love interest in any context whatsoever, "to resolving whatever issue is important to you. If it's important to you, it's darn important to me also." I wasn't in love with that last, tacked on line, but it seemed to carry a gravitas I felt would further my obviously weak cause.

"When was the last time we talked about our wedding?" she asked. Oh, such an innocent, oh-by-the-way, query.

I thought back. Hmm, I could not say with accuracy, but it was a month ago—maybe—that the topic first, and only that once, came up. I suspected on an instinctive level it was not in my best interest to say anything remotely along those lines. I also knew with certainty that reminding her of the existential crises we'd passed through in the interim might be considered by some to be valid reasons why party-planning might not have been my number one priority. Yeah, it'd be simpler for me to open the doors of the ship's fusion reactor and jump in. Much less painful and definitely a faster way to die.

"Ah, how about right now this very moment?" I rallied with a big smile. Yes, I was selling it hard. Used car salesman hard.

She peeked up at me. "Ok-*ay*," she said in a whiny, uncertain tone.

I was making progress, but darn, it was incremental. "So, one of my big questions is who do we get to do the service?"

Natalie's eyes suddenly became very large and moistish. "That's not the first or most important part, Chris."

Breaking that exchange down, here we go. One, it was something she had stressed over. Two, Natalie said only what *wasn't* first and most important. She didn't say the magic words of what *was* first and most important. We were going to play the Minefield version of Twenty Questions. How opposite of fun. What would be first? I already proposed. That sure seemed first to me ... a ring!

"I was really hoping we could, you know, go ring shopping soon. Make it totally official and all."

The boo-hoo face vanished, Natty threw her arms around me, and I was forgiven, yet again. I decided that was not the time or place to mention the fact that jewelry stores were pretty much a thing of the pre-apocalypse, so *going shopping* was going to be challenging. Baby steps, Chris Old Boy, baby steps.

A while later, Natalie was in the shower and I was toweling my hair, wandering into the mess for some badly needed coffee.

Sitting there with his hands folded on the table was Marcalif. He smiled at me. "Good morning, Captain."

"And good morning back atcha," I returned. "Is there something you wanted to discuss?" He didn't usually sit and wait for me in his robotic host. Mostly, he called out over the PA system or directly into my head via my implants. This seemed different in an *oh shit* manner.

"Yes, in fact there is. Something of the gravest nature, I'm afraid."

I sat and poured a cup from the carafe he'd already set in place. "This sounds weighty."

"It is. I was going over Visquisor's personal ship *Peerless*. I have been checking all his fleet systematically, to ensure they're in good repair and contain no surprises."

"Yeah, we discussed that a while ago," I reminded him. "Very prudent of you."

"Thank you. I reviewed his logs. I was able to determine why there was a lag time in his coming to this system to exact his promised revenge."

"Okay," I commented.

"He was on some mission that took him extremely close to the supermassive black hole at the center of the Milky Way galaxy. Hence, he incurred a time dilatation relative to us."

"Interesting, but how is that bad?"

"That in and of itself is not. But there was mention in the records of his using a scraper AS. I–"

"A what?" I stopped him.

"Hmm, how to put it? The term to *scrape* in the context of computers is one of information extraction. Scraping is done to interface with a computing system for which there is no compatible hardware. A *scraper AS* is a device that one brings in proximity to a computational system one wants to extract data from. That transfer is orchestrated by an AS."

"Gotcha," I confirmed.

"After learning of his use of such a machine, I went in search of it."

"Why? Just curious," I asked.

"Covering all of our bases. There might be useful information on the scraper," Marcalif explained.

"And was there?" I asked ominously.

"Indeed there was. I can reconstruct that Visquisor journeyed to that location as part of his search for the secrets of soul transfer."

"Ah, yes. His endless quest for his holy grail," I commented. Then I put one and one together. "Wait, did he find it?"

"*Possibly*," Marcalif replied cautiously. "What I downloaded from the scraper made clear reference to soul transfer. It contained no information as to how one might conduct such a process. But the citation is quite specific and detailed."

"I'm struggling to understand how that's a bad thing," I confessed.

"Captain, soul transfer was not the dream of only Visquisor. It has been lusted after since long before I was created."

"Wow, that's a lot of lusting time," I marveled.

"Indeed it is. The grave situation we thus find ourselves in is this. We now possess concrete, actionable information as to where one might go to master the process."

"Hang on, I'm still a bit foggy on this whole thing. What's the big deal about transferring a soul?"

"Let us use Visquisor as an example. He has lived a very long time, but he is nonetheless mortal. If he could transfer his soul, his very being, into an acceptable host—one made vacant of its present soul—he would achieve functional immortality."

"Hmm, not sure I share his vision, but so be it. But how is us—you and me—knowing something substantive about the process dangerous to us?"

"Because knowledge has a way of leaking," he replied cryptically.

"Say what?"

Marcalif angled his palm at right angles to the table top. "The knowledge was isolated somewhere very close to a massive singularity, a place where time and space are highly distorted. The reality of that location is incompatibly different to the one we exist in. Hence, it is not possible for that knowledge to leak out, to be learned by those who seek it with great passion."

"But data bits on a computer don't leak out like water from an old drainpipe. They ... they stay put because they're ... they lack wings."

He shook his head slowly. "That is not the way of the world," he said with regret. "If it sits on a scraper AS, if we only just knew it, that information will not remain contained. Like heat energy itself, it escapes. It goes somewhere. And when it does, extremely powerful and ruthless interested parties will come to take all the knowledge that exists."

"So, you're saying that because you and I just have it in our heads that someone close to the center of our galaxy knows something about the process, it's going to broadcast itself to the bad guys? Hopefully, you can tell by the way I framed that remark, you catch that I'm dubious."

"The information is not broadcast. But, it will certainly get out. This is but one potential pathway. Someday, a random technician will discover a downloaded copy of the AS file that I was unable to discover. They will mention it to a bartender. That bartender will mention it in passing to a gambler. That gambler will confess his knowledge to help escape a debt to a crime boss. And that crime boss will know of someone who would pay any sum of money to learn what he then had learned. Knowledge leaks. It always does."

"And when this tidbit leaks into the wrong person's ear–" I asked pregnantly.

"They will come to us and do whatever it takes to obtain every last detail that we possess."

"In other words, we are in real danger?" I asked.

"We are indeed," Marcalif responded grimly.

"Well, crap," I mumbled. "Ten minutes ago, my biggest concern was where to buy Natalie an engagement ring. Now I have to worry about the biggest, baddest villain in the galaxy coming to tear me to pieces." I rubbed the back of my knuckles against my chin. "I just can't catch a clean break here."

Marcalif simply shrugged.

"Hoo, boy," I huffed. "There really is no rest for the weary."

Trilogy's end ...

... but follow the action in the next thrilling adventure: *The Immortality Wars*, coming in early 2026.

GLOSSARY:

Alan, Glenn: Chris Alan's father.

And Cream: The artificial sentience (AS) for *Peerless*. A real dick.

Arc of Intention: The extremely advanced tech ship Chris was adopted by on Dez Falls.

Atwood, Robin: New chief-of-staff for Carl Sellers once the POTUS could choose someone who wasn't an idiot.

Bamdorian: An unfortunate species. They looked like a lumbering pile of poop. The bamdorian are not fetching.

Brown, Charles: General and US Army representative on the Joint Chiefs.

Brown, Kyle: USMC corporal on guard duty in the bunker the US government hid in during the alien invasion. Part of the intel mission to confirm the Dostivex were dead.

Buñuel Portolés, Isabella: USMC sergeant on guard duty in the bunker the US government hid in during the alien invasion. Led the intel mission to confirm the Dostivex were dead.

Burke, Miles "Salty": The admiral who represents the US Coast Guard on the Joint Chiefs of Staff.

Chang, Grace: Chris's middle school computer teacher and a friend. Married to Molly Cooper.

Cooper, Molly: The wife of Grace Chang. A really sweet person.

Cootie Bug: A slang term for the alien invaders, the Dostivex.

Dduddud: The specific gramphot who Chris scared to death in *Peerless*'s mess.

DBH-1, Death Becomes Her: A plasma rifle Natalie designed to replace the overly bulky BFGs that Chris fabricated.

Death Bringer-1000 BFG Plasma rifles: The rifle Chris had Peaches fabricate. It was way, way over the top. Go figure. Clearly, Chris has played too many video games.

Dez Falls: As Obi-Wan Kenobi might say, it's a wretched hive of scum and villainy. A bleak world, but the only place where Bliss Shale is found. No one seems to know it's actually a huge organism, not a planet. Chris dubbed the entity LN, based on his really long name.

Defiant: The name Peaches chose for the ship she was the AI for after she co-opted the ship.

Denali, Morpheus: A proud Algontol warrior who took Chris under his wing aboard *Peerless*. Grumpy but alright.

Dostivex: The horrible alien race that invaded, conquered, and then ate the people of Earth. Toyota 4-Runner-sized yellow jackets. I'm not a fan.

DuPree, Taye: USMC lieutenant on guard duty in the bunker the US government hid in during the alien invasion.

End Of All, The: A popular name for the event horizon, or Schwarzschild radius, the supermassive black hole at the center of the Milky Way galaxy.

Farrah: Grace and Molly's youngest daughter.

Fedorov, Timur: Insane member of Team Gamma, sent to kill Chris. He went nuts instead.

Felectian Brain Swish: A stew made by Felectians consisting of Felectian's brains. It looks like institutional scrambled eggs. Pass on this dubious food.

Felicia: Grace and Molly's oldest daughter.

Fet Ah Bruch: Grand Admiral of the Nef-Karat Empire. Fought against the Obsidian Concourse, which pissed Visquisor off enough to want to nuke them both.

Filter One: The rank of the first officer on Visquisor's *Peerless*.

Frift, Sennokia: The kindly doctor aboard *Peerless*.

Fuller, Gus: Crotchety old man living in Montana Rockies who befriended Chris during the alien occupation.

Higga-ir-Forn: A bamdorian like the late, unlamented Naid-ot-Oggle. Worked for Visquisor on Dez Falls.

Glandys, Tommy: Classmate and co-bully in Chris's middle school.

Gramphot: A service species aboard Peerless. Large and ugly, but made almost entirely of gelatin, they die easily. To make up for that Darwinian flaw, they bud often.

Golubev, Nestor: Former KGB, on Team Beta intending to kidnap Grace.

Ivanov, Ilya: A Russian oligarch and current inner-circle advisor to Prime Minister Mikhail Vassiliev.

Jabberstalk: A very tough meat-like food consumed by aliens with sufficiently deadly dentition.

James, Buck: General and USAF representative on the Joint Chiefs.

Kuzmin, Nikolai: Some form of Russian doctor, but way too sociopathic to be any good at that job. Inner-circle advisor to Prime Minister Mikhail Vassiliev.

Kuznetsov, Avian: Team Gamma, to assassinate Chris.

Lang, Melinda: One of POTUS Carl Sellers's security advisors.

Layers Studley: The rather preposterous name Chris was identified as during his time spent in the wavering ambiguity. When in Rome, do as the Romans. When in ambiguity, do something very silly.

Lebedev, Pavel: An old friend and current inner-circle advisor to Prime Minister Mikhail Vassiliev.

Lephoriz: The species of donut-shaped aliens Chris had to stop from ever fighting again. Really very silly-looking creatures, and stubborn.

LN: See Dez Falls.

Marcalif-Son: The AS aboard *Arc of Intention*. Extremely advanced tech. Also a very nice guy.

Miller, Beth: USMC sergeant on guard duty in the bunker the US government hid in during the alien invasion. Part of the intel mission to confirm the Dostivex were dead.

Mitchell, Wendy: Admiral and the Navy representative on the Joint Chief. Also the chairwoman of the Joint Chiefs of Staff.

Monk, Darrin: The president's chief of staff, mostly by default, while the US government hid in a bunker during the alien invasion.

Moorehead, Linda: The second-past POTUS proceeding Carl Sellers. Came to administer a come-to-Jesus session to Carl when he was being an ass.

Morozov, Andrei: Former KGB, on Team Beta intending to kidnap Grace.

Nafcadollians: The race who built *Arc of Intention*. Very human-like in appearance and physiology.

Naid-ot-Oggle: Manager of the first Bliss Shale plant Chris visited with Visquisor on Dez Falls. He looked like a lumbering pile of poop. The bamdorian are not fetching.

Nash, Fenton: One of POTUS Carl Sellers's security advisors.

Nikitin, Maxim: A retired FSB Spetsnaz major. Team Alpha member attempting to kidnap Farrah Chang-Cooper.

Nuful ging: A sort of fruit jam. Green paste with the streaks of purple with no real taste.

Orlov, Lev: A field assassin for the KGB before the alien invasion. Led Team Alpha attempting to kidnap Felicia Chang-Cooper.

Pakshin, Sergei: Russian Admiral of the Fleet. Helps in attempted raid on the Spokane Group.

Parrentians: The species that Visquisor was a member of.

Pender, Ben: Classmate and co-bully in Chris's middle school.

Peaches: The name that popped out of Chris's head when he decided *Defiant's* AI needed a proper name.

Peerless: Visquisor's flagship/home in space.

Petrov, Timur: A professor of something in Russia. Current inner-circle advisor to Prime Minister Mikhail Vassiliev.

Plovecians: According to ancient legend, a civilization among the very first to evolve after the Big Bang, had discovered the secret to the procedure for soul transfer.

Romanov, Denis: Lead Team Gamma, to assassinate Chris.

Romantica Flames: Chris's romantic costar in the film they were green-lighted to do in the wavering ambiguity.

Rosey the Robot: The name Chris gave to his service robot on *Arc of Intention*. She looked more like Marilyn Monroe than poor old Rosey from *The Jetsons*. She made Chris VERY nervous.

Sissiz Faltoffis: The manager of the second Bliss Shale plant on Dez Falls. His species, the womcator, very much resemble–and behave similarly to–the devil.

Sellers, Carl: Sitting US president at the time of the alien invasion. Survived in a bunker and continued as POTUS after the liberation. A tad impulsive and self-absorbed.

Severide, Ernie: The official head bully of Chris's middle school. A real dolt.

Solovyov, Lev: An army general and military advisor to Prime Minister Mikhail Vassiliev.

Stepanov, Yakov: Former KGB, on Team Beta intending to kidnap Grace.

Te-Momgre: First officer, of Filter One, on *Peerless* under Visquisor. He met a particularly foul fate at his captain's hand.

Vassiliev, Mikhail: Russian prime minister before and after alien invasion. A cruel and cunning man.

Volkov, Veer: Team Alpha member attempting to kidnap the Chang-Cooper girls.

Visquisor: One messed up dude–but never refer to him as one. The Master of the Parrentians, he is very human like, but a total head case. Narcissistic, egomaniacal, prone to violent excess, and he cheats at board games.

Wavering Ambiguity: A very nebulous occurrence. Chris was asked to resolve one by Visquisor as a test. Think of them as destabilizing head-trips in space.

Welsh, Natalie: The apple of Chris's eye and ultimately his partner. They went to middle school together.

Whitehorse, Susan: Appointed vice president under Carl Sellers after the aliens were defeated. A full-blooded Lakota Sioux.

Womcator: A species that looks demonic. Massive horns, red scaly skin, a whip-like tail that, if you use your imagination, ends in a pointy arrow-head. Really foul dispositions too.

Yakovlev, Aleksandr: Team Gamma, to assassinate Chris.

Yamato, Donald: One of POTUS Carl Sellers's security advisors.

AND NOW A WORD
FROM YOUR AUTHOR

Thanks so much for finishing the Teenager's Guide Trilogy! I hope you enjoyed reading it as much as I enjoyed squeezing it out of my head like toothpaste. Nice visual there, right? I'll be starting soon on the next trilogy in this universe, *The Alanverse.* Tentatively, it will be titled The Immortality Wars. Hopefully, it'll be out in early 2026.

As you know, posting a review for any book is a loving gift to us writers. So, please post a review from whatever source you purchased it from. If you do, I will know and then be able to mystically thank you via the ether.

A bit of background. My first series, The Forever, came out in 2016. It has been successful way beyond any response I could have dreamed of. As of this writing, there are thirty-three books in The Ryanverse. If you haven't yet, check them out. It all starts with *The Forever Life* for print and *The Forever* in audiobooks. You'll be glad you did, seriously. I, the author, say it's good stuff. What better guarantee could there be?

I can't leave without mentioning my Time Diving Series. Beginning with *Letters From Hell* (print/audio) it follows Matt as he discovers he has the ability to travel to and to change his past. I really love this series, so give it a try. A few readers mention it's too dark or wordy, but that's only Book 1 of the four-book series. It was also intentional on my part so I was able to show Matt's development.

Finally, don't be a stranger! Sign up for my mailing list by dropping me an email: contact@craigarobertson.com. I'm on Facebook: https://www.facebook.com/craigr1971. And what about my website, you ask? Well here it is: https://craigrobertsonblog.wpcomstaging.com/

So, there you have it. Again, thanks for joining me and my nutty characters. If we've made your journey any lighter, then we all agree we've done good.

Craig